# THE GIRL IN THE PAINTING

CALEB CROWE

INKUBATOR
BOOKS

Published by Inkubator Books
www.inkubatorbooks.com

ISBN (eBook): 978-1-83756-316-6
ISBN (Paperback): 978-1-83756-317-3
ISBN (Hardback): 978-1-83756-318-0

# PROLOGUE

The moment the car strikes the water is as violent a shock as anything she has ever experienced, like driving full speed into a dark slab of granite. Flying, then not flying. Her head pitches forward, slamming into the steering wheel, then the seat belt yanks her back so savagely that all the air leaves her body, jerking her into the seat with incredible force, before catapulting her forward again, so that her head smashes into the side window.

Then stillness. Calm. The car bobbing gently like a pedalo on a boating lake. Disoriented, Seline tries to catch her breath, work out where she is.

In a car. On water. An accident.

She moves her arm painfully, extending her fingers slowly to her temple. Wet. Blood. And what else? She tries to clear the muddiness in her head and work out what else she's injured. Her entire upper body is throbbing, but nothing feels broken. And her legs? Wet. Blood again? Oh Christ! Has she broken her legs? She looks down in the gloom, dreading what she might see.

Not blood.

Water. Freezing water, filling the footwell of the car, soaking her legs, covering her lap. Rising fast, sucking its way up her chest. By the time she fully comprehends what is going on, the water is licking her chin. Desperately, she takes a gasp of air before her mouth and nose are covered too.

Silence.

Now the car is full of water, perfectly balanced, like it could hang here weightlessly forever... before dipping forwards like a slow-motion diver, then listing steadily to one side, tumbling slowly downwards into the murky depths of the river – and she lifts again against the tethers of her seat belt, feeling like she is floating even though she knows she is sinking. The pressure of the water closes in around her.

Urgently, Seline scrabbles at the belt buckle, tugging at it in panic, somehow blindly manages to click it free. Still holding her breath, she gets one foot underneath her, pushes herself up, and in the relative weightlessness of the water enveloping her she manages to get her feet onto the steering wheel and forces herself over the headrest of the seat into the rear of the car. She braces her legs against the back of the driver's seat and squeezes her face against the rear window, finding a tiny pocket of air that has been trapped there. She gasps it in.

She nosedives ever deeper. The water closes around the car like a thick, opaque blanket. Sinking. Sinking. And a single thought forms like crystal in Seline's brain:

*This isn't an accident. This is deliberate. Someone wants me dead.*

# PART I

# 1

---

"Seline?"

"Yes, that's right."

The driver turns away from her, taps his phone briefly, then eases the taxi out of the otherwise empty station car park and onto the road.

Seline clicks her seat belt fast and twists around in the seat, craning her neck to look back at the receding grey-stone railway station, its windows shuttered and empty, its walls covered in moss as if nature is pulling the carved stone slowly back into the wild. The cobbled forecourt is deserted, save for a decaying picnic bench and a wooden planter built from railway sleepers which, presumably in the spring, is awash with pretty coloured flowers; but now, on this dreary September afternoon, it seems nothing more than a pointless soggy wooden box to house some soggy brown mud.

Who would choose this of all places to come for a picnic?

The train here had been almost equally deserted as it trundled its way across the Pennines, Seline eating her packed lunch of cheese and tomato sandwiches and ready-salted crisps, her carton of orange juice and an apple, like a child on a school trip, spreading her Tupperware and tin foil and napkin out on the seats next to her as a tactical defence – unnecessarily as it turned out – against anyone sitting near her. The only other people in her carriage were a couple who were on the train already when she got on in Manchester. Probably in their late sixties, the man thin and wearing a shabby grey trenchcoat and grey flat cap, his skin as grey as his clothes so he seemed sculpted out of ash; the woman buxom and contrastingly florid, in a rough canary-blue woollen coat buttoned up to her neck and a matching blue woollen hat, like a caricature couple taken from a comic sixties seaside postcard.

Seline boarded the train through the door right next to them, but they didn't look up or give any acknowledgement of her presence, as if she was a ghost entirely invisible to them, passing utterly undetected to the other end of the carriage. And so it continued, stop after stop, in an increasingly backwoods series of small, desolate stations. Only the couple's dog, a little ratty terrier of some sort, paid any attention to her at all, never taking his eyes off her for the whole journey. Though in truth Seline realised even the dog wasn't interested in her, but in her packed lunch, staring unblinkingly in the hope that a small morsel of bread or a sliver of potato crisp would fall unnoticed to the carriage floor and he might have some chance to retrieve it.

Seline had left home that day nervous but excited about the new adventure to come. A new job, her first ever, teaching art. A new place. A new beginning! But as the slow journey continued, the excitement began to subside and give way to worry, and then to an anxiety that formed like a stubborn knot in her stomach and wouldn't shift. Like the feeling she had before her piano exam when she was eight, or before the public speaking competition she'd foolishly entered when she was eleven, where her voice compressed into a small, dense knot in her throat, and she squeaked her way through her awful speech to the laughter of school-mates, and was convinced her knot of anxiety would literally choke her, and that she would fall down dead on the stage in front of everyone.

When the train arrives at Holts Hill station, sputtering and staggering to a standstill, Seline is the only one to get up and leave. The couple remain static, gazing into space, into nothing, and the dog following her with its unblinking and resentful stare as she steps down onto the platform.

And now here she is, in the back of a taxi, driving down the Holts Hill Road, deserted, as if there has been some kind of awful final apocalypse and she and the taxi driver are the last two people on Earth.

Seline pulls her arm back into the sleeve of her coat and grips the end of it with her curled fingers, then wipes at the condensation on her passenger window with the heel of her hand. An insurance broker. A drab tearoom. A hardware store. Alan's Chicken. A travel agent. The shops become less frequent and are replaced by small, uniform terraced houses. Very quickly, the cab approaches the edge of the small town, passing a brightly lit petrol station and then a stone mason's yard displaying on the pavement outside its gated entrance a jet black uninscribed gravestone, a small fountain, a marble column and – inexplicably – a large stoical ornamental gorilla, intended for the garden of someone who might consider this an amusing addition to the plain suburban lawn and raised beds – before the taxi turns off this road and out of the town.

Well, if that was Holts Hill, then what must Statheley Bridge be like, wonders Seline. Statheley Bridge where she is heading to begin her new teaching job, which she has never visited because her interview was conducted remotely via Zoom, a hangover of the post-lockdown protocols everyone's Health & Safety policies still demanded. Statheley Bridge, which must be even more uninspiring than the heady heights of Holts Hill, if Holts Hill has its own train station and Statheley Bridge doesn't.

Autumn has hit early and hard this year, and the landscape is already drear and uninviting. The car is now driving along a larger road which cuts its way through dark, cloddy fields fringed with sparse hedgerows and gnarled, spiny trees, or past uneven dry-stone walls behind which lurk sporadic clumps of miserable-looking sheep, sulking in groups of two or three like the rural equivalent of surly teenagers at a bus stop. Just looking at it all in the fading flat autumn light makes Seline feel cold. She pulls her coat around her and turns away from the window. She's never felt comfortable in the country – so very different from her home in Manchester. There's something odd about the countryside. The space just makes you feel small and insignificant. Even the sheep stare at you like you don't belong.

The taxi slows and Seline looks up to see, through the windscreen, a sign directing traffic to Statheley Bridge.

"Best view in the county," the driver pipes up from the front, the first time he's spoken since they left the station.

The car turns off the main road and immediately begins to dip down into the valley.

"Oh."

Under normal circumstances this would indeed be the

best view in the county, the car dropping down the steeply inclined road to reveal the other side of the valley like a magnificent wall of fields and trees, an idyllic backdrop from some kind of epic pastoral dream of rural perfection. But on this cold autumn day, the landscape is lost in a stubborn fog and the other side of the valley might as well not exist at all for all that can be seen of it through the claggy mist.

"Sorry, luv."

The car keeps going, disappearing behind the almost hard edge of the fog bank like an aeroplane descending into a thick blanket of cloud. Down the hill. Down towards the village of Statheley Bridge. Seline looks at the window again, and the small patch she has cleared in the condensation. She presses her face to the glass and peers out. But it's impossible to see anything clearly, just the rhythmic undulations of light and shadow as they drive past trees at the edge of the road. Though she can't see where they are going, her body tells her they are snaking from left to right, right to left. She digs her fingers into the cold plastic of the armrest on her door and hopes that the taxi driver has done this route so often he can pick his way down the snaking road practically unsighted. She's sure he has. Of course he has.

But the thought doesn't make her feel any easier. She was cold not five minutes ago. Now she notices her hands are sweating, her fingers slipping on the plastic she's gripping too hard. There it is again, that knot of anxiety in her stomach. With the car swinging left and right like a roller-coaster, she feels she might actually be sick.

She shouldn't have come here. She should have stayed in Manchester. This whole thing is a terrible mistake.

2

The fog lifts as they approach the village, and Seline is able to relax her vice-like grasp on the car's armrest and look out once again through the passenger window. The first thing she sees is a jumbled assortment of surprisingly lovely cottages clinging to the edge of the narrow, steep road which meanders its way like a tangle of string through the village outskirts – the sort of place you might see in a cosy Sunday afternoon television drama about cloth-capped vets or policemen on bicycles who only have the most trivial of crimes to investigate. Seline can imagine herself living in a cottage like this quite happily.

Disappointingly, the taxi motors on past the picturesque houses and begins to climb uphill again. The quaint cottages become fewer and fewer, and the gaps between them increasingly occupied by more modern properties, some quite grand, with stonework drives and two or three smart cars parked in front – others more shabby and sorry-looking, Nineteen-Thirties houses with low-pitched roofs and curved bay windows, looking weirdly suburban and out of place here in the depths of the countryside. But still the car drives on, until it rounds a corner with a high hedge and turns sharply onto a more modern-looking road, revealing a bland new-build estate as uninspiring in its architectural effect as the village-centre cottages had been quaint.

The taxi finally draws to a stop outside an ordinary-looking terraced house on an unprepossessing street. Seline's heart sinks a little as she realises that they have arrived.

She unbuckles her seat belt and steps out of the taxi. The driver is already out, by the open boot at the rear of the car, swinging Seline's small, light suitcases to the pavement.

"Sorry about that view."

"Not to worry. Thanks very much. I can manage."


SELINE IS MET by a small woman in her thirties, clearly flustered as she clutches a grumbling and wriggling toddler to her chest with one arm, while holding the door open with the other.

"Come in. Seline? Come in. It's feeding time at the zoo. It's chaos, sorry!"

The woman retreats down the narrow hallway and Seline enters, pulling in her cases as she does.

"Just leave those there. I'll show you your room in a minute. I'm Mary. This is Bertie. You found us then. Would you like a cup of tea?"

"Lovely, thanks – if you're sure?"

"No bother. Come in, come in!"

Mary heads back up the passageway. Seline follows her, glancing briefly at the pictures that line the walls: studio portraits of Mary and a man and two girls, twins maybe, in a variety of grouped poses, smiling awkwardly, the forced expressions of happiness as unconvincingly plastic as the plants on the coffee table in front of them.

Seline follows Mary to the kitchen, passing an open doorway to the lounge where the man from the photos sits on a boxy leather couch, reading a newspaper in front of a television quiz show he isn't watching. He doesn't look up to acknowledge Seline or seem to register her at all.

The kitchen is a mess, the work surfaces covered in a jumble of food packets, and swathes of children's clothes and bed sheets and tea towels hanging over radiators and the backs of seats. Mary wrestles the toddler into a high chair at a wooden table at which sit the children from the photographs in the hall, two girls of about seven.

"Sorry, it's always chaotic at this time." Mary flits around the kitchen, juggling a variety of tasks. Seline guesses that she's become adept at this domestic dance while the man in the other room lurks behind his newspaper, abdicating all responsibility.

"Claire!" Mary barks sharply at one of the girls. "He can't eat that if he's already got his mouth full."

The girl who's helping with the feeding sits balancing a tube of pasta on a yellow plastic spoon in front of the baby's face, making encouraging cooing noises. The baby chews away, smears of tomato sauce around his mouth like poorly applied lipstick. The other girl munches away on her pasta and keeps her head down, presumably to avoid getting roped into any chores.

Mary arrives with two mugs of insipid tea and plonks one in front of Seline. "Just taking his to Wayne. With you in a minute." And she leaves the kitchen.

"We've had pasta," chirps Claire. "Bertie loves pasta."

"Oooh, nice. It looks delicious. I'm Seline. Hello."

"This is Bertie. And this is Rose-Marie."

"Hello, Rose-Marie."

Rose-Marie looks up from her pasta. "You're in our room," she says flatly, before returning to her eating.

Seline doesn't know what to say. Fortunately, she's rescued from the awkward silence by Mary sweeping back into the kitchen.

"Right, let's show you your room. You can bring your tea. Claire, keep an eye on him."

Seline follows Mary up the stairs and onto the landing.

"Bathroom's here – just one, I'm afraid. It's carnage in the morning getting the girls off to school, but just elbow your way in. And here's you. I'll leave you to settle in."

Seline pushes the door open and wheels her cases into the room. It's a medium-sized featureless box, with a single bed, a wardrobe, a small desk, and a swivel office chair. The walls are cornflower blue – freshly painted, Seline can tell from the slight odour of fumes – apart from a feature wall behind the bed, which is covered in a wallpaper of wide white and yellow vertical stripes. The curtains at the window above the desk are also yellow, drawn closed. The lamp-shade is a large paper lantern that fills the room with a cold, hard light.

Seline lifts her suitcases onto the bed in turn, unzips them, takes out her clothes, and begins to put them away in the wardrobe, hanging the dresses and blouses and jackets on the rail, placing the underwear in the drawers under-neath. She thinks about taking her toiletries bag into the bathroom, but decides to keep it on the desk for now, next to a small cactus and a front door key. She places the smaller empty suitcase inside the larger one, lifts it onto the top of the wardrobe. The entire exercise takes her less than five minutes.

Her new home.

Seline sits on the bed and tries to imagine what it is going to be like living here. She notices a faint horizontal line on the wallpaper behind her, around five feet off the ground, running about the length of her bed. A slightly rough mark where something has rubbed against the wall.

Bunk beds.

This must have been where the girls slept, the room Rose-Marie suggested was theirs before Seline arrived like a cuckoo in the nest and ejected them. The house is small, so they must only be renting out a room because they need the money. Seline can't help concluding she's an inconvenience here, a financial necessity.

Now she's realised she's in the way, Seline feels awkward about leaving her room. She can hear the noises of life continuing in the spaces downstairs: chatter coming from the kitchen; the sound of the television rising up through the floor from the living room directly below. The ordinariness of the family going about their business makes her feel suddenly very lonely. What is she doing here? A stranger, hiding away like a shy teenager in her bedroom. She feels completely out of place with the whole thing – being here, in this house, in this room, her clothes folded in drawers as if she's in a hotel, just passing through. And about to start a new teaching job she feels woefully unprepared for.

Seline gets the horrible feeling she's caught in a kind of loop. She left her bedroom in Manchester this morning, where she's spent twenty-three years of her life, to start a new adventure. And after all that, where has she ended up?

Back in a kid's bedroom, feeling like a little kid, not completely comfortable where she is, but too afraid to venture out.

Seline looks at herself in the mirror on the wardrobe door. Grow up! That's the point, isn't it? The point of all this? The point of coming to a new place and starting her first job is to grow up and step out into the world.

Seline snatches up her coat and keys, crosses the landing and steps gingerly down the stairs. Quietly, so as not to disturb the family, and before she loses her nerve, she turns the latch and slips silently out through the front door and into the dusk.

## 3

Once they'd started climbing the hill, the cab ride hadn't seemed that long. But now, walking back down it, Seline realises they'd travelled further than she thought.

It's about twenty minutes before she finds herself walking past houses, and a further five before she feels she's entering the village proper, into civilisation. She zig-zags down a couple of deserted side streets with small houses on either side, the warm lights of televisions dancing behind people's curtains making her feel even more isolated. And then she turns off a street into the centre of the village itself.

It's a relief to be somewhere properly lit and Seline immediately feels less vulnerable. The village centre is larger and much prettier than she was expecting. A proper old English market town, its high street an impressively wide boulevard lined uniformly with mature plane trees and silver birch, with car parking on each side still leaving a vast space in the middle for traffic to pass through. This is where sheep and cattle would have been driven down from outlying farms for auction in the past, and which probably now plays host, some day in the week, to market stalls selling cheeses and meats and artisan breads and unusual relishes, chutneys and jams. The shops are all long shut now, but she can tell from the boutiques and pet beauty parlours that there's quite a bit of money here.

This isn't too bad at all. She keeps walking down the street, admiring the black gloss Victorian streetlights from which hang straggled loops of weather-worn bunting. There's a break in the run of shops and a tight pathway shrouded in shadow. Seline turns in to take a look. Her eyes rapidly adjust to the light in the narrow alleyway, and she sees a set of steep stone steps at the end of the path. She begins to climb them.

The steps finish at an iron railing and gate, which opens back onto level ground in the form of an unexpectedly large green, with tidy lawns and ornamental beds filled with neat evergreen shrubs. A tarmacked path winds its way across the green and ends at a stone arch which forms the entrance to an imposing Norman church. There are streetlights here too, but their sickly yellow light doesn't reveal much in comparison to the moon, nearly full, which hangs in the sky on a cushion of cloud just behind the square bell tower of the church, exactly like a scene out of an old black and white horror film.

Seline approaches. The moonlight is strong enough that the church casts a vast, cold shadow across the green. She reaches the arch and the church noticeboard, a wooden post covered in peeling white paint supporting a glass-covered display case. *St. Oswald's.* Seline pushes open the small waist-high wooden gate and walks through into the churchyard.

The plants are older here, and wilder than the ones on the green outside, the dark hues of yew and holly seeming almost black as Seline picks her way along the snaking gravel path. It's completely quiet and still, the only noise the crunch of the ground underfoot and the sweep of her coat brushing lightly against the holly. She keeps walking past the church on one side and the old graveyard on the other, its carved stones too dark to read under the shadowy canopy of the heavy trees. Then she turns away from the church and along another path by a small, thin trickling brook until she comes to a high fence behind which sits the building she's been looking for.

She can see it at a distance across a large playground – St. Oswald's, the school she'll be returning to tomorrow to commence her new teaching job. The path ends at a well-worn track carved into the grass by years of children's feet taking a shortcut through the church. Seline puts her hand against a tree and begins to make her way along it, careful not to fall should the mud be slippy.

The dirt track comes out through a gap between two shrubs. Seline steps onto the pavement. She can now see the school much better. It's a grand and imposing building, its red-brick walls punctuated by windows housed in ornately carved stone borders. The large main door in its stone-pillared arch looks more like the entrance to a castle than a village school. It feels very grown up and intimidating. This is where her new beginning really happens. Seline can't work out what it is she's feeling: cold, or excited, or nervous? Probably a bit of all three.

The lights in the lower windows are all off, like black sightless eyes fixed unblinking at the street ahead. But in one of the first-floor windows there appears to be some light.

Perhaps it's cleaners. But if it were cleaners, wouldn't there be lights on everywhere, not in just one room? Seline notices that all the other windows are uncovered, their cold black glass looking like dead space. But the window where the light is on has a vertical blind drawn closed, masking whatever is inside. Probably someone has been working in the room, then left and simply forgotten to turn the light out after them. That's exactly what she did just now, grabbing her coat and keys, rushing out and not turning off her bedroom light. That makes complete sense.

Even while Seline's reassuring herself with this thought, she sees the vertical blinds move.

There's someone in the room.

Instinctively she steps back a little, out of the glare of the streetlamp and into the shadow of a tree. She stares up at the window. She's sure she saw a movement. She's sure she did.

She waits.

Nothing.

Then the blind moves again, pulled back by a hand, revealing a figure at the window. They've stopped moving, and they're at the window, looking at her! At least she *thinks* they are. She can't be sure. Whoever it is can't be properly seen, silhouetted against the light of the room. Perhaps she is being watched. Or perhaps she just feels suddenly conspicuous, hiding here in the shadow of a tree.

Then the light goes out.

Seline turns and walks swiftly back up the road. She can't articulate for herself why, but she's unnerved. She scrabbles up the muddy track, but slips in her haste and gets mud on her hands and her knees. She crosses the churchyard and heads back towards the town. It's getting late and she has an early start tomorrow. She should be getting back.

·  ·  ·

THE WALK back up the hill is considerably more taxing than the walk down. Seline can feel her calves beginning to ache, and her hot breath comes quickly in cloudy plumes. The road is quiet and free of traffic, but after quarter of an hour or so of walking, Seline hears an engine noise from behind and realises there is a car approaching, at some speed.

The road has no path, and the number of dead wildfowl littering its fringes bear witness to the dangers of being hit by a car, so Seline squeezes herself as tight against the hedgerow as she can and looks down the hill to where the car is coming from. She can feel the hard, woody brambles digging into her back. Suddenly, a small sports car screeches around a bend, headlights dazzling her. She holds her breath and pushes herself even further back as the car thunders past her at what feels like a ridiculously reckless speed, just missing her by inches, the draft of the vehicle whipping her hair across her face.

And just as quickly it's gone, tyres squealing like some tortured animal as it vanishes around the next bend. Seline scrapes her hair out of her eyes, tears herself free of the thorns and wonders whether this entire walk was a foolish enterprise. She steps back onto the road and continues up the hill.

Soon she hears another car approaching, from ahead this time, coming down the hill. Again she prepares to press herself into the hedgerow, but it becomes clear from the engine note that this driver is sensibly slowing down. As the car approaches, it slows even more. As she sees its lights come around the bend in the road, it's going almost at walking pace.

As it draws alongside her, it comes to a complete stop. Neither she nor the car moves. She feels suddenly very isolated out here, in the middle of nowhere.

It sits there for a moment, the engine idling. Then the electric window slides down.

"Funny time to be out here on your own."

The voice is male, quite young. But Seline can't properly see the driver. Even though he's opened his window, he hasn't moved his head to talk to her, so his face is mostly lost in shadow inside the car.

"You shouldn't be out here this time of night on your own. Anything could happen to a girlie like you."

The statement could just be concern for her safety. But something about it makes Seline feel like it's threatening.

"It's dangerous out here. I can give you a lift if you like...?"

It *would* be sensible to get off this road. But then she looks properly at the car. Though she only saw it briefly, she's almost certain this is the same car that has just thundered past her at speed on the way up the hill, dark blue, or green, or black – it's hard to tell under the shadow of the trees. The man must have seen her in his headlights as he nearly hit her, then found some place to turn round, and has driven back specifically for her.

"I'm fine, thanks." Seline tries to sound as casual as possible, but she can hear a small catch of fear in her throat. Her heart is racing. She starts walking up the hill.

She hears the grinding of gears. The car begins to roll in reverse, creeps after her, at walking pace.

"You sure? Don't want you getting all smashed up like one of them badgers." The man laughs. "Besides, it's freezing out there. You'll catch your death. It's lovely and warm in here..."

Seline can hear the leering smile in the man's voice. She quickens her pace. "Really, I'm fine."

There's a pause. Then the man grinds the gears again and guns the engine.

"Suit yourself!" he barks in an angry tone and speeds away with incredible acceleration, screeching and squealing around the next corner, down the hill and out of sight.

Seline stops walking, tries to catch her breath. She listens for the note of the engine, making sure the driver has completely gone, and waits until the sound is thin and distant, and gets lost behind the thumping of her heart in her chest.

He's gone.

But what if he comes back? She feels a sense of dread rising in her. She starts walking again, briskly, and then begins to jog as fast as the steep hill will allow. She doesn't stop running until she's back in the safety of her little rented room.

# 4

Seline's brain was racing all night and she hadn't got much sleep. When she did nod off briefly, her fitful dreams were consumed with nameless terrors, lurking somewhere in the shadows, like that man's shadowy face inside the car, the panic of it all somehow more terrifying because she couldn't properly see or define it. And she awoke, fearful and anxious – a situation made even worse by sleeping in a strange bed and waking confused about where she was.

That horrible man on the road. That figure in the school window. The whole night completely unnerved her. Maybe she shouldn't have tried to start this new life; maybe she should have stayed where she was, safe in her bedroom back home.

Wayne is gone by breakfast to whatever job he does, and Seline manages to sneak into the bathroom in a small gap between Claire and Rose-Marie and Mary and Bertie, and gets herself smartly dressed for her first day of teaching –

which by now she is dreading. Luckily, Mary offers to drop her in town on the school run, so at least Seline is spared the walk down the hill again.

Perhaps because she is dreading it so much, the arrival at the school isn't nearly as bad as she had anticipated. The weather is one of those bright, crisp autumn days that makes her feel the world has magically sidestepped winter altogether and it's spring again. And instead of the desolate, abandoned street outside the school that unsettled her last night, the whole place is a throng of noisy, excited children catching up with each other after a long summer apart.

Seline enters the school and finds herself in a riot of children darting in all directions, like pedestrians on a busy Tokyo street crossing. She manages to identify herself as the new art teacher to a woman in reception and is directed into the school office for a brief induction. She's already emailed in a mass of paperwork from home, but apparently there is a pile more to go through, and a stack of Health & Safety protocols, Child Protection Policies and various other documents to sign for.

Clutching her bundle of papers, Seline is lead from the office for a guided tour of the school. Having been interviewed online, she anticipated there would be some kind of inset day. But instead, all she seems to be getting is a ten-minute race around the school from the overstretched and distracted secretary. When it's over, she's informed that the Head, Mrs Jessop, will meet with all the staff shortly, and follows directions upstairs to the staff room.

Entering the staff room itself feels bizarre. All through her teaching practice she could never quite get over the strangeness of coming into a school as an adult, and she still feels strangely out of place here. Seline has to do all she can to resist the urge to knock on the door. She opens it and goes in, feeling like a naughty kid who's been summoned for something she's done wrong.

It's a large room, with a couple of tired-looking sofas and some blocky chairs in bright blue, yellow and red, which might look more cheerful if they weren't old and saggy and faded where countless teachers have sat in them over the years. A couple of men in their mid-forties stand chatting by some plywood pigeonholes. Two older women and an older man are over by a sink, silently looking at a kettle as if they can intimidate it into boiling more speedily. A balding man in his fifties sits on his own at the side of the room flicking through a pile of exercise books. Seline feels conspicuous just standing by the door, so turns to her side and starts reading items pinned to the staff noticeboard, hoping to give the appearance she is doing something productive and isn't just the anxious new girl.

She scans the various official notices without really reading. Only one item draws her eye, a hand-written note scrawled in biro on a crumpled piece of paper with a ten-pound note pinned to it:

*All right its a new year. I'll be doing the lotery sindi-
cate again this year so if you want a krack at
winning your fortune then remember to bring you're
money in before Friday youve got to be in it to win it!
Heres a tenner you all won on the last draw of last
year so dont spend it all at once. Robbie.*

"Shocking, isn't it?"

Seline is interrupted by a voice over her shoulder.

"Hi. I'm Annie."

"Hello. I'm Seline, the new art teacher."

"Hi, Seline. I teach English. That note *isn't* by me or one of my students, before you ask. I do aim for a vague basic level of literacy!"

Annie is blonde and smiley and looks to be in her late twenties and immediately makes Seline feel more at ease.

"First days are horrible, but everyone's very nice here, on the whole. Come on, let's find you a mug."

Annie leads Seline over to the sink. She settles a large carrier bag full of textbooks onto the floor, squats down and starts clanking around in a cupboard, before emerging with a tea mug in hand. "This'll do, after a rinse."

Annie runs the mug under the tap for a bit, shakes it over the sink, then hands it to Seline. A legend on the front reads:

*You DO have to be mad to work here – and it DOESN'T help.*

Annie screws her nose up. "That's what passes for humour in these parts."

"Thanks."

"Make yourself a tea. I'll see you later. Welcome aboard."

Annie snatches her bookbag up and scuttles off.

Seline picks up the kettle and judges by the weight there's enough water for a cup of tea. She clicks it on to reboil, then takes a teabag out of a glass jar and drops it in her mug, pours on the boiling water. Annie's friendliness has made her feel a bit better. It's the first time she's smiled since

Manchester. She squeezes the teabag against the side of the mug, discards it and splashes in some milk. There's a plate of drab biscuits next to the kettle. Seline picks up a custard cream and crunches it.

The balding man who'd been marking the books walks past Seline on his way to the door. "It's two pounds a week for the tea and biscuits." And he's gone. His surly manner and unfriendly tone undoes all the good work Annie just did, and Seline feels unwelcome again.

Seline finds her pigeonhole. It's stuffed with yet more paperwork. There's a copy of the term timetable, a plan of the school with room numbers in tiny print, and an envelope with various official documents relating to her contract, pension scheme and some other things she decides she can read later. There's also a coloured envelope with her hand-written name on it that looks like a birthday card. When she opens it, it's a Good Luck card.

*Good luck on your first day in your new job. I'm sure you will be amazing. Best wishes, Michael.*

That's nice. Michael is an old friend of her father. Back in school the two were best mates, and kept in touch for quite a while after that, but kind of drifted apart when Seline was young – though Michael must have been following them on social media, because in the week Seline graduated from her teaching PGCE course, Michael sent her a message on Facebook saying he was a governor at a school looking for a new art teacher. She didn't have to apply anywhere else, her interview was a breeze – and now here she is. Thanks, Michael!

Suddenly the door bursts open and in comes a young man of about twenty-five.

"Alright, losers?"

Oh God.

Seline immediately recognises his voice as belonging to the man from last night, the man in the car, the one who nearly ran her down in the road and then tried to lure her into his car. She thought she hadn't been able to see his face properly in the shadows – but it's unmistakably him.

Does he work here?! She can feel her pulse beginning to quicken.

He begins to wander round the room, chatting to people as he goes. Seline can't hear what he's saying, but everyone seems happy to see him. He's shiny and confident, good-looking and charismatic. He exudes a positive energy that transforms the sombre mood of the staff room. He must be funny as well, because whatever he says elicits a laugh from whoever he's talking to. He looks bluff and manly with the men, but twinkly and cheeky with the women.

"That's Robbie." Annie has once again appeared at Seline's shoulder. "Robbie who wrote the note."

"Does he work here?"

"Kind of. He helps out here sometimes, does odd jobs, building maintenance stuff, I think – though I've never seen him actually do any work. He helps people out with stuff – like last year, I was having a bit of trouble with my car and couldn't get to the garage because of lessons, so Robbie drove it down there for me and got it sorted out. He's lived in the village forever. He knows people – he knows *everybody*. Whatever you want, he knows someone who knows someone who can get you one cheaper."

Robbie looks across the room, right at Seline, and smiles

a beaming, winning smile. She smiles back, instinctively. Even though she was so scared of him last night, he seems so different now, so attractive and full of life, she can't help but be drawn to him.

"Hi, Robbie!" Annie walks from behind Seline and across the room to Robbie.

Seline realises immediately that Robbie wasn't looking at her at all. He was looking at Annie. He hasn't even noticed Seline. He certainly hasn't recognised her from last night, that terrifying encounter on the road. It's as if she is invisible. She suddenly feels foolish and very small, and any confidence she had drains out of her. She watches Robbie continue to buzz around the room, chatting to everyone but her, before he makes an exit.

He's gone.

Seline is confused by her emotions. He really scared her last night – but now he's gone, she feels she's somehow missed a chance to talk to him. Lost her nerve, played it safe and stayed in her corner. All too familiar.

BEFORE LONG MRS JESSOP, the headteacher, arrives and gives a cheery welcome back to everyone. Seline is briefly introduced to the other members of staff, and she realises she's the only new person this year. There are a few announcements about the workings of the school which Seline doesn't understand, then everyone is allowed to head off to their first lessons.

"Er, Seline, could you hang back a minute?"

Mrs Jessop and Seline stand awkwardly in silence while they wait for the other teachers to leave the staff room. The Head gives Seline a fixed smile that conveys no warmth whatsoever. Eventually the final teacher leaves and it's just the two of them.

"We're very glad to have you here, Seline. We've recently made quite an investment in the Art Department, the facilities and resources and so forth, so it's quite a place to have landed for your first job."

"I'm looking forward to starting." Seline does her best to project confidence and enthusiasm, but feels sure her nerves are showing.

"This school is small, in a small village, but it has a long history and a fine reputation to maintain. I like to think of us all as guardians of that reputation. You're our one new addition this term. Most of the staff have been here for several years. We're a family. We're proud of what we do."

There's an awkward pause. Seline isn't sure if she's supposed to say something. But Mrs Jessop continues, her tone shifting, possibly with a hint of frustration.

"If I can be frank, getting the opportunity to head up a department, albeit a department of one, is quite an act of faith in someone with your level of experience. Your *inexperience,* I should say. It's unusual, highly unusual, and the way in which you... well... anyway..."

The Head trails off. Seline gets the impression she had a lot more to say, but has thought better of it.

"I don't know you, Seline, so I have to trust those who do, who have placed you in this position, and who tell me you're more than capable of executing your role to an extremely high standard. So I'm looking to YOU to step up and deliver excellent results. Good luck."

And with that, Mrs Jessop leaves.

Seline stands there, trying to work it out. It sounds like strings have been pulled and the Head isn't happy about it.

Does she mean Michael letting her know about the job? She though all he'd done was get her an interview. But did he use his influence, *make* the school employ her?

Any enthusiasm Seline has about her first day drains out of her. The school doesn't want her. She's as unwelcome here as she is in her rented bedroom up the hill.

## 5

Seline's trying to unpick what has just been said to her when the bell rings. Oh great. First lesson and she's already late. She rushes up the near-empty corridors, consulting her map of the school and trying to find her way to her class, too embarrassed to ask directions from any of the dawdling students who are also late – though at least they have the excuse of not being the teacher!

When she arrives at her classroom there's an unruly mob of fifteen-year-olds milling about outside, enjoying the chaos of their new start to the year. Seline bows her head and snakes her way through the crowd to the door, then lets herself and her students in. She makes a tactical decision not to admit any fault for the late start, remembering her training about establishing her authority – even if she doesn't really feel she has any.

"Sit down, please."

While the kids move slowly and noisily to their seats, Seline has a chance to take in the room. It's large, bright and fresh, and appears to be newly decorated. One side has a whole bank of large drawers for art storage, there's a well-stocked set of shelves with paper, card and paints – and she can see another room off this one that looks like it has drying racks for prints. She has a print room! This is all much nicer than she was anticipating.

Seline takes her laptop out, connects it to the projector, and steels herself to deliver the introduction she's been rehearsing for the last few weeks. After a couple of attempts, she manages to call the class to order.

"Hello. I'm Miss Henderson, your new art teacher... and I love art! It's an amazing form of self-expression which lets us communicate our thoughts, emotions, and experiences in ways that words simply can't capture. What's inside us? What do we think and feel? What do we hope and dream? Who *are* we?"

"We're Year 10, Miss – who the fuck are YOU?" The class laugh. The girl who has piped up, a stocky brunette with a messy uniform, thick black make-up lining her eyes and green streaks in her hair, stares defiantly at Seline, pleased with herself. Seline is thrown by the interruption, and even more so by the swearing. The girl is clearly looking for attention. Seline decides not to rise to it and carries on.

"This term we're going to look at self-portraits. Self-portraits are important because they give us an opportunity to understand ourselves and our inner world. They let us examine our own identity, our thoughts and hopes and dreams. And that's what we're going to do today – create self-portraits that capture the essence of who we are."

Seline clicks on the projector to show a reproduction of Van Gogh's self-portrait with the bandaged ear.

"Vincent Van Gogh lived in the late 19th century, and his

self-portraits are some of the most popular pieces of art ever produced. But why? Why do these paintings still capture so many people's imaginations? I'd say it's because he painted them with such rawness and emotion. He didn't hide his vulnerabilities and imperfections, or his bandaged ear, or his struggles with mental health. These aren't just pictures of his face. He used his paintings to show his inner turmoil."

"Reminds me of when my piercing went septic." It's the green-haired girl again. Seline can feel her face flushing, but rides the wave of laughter and pushes on.

"For me, it's the haunting expression in his eyes. I can feel the passion that drove him to paint, the way he poured his soul onto the canvas."

Snoring noises from Green Hair. Seline ignores them. She knows she's on the verge of losing the whole class so decides to push on to the end.

"So, I want each of you to create self-portraits that are true reflections of yourselves. It's not about creating a perfect painting of just what you look like. It's about expressing your thoughts, emotions, and experiences through art. These self-portraits are a chance for you to tell your own unique stories, to show the world who you really are."

Students begin to get up, move around the room, gathering materials from the paper and paint stores. Seline relaxes a little. At least she's begun. She gives them ten minutes or so to settle into their work. There's a general level of chatter, but it's not too disruptive, and she can see that people are doing things, looking into mirrors to study their faces, sharpening pencils, mixing paints, so she lets the talking continue. Then she begins to move around, looking at the work, offering words of encouragement or advice or asking questions as she goes.

Then she gets to Green Hair, who is sending texts on her phone.

"Phones away, please. Get on with your work."

"I've finished, Miss."

Seline looks at the sheet of A3 paper in front of the girl. There's a crudely drawn circle, with two dots for eyes and a line for a mouth. Probably ten seconds' work, if that. It's classic attention-seeking behaviour and Seline decides not to comment on it.

"Perhaps you can do another one then, dig a bit deeper into how you see yourself."

"No point, Miss. I think I've captured the absolute essence of me." This gets titters from the other kids in the immediate vicinity. Seline knows she needs to shut down this confrontation, fast.

"Give it a try. It doesn't have to be perfect. There's no wrong answers with art. It's just about taking risks."

Seline goes to take the stick-drawing and replace it with a fresh sheet of paper, but the moment she touches the work, the girl is up and out of her seat, grabbing Seline by the arm and wheeling her round so fast that she has her up against the wall before she knows what's going on. The girl is incredibly strong and determined, and Seline is taken so off-guard she freezes in a panic, her heart thumping in her chest. The girl leans into Seline with a face like thunder, icy, determined. She speaks in a hushed voice through gritted teeth.

"I could cut your fucking ear off."

What?

What?

Seline's mind races in terror.

It's a moment before she realises that the girl has walked away, is sitting back in her seat on her phone as if nothing had just happened. Slowly the muffling in Seline's head is replaced by the din of the class, all up on their feet and talking wildly, energised by the flash of violence they've just witnessed.

"What's your name?"

The girl just looks flatly at Seline, then returns to her texting.

"Right. With me, Head's office, now."

Seline grabs the girl – she knows she shouldn't have grabbed her, but too late – and the girl offers no resistance as she frog-marches her across the room to the door.

"Carry on with your work."

And they're out in the corridor. Seline turns and walks briskly, still holding the girl hard by the upper arm.

"Head's office is the other way." The girl looks at Seline, a disdainful smile on her lips. Seline turns and drags the girl the other way.

They both know who is in charge here, and it isn't Seline.

# 6

Seline sits miserably in the corner of the staff room, going over her terrible first day. That awful lesson, the general level of chaos and disruption she felt she was drowning in – and that vile loudmouth gobshite green-haired ringleader at the centre of it all, causing trouble, whipping up the others, swearing at her. Threatening her!

Of course, she'd denied it all once they'd got to Mrs Jessop's office. The Head asking lots of questions, her disappointment in Seline utterly apparent, as if that's exactly what she'd anticipated in their talk just minutes before, and Seline all twitchy and unsettled and barely under control – and the green-haired girl, Julie her name was, all smug and relaxed in comparison, and completely denying she'd said what she'd said.

*I could cut your fucking ear off!*

But no, Julie smiling, offering up that what she'd actually said was *I could draw you a Van Gogh.*

And then Seline doubting herself. Could she have misheard? She was *sure* she'd heard her correctly, she was positive – but she'd said it so quietly, and so calmly, and none of the other students would have heard it at that volume...

Then Mrs Jessop sending Julie off with a stern warning but no other punishment.

And sending Seline off with some kind of platitude about taking the week to bed herself in, and other things... Seline not even listening properly at this point.

AND SO HERE SHE SITS, wondering whether she's made the worst mistake of her life, feeling lonely and disheartened and a failure, just wanting to run back to the safety of her childhood bedroom and never come out again.

The door opens and Seline looks round, hoping for a brief moment that it might be Robbie again. But it's not. It's the balding man who told her off about needing to pay for the tea and biscuits.

He spots Seline, but doesn't come over, goes to a locker and starts loading in a few books and things. Eventually, even he must feel it's too awkward with both of them in here, in silence, so he wanders over to where Seline is sitting.

"Hullo. I'm Graham, Head of Science. You're Seline?"

"Seline. Yes. Hello."

"Would you like a cup of tea? You look like you could use one."

While Graham boils the kettle and makes the tea, Seline looks around at the other teachers who are beginning to come into the staff room, laughing and chatting, preparing to go home. No one else looks like they had a particularly challenging day.

"How has it been?"

"Oh, okay, I guess. It all feels a bit... real. But I'm sure I'll get used to it. I've got a nice room anyway."

"Yes?"

"Yes. Much better equipped than I was expecting. The print room is better than the one I had at art college!"

"Yes, there's been a real investment in art over the summer."

Graham hands Seline her tea.

"Thanks."

"That used to be my classroom actually."

"What?"

"Yes, my room – and then the room at the back was my chemicals store. We've been squeezed in around the corner now. But good to make way for something that's been under-invested in. Science's loss is art's gain."

"Oh. Sorry."

Graham seems to be making light of it, but Seline thinks there's a bitter tone under the jokiness. God, he must resent her.

She's relieved to be rescued from this line of conversation when Annie comes over and asks how her first day has gone. She starts making a few general comments, but she can't shake the feeling of hopeless inadequacy. The more she talks, the more upset she can feel herself getting, about how hard it was to control the class, how depressing it was to have something she thought she'd prepared well, on a subject she loves, getting so roundly ridiculed.

"Sorry, which class is this?" Annie looks concerned. Seline explains it was her first class of the day, the Year 10s.

"Oh! Them!" Annie lets go of the tension in her voice. "God, in that case, don't worry. They're a proper handful.

Everyone has a problem with them. At best, morose, at worst, feral."

Seline looks at the other teachers, who are nodding in agreement. So maybe it's not her. Maybe it's them, those kids. With their snide comments and mocking laughter and refusal to engage with the work in case it makes them look foolish in front of their mates. Seline begins to warm to her theme, talking about how the lesson went from bad to worse – and driven mainly by one pupil in particular, Julie: a horrible, nasty, sneering girl with a smug, supercilious expression on her face, a mess of dyed green hair and make-up and piercings in the most crass and obvious authority-challenging way. Pathetic really. Such a cliché. Sad even...

Seline stops her rant and notices the room has gone quiet. She spots Graham leaving the staff room. Annie leans over to her in a hushed voice.

"Julie in Year 10 – that's Graham's daughter."

Oh God. It's only her first day and she's already made an enemy.

Seline waits in the staff room for everyone else to leave. She just doesn't have the energy to talk to anyone. Well, almost anyone.

"Oh, hi, luv. I didn't expect to hear from you so early. How did it go?"

It's her mum. Seline promised to call that evening to fill her in on her first day. But she's feeling lost and lonely and really needs to hear a comforting voice now.

"Yeah, really well," she lies. She can't bring herself to tell her mum the truth – that her first twenty-four hours have been far from idyllic.

She knows her parents have been worried about her coming away to this place. For some reason she doesn't fully understand, she's always been quiet and cautious, slow to make friends and happier on her own, doing her art, than out with other people. She's always been wildly imaginative. An only child, she spent large chunks of her childhood alone, locked away in her bedroom, disappearing into her fantasy world full of vividly real imaginary friends and drawing them over and over. Looking back now, she finds it hard to distinguish what in her childhood was real from what was imagined.

When she told her parents about the message she'd had from Michael, mentioning this school, her mum had been weird with her, and even tried to persuade her not to take the job. Seline has the sense her mum doesn't trust her to be able to do it, that she thinks being here will be too much for her. It's made Seline all the more determined to make this move away from home and her teaching a success. It feels like there's a lot at stake, coming out into the world. She wants to make her parents proud. She needs to make a go of it at all costs, whatever the odds, and prove to them she can do it.

The two of them chat for a while, not saying that much – her mum fishing for details about the school, and her accommodation, and whether she's heard from Michael yet, and Seline answering breezily but giving away as little as possible.

"You know, luv, if you find you don't like it, you're always welcome back home with us."

"What do you mean?"

"Only that you shouldn't feel you have to prove anything to anyone. Your dad and I wouldn't think anything bad of you."

Seline bites her tongue. Do her parents really think she's so incapable of making a go of this that she'll come running home with her tail between her legs after a day?

"Thanks, Mum. But it's great. I'm really enjoying it."

She's been on the phone for ten minutes or so and feels confident that everyone else will have left and she can sneak out alone, so she says her goodbyes and ends the call.

She gathers her things up and prepares for the long walk back through town and up the hill. She looks out of the staff room window to check if the coast is clear.

The playground below is pretty empty by now. A few kids hang about in groups: some boys kicking a ball near a makeshift goal marked in chalk against a wall; a group of girls on a bench laughing over something they're watching on a phone – including the awful green-haired Julie. They're probably all waiting to be picked up by parents, or enjoying their last few minutes of freedom between school and home; or in Julie's case, plotting some kind of teenage antisocial abomination. Seline dreads what will happen if she crosses the playground alone with that girl down there. She decides she'll just have to wait up here, effectively trapped, until Green Hair leaves.

Then in through the gates roars a car. It's a shabby old dark blue sports number. Seline immediately recognises it as the one that nearly hit her on the road last night, the one Robbie tried to lure her into. The car swings round into the staff car park with a squeal of tyres she can hear even at this distance and pulls to a sudden halt with a screech of brakes.

The commotion gets the attention of the kids in the playground, who stop what they're doing and head towards it. This leaves the way entirely clear for Seline to leave – but instead she squats down by the window, watching intently as Robbie gets out of the car, starts chatting to the boys, pops the bonnet of his vehicle to show them the engine. She can't hear any of what's being said, but she can see he's enjoying showing off to the boys, and that he's flirting completely inappropriately with the girls, none of whom can be any older than fifteen, him swaggering away and them giggling hysterically with each other.

She knows she should go, but for some reason she can't tear herself away. She can't abide seeing Julie and Robbie talking. She could run and hide like she feels she's always done – or she can do something different, take a chance, really do something new.

She sees the boys and girls begin to drift away from the car.

Before she knows it, she snatches up her things, is across the room and crashing out of the staff room door. She races up the corridor and tears down the stairs, crosses the reception area and bursts out through the main door and into the cold playground. She checks that there's no sign of Julie. She slows her step so as not to look like she's running, but walks briskly towards the car. She can see Robbie is moving away, his back towards her. She quickens her pace a little, lengthens her stride and marches towards him until she's within earshot.

"Hey! Excuse me! Hello!"

Robbie turns and waits for her to arrive.

She gets to him and stops. She tries to appear casual, but she can feel herself breathing heavily from the exertion of the run. Robbie just stares at her. She sees his eyes briefly scan up and down, taking her in. Does she look red from hurrying, she wonders. She looks at him too. He's incredibly attractive and she feels shy and tongue-tied, like a teenager fancying a boy at a school dance.

"Yeah?" He doesn't have a clue what she's after. He sounds vaguely annoyed to have been stopped. Whatever he's thinking, he shows absolutely no signs of recognising her from the night before on the road. He's waiting for her to continue and make sense of why she's stopped him.

"I wanted to ask you about the lottery syndicate. What do

I need to do to join?" Seline knows it isn't a great opening, but it's the only thing she can think of that gives her a legitimate opportunity to talk to this man she fancies.

"Oh, right. Well, you can start whenever. Just give me five pounds in the week and I'll pop you on the list. You're new here."

"Yes, I'm Seline, the new art teacher. And you're... Robbie, right?"

"Right."

Seline feels an awkward silence develop.

"Well, like I say, just bung me a fiver in the week and you're good to go. I'm in and out doing bits and pieces most weeks."

"Oh, good. Well... thanks." Seline doesn't know what else to say. She's broken the ice, but hasn't got very far. Fortunately, Robbie picks up the conversation.

"I can text you the numbers if you want. Gimme your phone."

"Oh, right." Seline digs into her coat pocket and pulls out her mobile. She nervously hands it over to Robbie. It seems odd to be giving a complete stranger her phone.

"What's your passcode?"

She doesn't feel comfortable giving him the code to her phone. But he's holding it now, standing there staring at her. She doesn't feel she has an option. "Seven eight one nine two nine."

Robbie punches the number in, scrolls through a couple of her apps, starts typing something. After a moment his own phone rings. He takes out his phone and cancels the call, then hands Seline her mobile back.

"Right. Now you've got my number – and I've got yours."

Seline isn't sure what she expected when she ran down

from the staff room, but things seem to be moving at quite a pace. This strange man has her number. She feels a fizz of excitement. She wonders whether she's foolishly jumped in too fast without thinking. She gives a little shiver, though she's not sure whether it's because she doesn't have her coat on or it's from nervousness. Robbie notices.

"Cold? Where are you headed now?"

"Oh, just back home."

"Right." He just looks at her.

Seline smiles weakly and doesn't know what to say. Why is she so hopeless with boys? Why didn't she practice more when she was younger, so she'd be funny and flirty now, when it matters? She begins to turn away to head off, but before she can, Robbie swings the door of his car open.

"I'll give you a lift."

"Really, it's no bother..." a flustered Seline stutters. Maybe he does fancy her?

"I insist." Robbie stands there, holding the car door open, staring flatly at her. He's not going to take no for an answer.

Seline has no idea what she's doing as she climbs nervously into the strange man's car.

## 8

Seline checks her seat belt is secure as the car swings out of the school and onto the road. She's seen how Robbie drives when he's on his own, like a lunatic, so God alone knows how he'll drive when he has someone else in the car. Maybe he'll calm down with a passenger. Maybe. Though Seline rather suspects that he's the sort who'll show off if he has someone in the car with him, some new girl he's trying to impress.

Robbie threads the car through the town with one hand on the steering wheel and one hand permanently on the gear lever. Seline has only recently passed her driving test, and the correct rules of driving are hard-wired into her brain. Within five minutes Robbie has broken pretty much all of them. He accelerates too hard, brakes too hard, sits within a meter or two of the car in front. He's the sort of bad driver who thinks he's a tremendous driver and everyone else on the road is an idiot, put there to get in his way. There's aggression in every move he makes.

Seline has given Robbie her new address, and he leaves

town that way as he heads up the hill. But after a couple of minutes, he steers hard and unexpectedly off the road and down an even narrower lane that takes them away from their destination.

"Let's show you what this can really do," smirks Robbie. She assumes this is offered as an exciting opportunity, but it feels more like a threat of upsetting incidents to come.

Seline has a sudden flashback to when she was a child of fourteen, taken to an amusement park and onto a roller-coaster which had looked fun and exciting from a distance but, as she approached it, clearly elicited more screams than laughs. Standing in the queue, the anxiety had steadily risen up in her – the horrible anticipation. And by the time she was sitting in its hard wooden seat, strapped in, being trundled slowly upwards with no chance of escape, a wave of cold dread swept over her body. She'd have given anything to go back, to get off, to escape – but it was too late. And that's just how she feels now as Robbie guns the engine and races off even faster. Too late to go back now.

It doesn't take long for Seline to learn she was right about the showing off. Robbie takes the sweeping bends as fast as possible, lessening the impact of the turns by ignoring the white lines dividing the lanes, driving on the left, then the right, then the left. She prays they don't meet someone head-on coming unsuspectingly round a corner. The worn leather sports seats of the car support her as they take the turns, but not enough to prevent her swinging from left to right to left as well. On one particularly tight bend, the rear-view mirror comes flying off and falls into the footwell by Robbie's feet. He leans down, taking his eyes off the road to retrieve it, then jams the stalk of the mirror back in the hole above the windscreen. Christ, if the inside of the car is falling apart like this, maybe the same could be happening to the brakes.

Robbie can no doubt sense her nervousness. She stares fixedly ahead, on high alert for the next car or tree or hedge she's convinced they'll hit, while out of the corner of her eye she can see Robbie occasionally turn and gawp at her, a grin on his face. He accelerates violently, and every now and then she hears the grind of the gears and can smell something in the heat of the car which she guesses must be tyre smoke or the burning clutch. He's reckless, utterly careless, it seems to Seline, of whether he destroys the car, or them, or both.

When they round a particularly sharp left-hand bend she's thrown to her right. She gives a small involuntary cry and puts out her hand to steady herself, but she misses the seat and instead grasps at Robbie's leg. She pulls her hand away immediately. Underneath the fear of the moment, she can't help feeling embarrassment as well, the embarrassment of her hand, high on Robbie's thigh.

The drive carries on like this for some minutes, a heady cocktail of fear and exhilaration, until the car rounds another corner and the road opens out onto a view, one side of a lake. It's getting into the gloom of the early evening now, but the open vista is a relief after the claustrophobia of barrelling down the tight country lanes like a bullet. She can feel the car slowing. Thank Christ.

Robbie yanks the steering wheel one more time and they swing off the road into a lay-by, the tyres throwing up a hammering of gravel against the underside of the car as they skid to a halt.

Seline can't relax immediately. She notices how rigidly she's sitting. Her heart is racing, pumping chemicals around her body and into her brain: adrenaline, dopamine... The fear of the drive gives way to the relief of stopping and she suddenly feels an explosion of endorphins and euphoria. She's convinced she's had a near-death experience and now it seems to her she's never felt so alive. The trees look the greenest green she's ever seen, she's fizzing with excitement.

Before she can move, Robbie undoes his seat belt and leans across towards her. His face is close to hers, he's kissing her, his hand is holding her shoulder, pulling her towards him, grabbing at her breast, his tongue in her mouth. She can't stop him. She doesn't want to stop him. It all feels like the same roller-coaster surge of emotions, fear and excitement and body-tingling hyper-awareness. This is happening. Happening now. She's never felt so alive, and she lets herself go, loses herself, lost, and she's his for the asking.

## 9

After half an hour or so of kissing and groping in a lay-by like teenagers, Seline pulls herself back from the adrenaline rush of this whole encounter and persuades Robbie to drive her back to her digs. But now she's sitting here outside the door, engine idling, she really can't face the idea of going into the strangers' house, her grim pokey room, the vague sadness of it all. It seems so drab and ordinary in comparison to the crazy adventure she's just had.

"You getting out or what?"

"Wait here," she says, opening the car door, running up the path to the house.

And minutes later, she's running back down, slipping into the passenger seat, with a small canvas tote bag on her lap, in which she's hurriedly packed some make-up, her toothbrush, a change of underwear.

"Let's go."

Robbie laughs and without looking at her, slips the car into gear and drives off.

·   ·   ·

AFTER PARKING the car on a broken piece of waste ground behind a row of shops, the two of them walk round to the street and Robbie opens the scratched and dented door next door to a fish and chip shop, its large greasy window misted up from frying. They step into the gloomy hallway, trampling over a mat of junk mail and flyers, and she follows Robbie up the narrow uncarpeted stairs.

The flat itself is equally gloomy, and not much brighter when Robbie flicks on the dull bare bulb in the ceiling, revealing a room of rented tat. There's a three-piece suite that's too large for the space, grey and saggy – the sofa facing an absurdly large television, one fat armchair shoved into a shadowy corner and the other one wedged uncomfortably under the window, like a Japanese commuter crammed into a subway train. A cheap veneered coffee table sits between the sofa and the TV, adorned with an assortment of beer cans, ashtrays and a couple of Happy Fryer takeaway cartons, presumably from the fish shop below.

Robbie takes the bag from Seline's hand and throws it onto one of the chairs, grabs her roughly and starts kissing her again. It's all happening so fast, it's quite surreal, and Seline has the sense of looking down on herself doing all this, so out of character, as if she's watching a completely different person in action. Her face keeps kissing, but out of the corner of her eye she can see her bag on the armchair has fallen over on its side, and a tube of mascara has rolled out and onto the floor. She must remember to pick it up.

He grabs her hand and tugs her through a door off the living room. This is his bedroom. This isn't much more inviting than the room they've just left. The bed is unmade, and the floor around it littered with crumpled clothes, coffee mugs and old copies of *The Racing Post*. A wardrobe stands against the wall, one door missing, revealing a heaving mass of designer leisure-wear clothes. Against the wall by the wardrobe are multiple boxes of trainers, maybe fifty at a guess. The whole place smells vaguely of chip fat. Robbie swings Seline round and pushes her backwards onto the bed. It's incredibly soft and she sinks into it and springs up before wobbling still, like a kid on a bouncy castle. The whole thing is comical somehow and she can't help giving a loud laugh.

"What?" He's smiling but he is clearly confused by the laugh.

"Nothing, don't worry. Come here..." Seline reaches up, takes Robbie's hand and pulls him down onto the bed next to her.

She has no idea why she laughed. Nerves probably. The whole experience is so completely unlike her that she can't take it seriously, like it isn't her doing it. She's here, with a complete stranger, in his utter tip of a flat, about to – who knows what? Have sex, she supposes. Well, she wanted a new start and she's certainly having one of those. It's surprising, and exhilarating, and she decides to throw her usual reserve to the wind and see where the tide takes her.

She's slept with people before, at college, and even had a semi-serious boyfriend for a few months: Jamie, a very intense, sensitive overseas student doing biology. But when he graduated and moved back to Hong Kong to do research, she couldn't find the energy to get involved with anyone else again, couldn't imagine herself going through all the drama and heartache and intense angst-ridden talks, and so threw herself back into her artwork instead.

But with Robbie it's different. It's rough and messy and passionate. He's a fumbling, clumsy lover, but there's something about how driven and consumed by it he is that means she can just let go and be carried where he takes her. It's a bit scary – but the newness of it all is liberating and she feels present and alive. A strange thought comes into her head: that it feels like something a grown-up would do. She feels suddenly grown up. Forty-eight hours ago she could never have predicted that she'd be here.

ROBBIE PULLS on some boxers and a t-shirt. "I'm starving." He kisses her sweetly, gets up and wanders out of the room, to the kitchen she assumes. She sits up in the bed and pulls the crumpled duvet over herself to cover her nakedness against the chill of the flat, leans back against the wall where the bed might be expected to have a headboard but doesn't. She can hear him running a tap, opening and closing cupboards, the rustling of some food packet or other. She absorbs the thrill of the situation, lying in her lover's bed while he moves about the flat.

After a while, Robbie comes back in with a couple of bowls and hands her one and a fork. He's made some kind of pasta concoction. A heap of limp greasy pasta, wilting tubes loaded with flakes of tinned tuna in a thin, oily sauce – maybe just the oil from the pasta tin – covered with a handful of grated cheddar cheese. He sits on the end of the bed, shovelling it in.

Now the frenetic madness of the driving and the sex are over, Robbie seems calmer. He no longer feels he has to show off, and he's sweet. Seline watches him while he eats. He's handsome, with an almost pretty boyish face. His tousled hair and stubble give him a rakish quality. His eyes twinkle and he has a natural, winning smile. Yes, she definitely fancies him. Seline feels herself calming down too, feels quite relaxed despite the unfamiliarity of the situation.

While they eat, they begin to chat. There's an ease between them. Robbie is twenty-eight. He has lived in the village all his life. He has siblings who sound a bit rough, all of whom have moved away, apart from his older brother, who died. She puts her plate down, wraps the duvet around her and shuffles over to him, gives him a sympathetic hug, lays her head in his lap. He doesn't say much about his parents and Seline can't work out whether they still live here in the village, whether they're alive even, but something in the way he talks about them makes her feel it's better not to ask. He strokes her hair tenderly as he talks. He went to St. Oswald's school himself when he was a kid; or rather, he attended when it suited him. She gets the feeling that school lost his interest and he pulled away from it as early as possible. He left when he was fifteen – she wonders whether kids can legally do this, but Robbie did apparently – and started working on a few jobs here and there. Robbie's not at all ashamed about leaving school; the way he tells it, all the other idiot kids were stuck getting bored for nothing while he was out earning money.

Seline needs the loo. She feels suddenly awkward about being naked and wonders if she can pull on her underwear to get up and go to the bathroom, but she doesn't know how to do it without looking self-conscious. She decides to brazen it out and just get up, pretending to be more at ease with her nakedness than she actually is. She can feel him admiring her as she leaves the room, which gives her a boost of confidence.

"End of the passage," he calls after her from the bedroom.

She walks briskly up the chill corridor, pausing briefly to peek in the kitchen. The light is off, but the streetlight comes in through the window, throwing a diagonal floodlight across the sink, piled high with greasy dishes and mugs, the volcano of a bin erupting rubbish onto the floor.

She grasps the bathroom door handle and turns it, but it's stiff and she can't get the door open. She tries again; maybe there's a knack to it. But no, she just can't seem to shift it. How embarrassing. She stands there, completely nude in a relative stranger's hallway, feeling like a fool, and really needing to pee! She rattles the handle again, but it's definitely not budging.

She can't just stand here forever.

"Robbie?"

"Hmm?"

"I can't get in the bathroom." She giggles.

"Christ!" He's amused. "Hang on…"

With the clank of a spring she hears him shift on the bed. Robbie appears at the bedroom door to see what she's up to.

"Not that one!" he roars. He leaps from the bedroom and races down the passageway at such a pace it surprises her. She instinctively steps back against the wall, almost as if she's back on the road and he's charging at her in his car. He grabs the door handle she was trying and rattles it violently – but she can tell he's checking it is still locked rather than trying to open it.

"*That* one." Robbie gestures at another door off to the side, masked slightly by a large black puffer jacket on a hook. He puffs out a breath, calms down. He stares at her flatly.

Seline pushes this second door and goes into the bathroom. She moves the doorstop, an old football trophy Robbie must have won at school or in some Sunday pub league, and closes the creaky door. She pees and flushes the toilet. She runs the tap in the sink, puts the toilet lid down and sits, wondering what has just happened, how the mood has suddenly shifted.

It brings her back to reality, like a drunk suddenly sobering up in the cold air. What is she doing? How has she found herself in this man's flat? Why has she gone off on this wild encounter with a stranger? And why did he bark at her like that? The sense of being worried by him, just like she was on the road, begins to rise in her again. There was a flash of something then, in his voice, in his eyes... a flash of something dangerous.

And what the hell has he got in that locked room he's so twitchy about?

## 10

The following morning Seline rose quietly, tiptoed out of the bedroom with her clothes bundled under her arm and got dressed in the living room so as not to wake Robbie, who lay sprawled and unconscious on the dishevelled bed. She couldn't face the mildewed bathroom, so snuck out of the flat, down the stairs and onto the street, then made the twenty-minute walk to school, navigating by the flag on the top of St. Oswald's church in the distance. Once at the school, she nipped into the staff toilets, washed her face and cleaned her teeth. She hoped no one would spot she was wearing yesterday's clothes. Yet at the same time, she felt ludicrously excited to be carrying around such a secret.

That was Tuesday.

Today is Friday – and there has been no sign of Robbie or contact from him since. Not hearing from him has made her nervous and agitated, like a teenager, and the thought of how attracted she is to him has grown in her mind with the torturously slow passing of each unbearable hour. On occasions through the week, Seline has reached for her phone, thrilled to hear it vibrate in her bag or pocket, only to discover she's imagined it. Once or twice she's looked at his number, which he typed into her contacts list that time in the playground, but she decides not to ring him, not wanting to mess things up by seeming over-keen. Can he really have dropped her so easily? The thought of it lodges like an ache in the pit of her stomach. Every lunchtime she goes to the canteen and pokes food around her plate with her fork, but she can't bring herself to eat.

Annoyed with herself for being so feeble about it all, Seline resolves to do something constructive instead, and occupies her time with her painting. At the end of the school day, once all the pupils have left and the staff have drifted home, she goes back down into her classroom to work on her art. She hasn't managed to get her hands on any canvasses yet, or her usual oils, which she has ordered and will arrive next week. So for now she sets up an area for herself in the print room and makes a series of preliminary charcoal drawings for later paintings. On the first evening, she was interrupted by a rather surly security guard, questioning why she was still in the building when everyone else had left. But once they'd got chatting he softened, introduced himself as Dave, and said it was fine for her to stay, and that he'd come and unlock for her when she's finished.

Drawing calms her immediately, makes her feel herself again. As always, her work depicts female figures, often alone in quiet meditation in their own domestic spaces. She's drawn these figures for so long now that she can do it almost without thinking. Indeed, she loves the feeling of letting her brain switch off and her hand take over, almost surprised by what emerges on the paper, as if it's not her doing it at all, that she's a witness to someone else's drawing.

She works fast and fluidly and has built up quite a few drawings across the week so far – successfully distracting herself from thinking about Robbie. So at least she has him to thank for that.

As she stands at the tea station, checking her phone for the umpteenth time that morning, Graham comes into the staff room. She hasn't spoken to him since her awkward rant earlier in the week about his disruptive daughter Julie. The incident has played on her mind because she desperately needs to have a successful time teaching here and doesn't want there to be any bad blood that gets in the way. She knows what she's like – she can't just put it behind her, and knows that her worry about what he thinks of her will lodge in her brain and grow until it gets in the way of everything. Rather than let it fester over the weekend, Seline decides to bite the bullet and do something about it.

"Graham? Can I have a word?" She's gone over to where he's sitting in the corner, his head down in a pile of marking, a book open on a page which appears to contain more of his angry red-scrawled comments than it does student writing.

"Yes?" He looks up at her quizzically over the rim of his glasses.

She sits down next to him.

"Look, I just wanted to clear the air about all that stuff with your daughter. It was my first day and I was in a bit of a state and I said a load of stuff I shouldn't have said. I'm sorry."

"That's fine."

"I had no idea she was your daughter, and I didn't mean to offend you. As I say, I'm sorry."

Graham properly turns to her from his work. He regards her full-on. She's expecting him to push back at her, but he looks at her kindly.

"Really, it's fine. Kids can be proper shits if they see an opportunity with a new teacher. They're like the velociraptors in Jurassic Park, testing the electric fences for signs of weakness."

Seline laughs.

"As for Julie, you didn't say anything that every other teacher here hasn't said about her before, or that I haven't thought pretty much every day for the last fifteen years."

"Okay. Thanks." She gets up to leave, relieved to have got any ill-will out of the way.

"Seline?"

"Yes?"

"You'll be okay, you know. You will. Just give it time."

"Thanks, Graham."


By the time Seline gets to her classroom there's the usual bunch of noisy chattering kids outside, but she's feeling much better about everything, so she decides to let their yabbering pass without comment.

"Is that your boyfriend, Miss?"

"Sorry?"

"Your boyfriend's here!" A grinning ginger boy indicates the classroom with his thumb. Hysterical laughter erupts from the rest of the children.

Seline looks into the class through the window in the door. She's thrilled to see Robbie's in there, sitting on the edge of the desk. She tries to gather her thoughts, checks her watch – it's noon, the middle of the school day; she should be teaching.

"Wait here – quietly." Seline enters the classroom, choosing to ignore the loud chorus of provocative *ooohs* as she does so.

Robbie hears her come in and stands to face her. He beams his cheeky grin. She feels herself melt, but tries to hold it together. She wants to grab hold of him, but doesn't.

"What are you doing here? I have a lesson!"

"Just came to say sorry for not ringing. I've been busy. I've wanted to see you. Here."

He picks up a bunch of flowers from the desk and offers them to her. They look like he's stolen them from someone's garden, or off a grave. Nonetheless, she's inordinately touched by the gesture. He hadn't struck her as the sort who'd ever think to give a girl flowers.

"Thanks. They're lovely. But you have to go now."

Could she grab him? Are the kids watching from the hallway? Could she touch his arm without them seeing?

"Also, I wanted to say I'm sorry for yelling at you at the flat. That room – it's where I keep my brother's stuff. I don't like people to go in there. But I really shouldn't have shouted."

She feels a surge of relief. It makes complete sense he'd get upset if someone was messing with his dead brother's things.

"I'm sorry, that's my fault. And it's so sweet of you to say that, and to come here. But you really have to go now."

"I know. I'll see you later? Pick you up after work?"

"Oh yes, that would be lovely. See you later."

He leans in and kisses her. She can hear the riot of noise from the kids watching this through the window in the door, but she doesn't care.

She watches Robbie walk out past her giggling class, hides her flowers under her desk, then ushers them in.

The kids make jokes about Robbie for a while, but soon get bored and settle down to their work. But Seline doesn't settle down. For the whole lesson she's distracted. She can't stop thinking about Robbie, about that kiss, can't stop thinking about the flowers under her desk, and about seeing him later.

She had been afraid that her surprising adventure with Robbie was over – but it seems Robbie hasn't finished with her yet.

ONCE THE FINAL bell of the day has rung, Seline sits in the staff room pretending to make some notes towards lesson plans. In reality, she's waiting for everyone to go before she goes out to meet Robbie – she really doesn't want anyone knowing her business, knowing that she's seeing him. It was bad enough that class of kids saw him in her room; she can't imagine what her colleagues will think of her if they learn she's started some fling with him in her first week. She's struggling to appear professional as it is without that. And in any case, there's something unimaginably exciting about having this thrilling secret to herself.

People wish each other a nice weekend and drift away. At last, it's just her. She grabs her things and heads out of the staff room and back down to her class to get her bag and computer. The sun won't be setting for a good while yet, but it's one of those horribly overcast autumn days when it never gets properly light and you know the summer is over for good. The lights are on in all the corridors, but as she wasn't teaching for the last hour of the day, Seline's class is in relative darkness. She walks in briskly, not bothering to flick on the light switch, as she only has to grab her bag from her desk. She picks up her things – and then notices that the door to the print room is open a chink and the light is on. She knows she didn't put the light on in there this afternoon, and that she closed the door when she left.

Someone has been in there.

Seline crosses the gloomy classroom and pushes the print room door open slowly. By contrast, the light is bright and hard in here and makes her squint a little now her eyes have adjusted to the darkness of the main classroom. The room is empty. The long worktable in the centre of the room is scattered with sheets of A2 and A3 drawing paper. The paper is blank but for smudges of charcoal fingerprints, and Seline knows what they are immediately – her drawings.

She turns the pages over slowly, one by one. Yes, these are the drawings she has been doing through the week, of various figures in a variety of poses – except that now the faces of the figures have been scribbled on crudely in black marker pen, faces crossed out, eyes scrawled on to make two sightless pits staring blindly up in anguish from the paper. Other drawings have been ripped in half. One of them, a large study of a head, has been torn down one side so that the face is now missing an ear.

This isn't casual or accidental damage. This is brutal, violent, sadistic. It's more than vandalism. Seline feels like she's been attacked personally, like this attack on the figures in her work is effectively an attack on herself. This is her art, where she pours out the deepest, most secret part of herself – and now that has been assaulted, violated.

Whoever has done this must truly hate her.

## 11

_____

Robbie is waiting in his car in the staff car park when Seline comes out of the school. She gets in and buckles up, anticipating his usual wild driving, but as they move off she notes with surprise that he's driving very sedately. Maybe he no longer feels the need to show off to her. She remembers she's forgotten the flowers Robbie brought her. Damn.

She can't contain the agitation she's feeling. She starts to tell him all about what has happened to her drawings, on the verge of tears, the awfulness of it spilling out of her. To her relief, he is sympathetic and comforting, putting his hand on her leg as he drives. She talks to him about leaving Manchester, how closeted away she's felt up to this point, the pressure she feels she's under to succeed, to show her parents she can make it on her own in the outside world. She hasn't realised quite how much pressure she feels until she starts saying it out loud. Just telling him about it seems to release the pressure valve somehow, as it all floods out. She starts to feel better as she talks, distracted from her concern by the pleasurable weight of his hand moving on and off her thigh between gear changes.

After five minutes she realises she has no idea where they are going – certainly not to Robbie's flat or back to her digs. They're on a road she doesn't recognise, and Robbie hasn't told her where they're headed. They slip into silence.

She doesn't bother to ask where they're going. She's actually glad of the drive and the silence, as it gives her a chance to process her eventful first week of teaching and everything that has happened. She knew it might be tough, but she hadn't anticipated being threatened by a student on her first day! Or having her personal belongings vandalised. Who could have done it? She's certain that girl Julie threatened to cut her ear off – and then one of the destroyed drawings had an ear ripped off – but is that too obvious? Maybe Graham was pretending to be nice to her and he did it after she'd insulted his daughter and thrown him out of his old classroom. But that's absurd, and anyway, he hardly seems the sort.

She'd rather know who it was. That would be better than this – knowing there's someone out there who has targeted her. She should probably go and see Mrs Jessop about it – but the Head has been so cold to her all week, Seline doesn't feel she will get any real support there. She goes over and over it in her mind and can feel the anxiety welling up in her again.

Robbie must feel her tense up. He gives her leg a firmer squeeze. "If I find out who did that to your drawings, I'll fucking kill them."

It's supposed to be reassuring, but it's actually unnerving. There's something in his tone that makes her sure this isn't just a figure of speech. He means it.

After about twenty minutes the car pulls off the main road towards a village – Seline doesn't know what it's called as they've turned before she can see the road sign. They drive for a mile or so further and then pull into a completely empty pub car park. The Black Swan.

Robbie switches the engine off. "Drink?" He's smiley and breezy again. "Sounds like you need one after the shit day you've had."

He's a strange one, she thinks. He seems a bit of a rough diamond, but then he comes up with these little romantic gestures. The flowers. This pub. She can't quite figure him out.

They get out and go inside.

She's assumed they've driven out of town because this is a particularly lovely place for a drink, but when they enter the pub Seline is struck by its ordinariness. It's a drab room that has seen better days. It doesn't look like it's been decorated in living memory. The walls are a yellowy cream that falls halfway between a paint shade and the nicotine staining from when smoking inside was allowed. The patterned carpet somehow manages to be gaudy and depressing at the same time, with a threadbare track worn from the door they've just entered to the bar.

Robbie gestures towards the table in a murky corner, indicating that Seline should sit down. "What do you want?"

"White wine, please." She takes in more of the room. "Er, actually, gin and tonic might be a safer bet."

Robbie heads to the bar, where a shabby-looking balding man sits on a bar stool reading a newspaper. The man gets up, goes around behind the bar and takes Robbie's order. Seline occupies herself by trying to de-wobble the table with a folded beer mat. In this corner of the room there's a vague smell of urine from the toilets. Robbie returns with a gin and tonic and a pint of lager for himself.

"Sorry this place is a bit shit. I wanted to take you for a drink, but I've got to do a bit of business."

He sits down, takes his phone out and begins texting. "Just got to see a man about a dog." His face clouds over as he taps away for some time, his stern face illuminated by his screen.

Once he's finished sending his text, Robbie puts his phone down on the table and gives her his full attention. His face lights up immediately. When she first saw him, she thought he had the most captivating natural charm – but now she can see that it's something he switches in and out of, like someone going into a darkened room and switching all the lights on. But she's happy to be here with him now, and looking forward to their drink together – their first proper date.

"So then, Miss, here's to your first week teaching."

They chink glasses.

"Other than the vandalism and the casual threats of violence, how's it been?"

"Honestly?" Seline gives a pained laugh. "Awful!"

She gulps down a mouthful of drink and begins to unload more about her week: her miserable rented room; the Head suggesting she's got the job through some kind of favour for someone; her run-in with Julie; her overwhelming sense of impostor syndrome and the feeling she's not really cutting it as a teacher. Even though the stuff she's talking about is upsetting, it feels good to be telling someone about it. To be telling Robbie about it.

"It has had its nicer moments as well," she says flirtatiously, remembering the two of them curled up in his bed.

While she's talking, Robbie's phone lights up with an incoming text. He reads it and stands up.

"Sorry, sweetheart. Won't be a minute. Get us another one. I'll be right back." And he's gone out of the door.

Seline sips her drink, feeling awkward that she's been abandoned and is the only person in the room now, apart from the balding barman – though he's returned to his stool with his back to her, paying her no heed whatsoever, nose buried in his paper. Once she's finished her drink Seline goes over, orders another for herself and a pint for Robbie, takes them back to the table. There's a window near her table and before she sits down she can see out to the car park, where a white car has pulled up directly next to Robbie's car. The boots of both cars are open, and Robbie and the other driver must be standing behind them, obscured from her view. It's cold out there. What sort of business can Robbie be doing in the carpark of a pub in the middle of nowhere? She stands watching for as long as she can before it feels odd, then she sits down.

It's about ten minutes before Robbie comes back. He stands at the table and downs his pint in one.

"It's a bit dead in here, isn't it?" he says breezily. "Come on. Let's go."

Once they're in the car and driving back towards town, Robbie's returned to his old self, hurling the car full-pelt around the bends, chatting away non-stop, joking, telling anecdotes about his own school experiences and making Seline feel better about her week.

It's odd. Even while she's laughing, she can't help the growing feeling that he's like two completely different people – the charming, gregarious guy she fancies, and this darker, secretive, rather dangerous figure. It makes her wonder something about herself too: whether the dangerous side is one of the reasons she finds him so attractive.

As they're approaching town, Robbie stops talking and starts paying closer attention to his driving. At first, Seline thinks he must have noticed her clinging onto the edge of her seat, and is slowing down for her sake. But then she realises he's not looking at her at all – he's flicking his eyes constantly between the road ahead and his rear-view mirror. Without turning round, Seline can tell there's now a car behind them, because its headlights are hitting the mirror and lighting up Robbie's impassive face.

Without indicating, Robbie turns left onto a narrow track and slows the car to a stop. Seline's not sure what's happening. They wait in silence for a few seconds until the car that was behind them carries on along the road into town.

Robbie pipes up casually, "There's another nice pub down this way, but actually it's a bit of a trot, so let's not go there."

He reverses back onto the road and keeps driving the way they were heading, staying at a steady pace. Seline isn't sure what's just happened. Did he think he was being followed? *Was* he being followed? Or did he really just want to go to another pub and then change his mind?

Robbie drives in a conservative manner all the way back to town and to his flat. He parks up on the waste ground round the back.

"I'm hungry, actually. Okay if we don't go for that drink?"

He hasn't even asked Seline – just presumed that his flat is where they're going to end up. She likes the fact he assumes they have that kind of relationship, so she just goes with the flow.

When they're in the flat, Robbie takes her straight into

the bedroom, but to her surprise he doesn't pounce on her immediately. Instead he shows her the scrappy flat-pack chest of drawers against the wall. He opens the bottom drawer. It's empty.

"I thought you might want to leave some stuff here. For if you stay over."

They've only hung out twice, but she's relieved that he can feel it too, the possibility that there might be something going on between them, that she might be a regular visitor here. It's just a flat-pack drawer, but it feels like it could be the beginning of something. She kisses him passionately. He kisses her too, then steps back.

"You sort yourself in here. I'll just be a minute." He smiles at her sweetly and leaves the room.

She hears him walk down the corridor and assumes he's going to the bathroom, but then she hears him go out of the front door. His footsteps fade as he goes down the stairs and onto the street.

Why has he brought her home and immediately gone out? That's weird. If he was going out for something, why didn't he say? That business on the drive back has made her nervous. Something doesn't feel right. Or maybe she's just on edge and being paranoid. Maybe he just went out for fish and chips from downstairs.

She isn't sure what to do now. She doesn't have anything with her to put in her drawer, so she sits on the bed and waits. After a couple of minutes, she hears him coming up the stairs again, then through the front door, which he closes. She hears the bathroom door creak closed. Then she hears a key in a lock. Is he locking the front door? She gets up and creeps to the bedroom door, presses her eye close to where the door hinges against the wall, looking down the passage through the chink between the door and the architrave.

No. He's unlocking the locked door. The one he got so weird about her touching.

He's brought something upstairs and is now taking it into the locked room. But if that's the room where he keeps the stuff that belonged to his dead brother, what would he be taking in there? And where did it come from? The boot of his car maybe?

After a minute or so he comes back out into the passage and locks the door. Seline steps back and moves as quietly as she can back to sit on the bed. She doesn't want him to know she's been spying on him.

The bathroom door creaks again. He must be going to the loo. She thinks about getting up to sneak another look, but he's suddenly at the doorway.

"Right. Dinner. What do you fancy?" His beaming face is poking round the door again, like everything's normal, like he hasn't been up to anything remotely suspicious, like all this behaviour is completely normal.

He didn't go for fish and chips anyway. So what *was* he up to?

## 12

She goes back to her digs for about fifteen minutes all weekend, and that only to run upstairs and past the twins' bedroom to throw a few things into a bag, before coming down again to where Robbie is waiting, bumped up on the kerb outside the house, engine still running. Robbie simply proceeds on the absolute assumption that Seline will be doing everything with him, staying at his, and she finds herself caught up in the momentum of it all, drunk on the excitement of this bewitching new relationship, somehow powerless to resist his charms, whatever nagging doubts she may have about him.

On Saturday night they stay in with a takeaway from downstairs and watch the lottery draw live, Seline on her phone checking the numbers Robbie has texted everyone in the syndicate earlier that day. No winning lines whatsoever. Seline has never played the lottery before and is surprised by the feeling of disappointment she has at not winning, as if becoming a millionaire has been stolen away from her. Robbie on the other hand seems delighted that no one in the school has won anything, as if their bad luck reflects more favourably on his own lowly fortunes.

And there's sex, of course. It's wild and exciting and Seline lets herself be carried away in the moment, finding it liberating to give in to wherever Robbie leads her. The fact that she's been so abandoned with him makes her slightly shy afterwards, lying nude in the bed of a relative stranger. She tries to look as casual as possible as she pulls the covers around her to hide her nakedness, but sometimes Robbie notices and tugs the covers away, or asks her to let them go so he can look at her.

"What are you being shy for? You're beautiful. Here—"

He reaches for his phone and begins to take photos of her. She is shy at first, and can't take the whole thing seriously, but as he tells her how sexy she looks, she begins to feel more confident and starts striking poses she remembers from pretty girls she's seen on Instagram. The two of them giggle together as her posturing becomes more confident and outrageous and she starts to ham it up. It's silly, and the fun they're having makes her more relaxed and playful.

"See." He shows her some of the photographs he's taken. "Proper gorgeous."

She looks at the photos and begins to see herself how he sees her. She starts to really enjoy the way he looks at her. She feels sexy.

Though they have a lot of fun throughout the weekend, whenever she goes to the bathroom, she can't help casting a look at the locked room and wondering what is hidden in there that Robbie hasn't been entirely honest about. But she reminds herself that she's probably just worrying about nothing, that her uneasiness is a natural result of leaving Manchester and coming here to step out of her comfort zone. That the unpredictable rush of everything she's experiencing is exactly the reason she took the risk of leaving home, and she should embrace it.

Through the next couple of weeks she stays almost every night at Robbie's. She brings more of her clothes round and crams them into the drawer he's allocated for her. She doesn't trust the look of his ancient washing machine, fearing it may leave the clothes dirtier than they were when she put them in, so on a couple of occasions she goes back to her digs and cheekily does a couple of loads of washing before leaving again, always trying to sneak in and out without anyone seeing her. Mary doesn't say anything about her comings and goings, but Seline can imagine what she thinks. Ah well, it's easy money for them anyway, renting a room that never gets used by someone who's never there.

It's not just the washing machine she's wary of. Seline shares the same scepticism about Robbie's grimy bathroom. She's started going into school early and using the showers next to the gymnasium. Sometimes Dave the security guard, the one who was sniffy about her staying late to paint, sees her early in the morning as he's finishing his shift. Then he often sees her working late in her art room when he's starting his evening shift again.

She begins to settle into a rhythm at school. She still feels anxious when she thinks about her drawings being vandalised, but nothing like it has happened since – and when she thinks of some of the horror stories people told on her teacher training course, she puts it down to the sort of stupid thing some kids get up to in schools.

She has no option but to use Robbie's bathroom last thing at night, frequently without putting the light on so she doesn't have to see the full squalor, and once stubbing her toe so hard on that stupid football trophy doorstop that her nail comes up all tender and black. She can't abide the idea of her toothbrush sitting in the room all day and night on the sill pock-marked with black mould, next to the mildew-ridden window running with condensation – so she buys a massive supply of cheap toothbrushes, all the same colour, and hides them at the back of her drawer. Every time she cleans her teeth at night she opens a new toothbrush and hides the old one in her work bag, taking it into school to throw it away there.

She doesn't want Robbie to notice, to think she's judging him. He can be very thin-skinned, very changeable. On one occasion when he spots her coming in with a lot of cleaning products he blows up at her and accuses her of disrespecting him and suggesting he's a dirty slob. She's taken aback by how fast he flares up over something so trivial. But after half an hour of sulking he's back to normal, and is full of apologies and hugs and kisses.

The longer she spends with Robbie, the more she notices a change in him. She tells herself it's the inevitable cooling of a honeymoon period – though the cooling is happening quicker than she expects it should. He stops commenting on her cleaning, and she assumes it's because he'd probably rather have the place clean as well but can't be bothered to do it himself.

Robbie doesn't seem to operate by any kind of regular timetable. He's often sending or receiving texts at odd hours and needing to go out suddenly. She notices that he's sometimes using a different phone – she's spotted three different phones he uses so far. He apologises for his absences but doesn't ever say who's calling when he gets these messages, and disappears off at any hour, without saying where he's going or when he'll be back. Once or twice in the early stages, Seline asks when he plans to come home, but he's quite short with her and she doesn't ask again.

They still have fun times, go out on dates, he's still funny and rakishly charming and she still fancies him like crazy. But around the flat he's prone to dramatic switches of mood. Maybe it was a mistake, moving in here so fast. Dating is exciting, but there's something about living together that brings in an element of domestic ordinariness, exposed to each other in the boring bits of life that live in between the exciting bits. She reasons with herself that it's inevitable people stop making such an effort with each other, start taking each other a little for granted. Plus, whenever he loses his temper or becomes surly and uncommunicative, he eventually calms down and apologises, and wins her over again. She vows to make a bit more effort herself, and thinks that might create the right atmosphere for Robbie to do so too.


IT'S ANOTHER DULL, rainy Wednesday evening and Seline's sitting in the gloom of Robbie's flat. He's only been home for ten minutes before one of his phones rings. Seline can hear him mumbling indistinctly in the bathroom, before he bursts into the room and gathers her up in a hug.

"Sorry, sweetheart, duty calls. I have to go out again. See you soon."

That was two hours ago.

She fills a bit of the time by giving her mum a call, as she does every few days. She usually overplays how well she's doing at school, how comfortably she's settled in. It's true that things have calmed down and fallen into a decent routine with her teaching. Her lessons are going okay, and she's carefully given Green Hair a wide berth, so there have been no more awkward confrontations. But Seline's sure she can always detect a note of anxiety in her mum's voice, the sense her mum assumes things can't be going entirely well, which makes Seline exaggerate what a success she's making of everything. She hasn't told her mum anything about Robbie, because she's sure she'll worry at this distance. Maybe she'll tell her all about it when she goes home at half term. Maybe.

She ends the call. Not knowing when Robbie's coming back, Seline gives in to the pangs of hunger and decides to make some food. It's too wet to go out to shop, the rain hammering off the kitchen window like a car wash. She could just about make it to the chip shop below, but she can't face fish and chips again as it's what they seem to eat every other day.

It would be lovely to make them a romantic dinner. She opens the fridge and cupboards, pokes about pessimistically looking for food she suspects won't be there. After a thorough search, she's made a sad pile of things on the work surface: a withered onion; half a pack of butter; a sachet of easy-cook savoury rice; a lump of cheddar cheese so old its surface is cracked like a dry river bed; an old takeaway box containing some wild mushrooms; a stock cube. She figures this could work; she can make a bastardised risotto with what she has.

She takes her time cooking, sweating off the onions, chopping the mushrooms into rustic chunks and frying them in butter, boiling the kettle and dissolving the stock cube, stirring it into the packet of rice. She's pleased with how it smells. While the food cooks, she scrabbles about in the cupboard under the sink, finds a couple of old candles and sets the table up as well as she can for a romantic dinner for two.

Even though she dawdles and drags the task out, by the time it's ready there is still no sign of Robbie. She waits as long as she can, until the risotto is barely tepid, then spoons half of it into a bowl for herself and puts a lid on the saucepan with the rest, in case Robbie's hungry when he gets back.

She sits at the table, forking in mouthfuls of risotto and feeling rather pleased with how tasty it has turned out. She hopes Robbie will be back soon, and that he hasn't eaten while he's out. She can warm his up again in the pan.

IT'S BEEN HALF an hour since she finished eating – and still no Robbie. She's used to him disappearing like this, but for some reason this evening is different. Maybe it's because she's made such an effort with the food, has been feeling romantic and loving, and looking forward to seeing him. She's been sitting at this table for hours now, thinking about nothing else, and her head is beginning to throb from the stress of it all. She stares down at the table in front of her, at a single grain of rice that has fallen from her plate, coated in its artificially yellow sauce. The darkness of the evening has properly set in, but she hasn't turned the ceiling light on, or lit the candles, so the room is illuminated by the artificial glow of the streetlight coming in through the kitchen window, giving everything an otherworldly brilliance. The light is refracted through the rain on the window, cascading across the kitchen like a nightclub glitterball. The grain of rice seems to shine with an internal vibrancy, giving the kitchen an ethereal quality.

Seline traces her fingertips along the worn countertop. She's hyper-aware of this space, the cold, hard surface, and suddenly has the dispiriting sense she's made an awful mistake being here, that she's trapped in a prison cell. Her skin prickles with goosebumps. The smell of the risotto combines with the ubiquitous odour of chip-fat, ashtrays and beer cans, like some horrible perfume. She can hardly breathe it is so overwhelming.

It dawns on her that the silence of the room isn't silence at all. The rain drumming on the window, the ticking of her watch, the incessant hum of the fridge compressor fill her muddled head so that she can't think straight. *Tick tick tick.*

Her thoughts begin to wander, taking unexpected turns and tangents. She doesn't know what she's thinking. Ideas, memories, and emotions tumble over each other, creating a swirling tapestry. *Tick tick tick.* Time itself becomes elastic. She has the sense she's been sitting in this room for her whole life, waiting.

*Tick tick tick.* There's something else in the symphony of noises. She gets up sleepily and drifts from the kitchen into the dark passageway, towards where the noise is coming from.

There it is again. Scratching and whispering. In the darkness. Like a creature waiting by the front door.

The room. The locked room. The noise is coming from inside the locked room.

Seline rushes up the corridor and presses her ear against the door. She can hear movement, like something heavy being dragged slowly across the floor. Scratching against the door, like an animal pleading to be let out. And whispering –

quiet, urgent, unintelligible. She presses her eye to the keyhole and can see light inside, moving light, like an aurora borealis trapped in a box. And something else. Some other movement.

A person.

Christ.

Oh Christ. He's got someone locked in there!

# 13

eline starts yelling, hammering at the door. There's someone trapped in that room and she has to get them out. She knows there's something not right with Robbie – but she never expected this! She can still hear them whispering, sounding terribly weak. How long have they been in there? She pushes desperately – but the door is heavy and thick and the lock won't budge. She attempts to barge the door with her shoulder, but she can't shift it.

She runs to the kitchen, grabs a chair, and runs back down the dark passage. She starts to slam the chair against the door, trying to break it down. One of the thin tubular legs of the chair bends and folds against the door. She swings the chair again with all her strength, gives another thump. A corner of the plywood seat cracks off. The door doesn't budge.

The passageway explodes into light.

It's Robbie!

He's come in through the front door, flicked the light on, and is staring agog at Seline, who stands stock-still with the damaged chair above her head, ready to strike the door again. Robbie launches himself at her and she goes to swing the chair at him, to defend herself, but he's grabbed her before she has the chance. He pushes her with incredible force up the corridor and she stumbles backwards, falling heavily and painfully onto her back. The chair she's still holding comes down after her and catches her a painful blow above the left eye.

Robbie ignores her and grabs the door handle of the locked room. He must be checking whether the person inside has escaped or is still captive. He rattles the handle violently a few times and leans his weight against the door. Once he's confident it's secure, he turns towards Seline, thunders towards her and hauls her roughly from the ground, crushing her shoulder and pinching her skin so hard she yells out in pain.

"What the fuck are you doing with that room!?" He kicks the chair away from her, pushes her so hard that she stumbles backwards and into the kitchen. It's only the fact that she crashes into the kitchen table that stops her falling to the floor again. The edge of it stabs her hard in the back.

Her senses are on overload. Robbie's kidnapped someone, now she's found out, and he's furious. She's in terrible danger. She can feel blood trickling down her forehead from where the chair hit her. From the fury in Robbie's eyes, he's about to do a lot worse.

Her eyes dart round the room for something she can use to defend herself: the risotto pan on the stove; the knife she used to chop the mushrooms! Robbie's eyes follow her eyeline. She launches herself across the room and grabs the knife – but he's moved fast too, grabs her wrist. She tries to twist away from him as they struggle, knocking the chopping board from the work surface, sending the onion skin and the remains of the mushrooms in the takeaway carton skittering across the floor. Her wrist stabs in excruciating pain as he bends it back violently and she hears something crack, which she thinks must be her wrist breaking, before she realises it is the sound of the knife hitting the floor.

Robbie grabs her hair and holds her at a distance while he leans down to pick up the knife. Her scalp burns as he clenches a handful of her hair roughly in his fist. He holds her still while he looks at the mess on the floor.

"What have you done with them mushrooms?"

He follows her gaze to the pan on the stove. What's he thinking? Is he planning to hit her with it, cave her skull in, kill her here and now in his kitchen? He's got hold of her wrist again. It hurts so much she thinks she might faint. He stands there, thinking, like some kind of mad doctor taking her pulse.

After a moment he rights a chair that has been knocked over in the scuffle, sits her down hard on it and leans in close to her face. "Wait here."

She's terrified. She can see out of the corner of her eye that he's still holding the knife. Now isn't the time to cross him. She sits tight as he leaves the kitchen. She touches her fingers to her stinging forehead where the chair hit her and feels a lump already forming. She looks at her fingers. Blood.

She can hear him at the end of the passage. She thinks he's going to the bathroom and wonders if she can make a run for it through the front door, but then she hears him putting his key in the lock and opening the room. She listens hard for voices. Whatever monstrous thing he's doing to the person inside, he's doing it quietly. Seline couldn't run if she wanted to – she's frozen to the chair in fear.

After a second he comes out, locking up again. He comes back into the kitchen, picks up another chair and swings it around to face hers. He sits down and leans in close to her face. Seline recoils, terrified of what he's about to do to her. He puts the knife down on the table – out of her reach, but thankfully no longer in his hand. When he eventually speaks, all traces of anger in him have gone. He's surprisingly soft and calm.

"You've taken magic mushrooms. Too many. You're having a bad trip. You're freaked out now, but you're going to be okay. I'll look after you."

She tries to process what he's saying. She feels like she's spinning, like the room is spinning and she's spinning with it. She doesn't know what to think.

"Here. Drink this." He's got up and crossed back from the sink with a large glass of water. She takes it from him and drinks, large gulping mouthfuls. The dryness in her mouth gives way to a wave of nausea.

"Who have you got in that room?"

He ignores her question, holds his hand out. "Take these." He puts a couple of tablets into her hand. She doesn't recognise the shape of them – they're not paracetamol or aspirin or any tablets she's seen before.

"What are they?"

"Don't worry about that. They'll help." His tone is unbelievably reassuring. He's not threatening her or hurting her. He's looking after her. She can already feel her agitation subsiding. Without thinking, she takes the tablets with another glug of water.

He leads her from the kitchen to the bedroom and lays her on the bed. He slips her out of her clothes gently – not the usual pulling and tugging that acts as prelude to their bouts of rough sex, but softly and gently, like a parent undressing a child. He pulls the covers over her.

"Sleep. You'll feel better after sleep. There's a bowl by the bed if you feel sick. I'll sleep here."

He goes to the chair in the corner of the room, piled high with clothes like a makeshift wardrobe. He pushes the clothes to the floor and sits down.

Her brain feels foggy. She can still hear the ticking of her watch, but the whispering and scratching from the locked room have gone quiet now, and Robbie's rhythmic breathing has taken its place. It's late. Perhaps the person in the room has gone to sleep. She can ask Robbie in the morning.

She listens to her watch, and Robbie's breathing, and the two of them mesh in rhythm, a calming rhythmic lullaby. *Tick tick tick.* Her brain clears of any other thoughts. She just focuses on the ticking as she drifts into sleep.

When she wakes in the morning the chair in the corner of the room is empty. Seline's head is throbbing like a bad hangover, but then she remembers the blow to her head and reaches up to feel a hardboiled-egg-sized lump. She can't remember much about yesterday, tries to piece it together. She does remember Robbie saying something about magic mushrooms, and though she's hazy on most of the details, the mushroom thing sounds right.

Robbie comes in holding a couple of cups of tea. He sits on the bed and passes her one.

"Quite a night."

Seline sips the tea and is glad that she no longer feels sick. Robbie stares at the floor for a while, then looks at her.

"Look, I'm sorry. I was out with a mate the other day,

walking his dog. We came across some wild mushrooms and I brought them home. Only, they must have been magic mushrooms. It was a bloody stupid thing to do. I'm just glad they weren't poisonous."

Seline sips her tea, taking this in.

"Anyway, I know a bit about shrooms. You were hallucinating, going on about someone being locked in that room. You were hearing things, seeing things probably. You had a fucking massive dose. Those things can be great but they can make you paranoid as fuck as well. You must feel like shit. I've called the school, told them you're sick and you won't be in."

"Right."

"You'll feel better today. The good thing is, they wear off fast – physically anyway. But your head might be messed up for a bit. Things might seem odd, and your head might play tricks on you for a bit. Your moods'll be up and down. Just give yourself a bit of time. Okay?"

He leans over and kisses her tenderly on the forehead. It hurts where he presses the lump on her head.

"Okay. Thanks."

FOR THE REST of the day Robbie acts really sweet, looking after her, getting her food and drinks while she stays in bed and rests up. She spends the gaps in the day when he's not in the bedroom trying to think things through. She can see how she was imagining those noises in that room. *Of course* he doesn't have someone locked up in there. That was just a paranoid delusion.

She plugs her phone into its charger and looks up everything she can find about magic mushrooms. Eating so many of them will have made her paranoid – and the psychedelic effects will have made her imagine all sorts of stuff, all that scratching and whispering. Everything she reads makes sense of what she thought was going on. She was overworried and hypersensitive and imagining all sorts of threats and dangers. It's completely textbook.

But she knows what she *didn't* imagine: Robbie's face, when he first came in and saw her trying to break the door down, how violently he'd reacted. How he shoved her to the floor, pulled her hair, practically broke her wrist, kept hold of that knife.

She keeps reading. It's extremely common that the physical effects of the drugs wear off in a few hours, but the psychological impact can go on for a lot longer. So any anxiety she's feeling now could just be a result of the drugs.

Except she admits to herself now how uneasy and suspicious she was beginning to feel long before last night. And Robbie hardly strikes her as the sort of person who goes foraging for wild mushrooms in the woods. He *knew* those were magic mushrooms. He's probably dealing them – dealing other drugs as well.

Maybe her paranoia is an illusion.

Or maybe it isn't.

He hasn't got a person in that room. But he's got *something* in that room he really doesn't want her to know about.

What the hell has she got herself into?

## 14

Seline goes into school the following day with her story all prepared, anticipating the questions she knows she'll be asked. She was out for a run, feeling a bit ill, coming down with something viral. She thought she could sweat it out, but stupidly she didn't eat when she should have, came over all weak and slipped while she was running, banging her head against a lamp post of all things. Yes, go ahead and laugh. It looks worse than it is. She realised she should be sensible, rested up for twenty-four hours, and now she's feeling much better, thanks.

She doesn't mention the massive bruise on her throbbing wrist, the pain in her kidneys that makes her gasp every time she moves, from where she was slammed into the table.

She hears herself telling the story to a series of people and thinks she's over-elaborating the lie – but no one questions it at all. By lunchtime there's even a Get Well Soon card in her pigeonhole from Annie, which Seline appreciates, even though it makes her feel guilty about lying. There's another card too – but when she opens it she sees it's an invitation to Sunday lunch with Michael, her dad's old school friend who helped her get this job, at his house, with his family. She makes a mental note to tell her mum, as she often asks whether Michael has been around, so she's bound to be pleased.

She manages to get through the day, but teaching feels like a slog and she can't focus on it. She keeps thinking about what happened at Robbie's and wondering what she's going to do about it. Her classes spot her lack of focus and take advantage, all of them being more disruptive than normal and sapping her energy. She somehow manages to make it through the end of her final lesson.

As she leaves for the day to walk back to the flat, she discovers that Robbie is waiting in his car for her. Feeling as tired as she is, it's a relief that he's come to save her the twenty-minute walk.

She manoeuvres her aching body into the passenger seat as carefully as she can. He leans over and gives her a kiss.

"You okay, sweetheart?"

"Yeah. Tired. Thanks for coming to get me."

"No worries. You've had a bit of a time of it. Got to look after you, haven't we?"

He drives the car out of the car park, carefully for once. They head back towards the flat for a while in silence, his hand on her leg. For the first time that day, Seline finds herself beginning to relax.

"And people believed you, did they, about how you hurt your head?"

She can't read his tone. Maybe he genuinely is concerned about her. Or maybe he's checking what the fallout might be for him, whether people might know or suspect he's the one behind her injuries.

"Yeah."

"Good. That's good."

His voice is smiling. He gives her leg a warm squeeze. Seline can feel herself tensing up again. Robbie's just being nice to her because he doesn't want her giving away he's messing about with drugs. Even when he looked after her, when he found her off her head, he was only being nice because that's what you do to someone on a trip if you don't want them to get worse. He didn't want her to make a scene and show *him* up.

ONCE THEY GET BACK to the flat her body's instincts kick in and she falls into a doze on the sofa. The act of putting a brave face on things all day has knocked the wind out of her, and she desperately needs sleep to recharge. She can vaguely hear him in the flat, and the television, as she drifts in and out of consciousness. She's not sure how long she's crashed out for, and she doesn't properly wake up again until a few hours later, when Robbie gently shakes her shoulder to rouse her, and presents her with a plate of takeaway.

They're watching something mindless on the telly when Robbie mentions her dinner with Michael and says he'll come along with her.

She looks up from the television in shock.

"How the hell do you know about that?"

He must have gone through her bag while she was asleep and found the invitation.

"Have you been in my bag?"

She's so taken aback that she's confronted Robbie before she even realises. To her surprise, Robbie seems wrong-footed. He looks confused.

"I didn't look in your bag."

"How do you know about it then?" She's confrontational and strident. It's like all the pent-up doubts she's had about him have finally broken down the dam and now she's really showing the feelings she's been bottling up. She's almost as surprised by herself as he is.

"You told me an hour ago, when we got in. I don't even know where your bag is."

"That's bollocks."

She *knows* she hasn't told him. She was asleep. Seline gets up angrily and stomps around the flat looking for her bag. He just sits on the sofa, watching her flatly. She can't find it.

Then she remembers the end of the day in the staff room, exhausted, moving round like a zombie, packing her bag, going to leave, realising she'd forgotten her coat, putting her bag down to put her coat on – and she forgot to pick the bag up when she left school. She can picture it now, on the chair in the staff room where she left it.

So she *must* have told Robbie – briefly woken up from her sleep and had a conversation – though she can't remember it at all. She can't have properly recovered from what happened yesterday. She's so muddled, she can't concentrate on anything.

"I'm sorry, Robbie."

"Forget it."

He sits watching the television, deliberately not looking at her. It's obvious he's angry. The atmosphere is strained and awkward.

And however he knows about it, Robbie has invited himself along to her lunch with Michael.

## 15

By the time Sunday arrives and she is due to go to Michael and his family for lunch, she's excited to be meeting her parents' old family friend at last. But Robbie takes the shine off the anticipation by acting oddly, on edge somehow. He gets more dressed up than usual, irons a shirt and wears some smart shoes she's never seen before, rather than his usual designer trainers. Maybe he's even bought them for the occasion. He moans about having to go, and how it'll probably be "all posey and poncy," which Seline thinks is a bit rich, given that he invited himself in the first place. He takes an interest in how she's dressed too, which she finds flattering at first, until she gets the sense there's another side to his curiosity. He doesn't go as far as telling her what she should wear, but she can sense him looking her up and down, scrutinising her outfit to judge whether it's acceptable.

Michael's address is a bit of a way out of town, and Robbie gets twitchy about them leaving on time so they won't be late – so much so that they arrive ten minutes early, and he parks up half a mile down the road and makes them wait, so they'll arrive exactly on time. She makes fun of him about it, but he doesn't rise to her gentle mockery.

They drive up the slope of the valley and then turn at a crossroad and drive about half a mile down a single-lane track before turning through a pair of monumental fence posts that signal the grandeur of what lies beyond. The house is a beautiful old barn conversion on the fringes of what must once have been a working farm. They pull the car up next to a swish-looking limo and a vast four-by-four, then go up some ancient worn stone steps to the imposing front door. Robbie lifts and drops the heavy metal doorknocker to announce their arrival.

The door is opened by a smart-looking man Seline recognises from his social media posts. Michael.

"Seline! Welcome, welcome!"

He swings the heavy door open and makes an expansive gesture to invite them in. Seline steps inside and goes to take his hand to shake it, but he leans in warmly to give her a hug, which she returns somewhat awkwardly.

"Thanks. I hope you don't mind but I brought my... a friend of mine, Robbie."

Michael looks at Robbie in the doorway. "Oh, I know Robbie. Come in, lad."

Robbie steps into the house and shakes Michael's hand deferentially. "Mr Lockwood."

Seline's confused. Robbie knows Michael? Of course, now she thinks about it, it makes complete sense. It's a small place, it's that kind of village, people know people – and Seline remembers what she was told about Robbie on her first day: that he knows everybody. But even so, it has thrown her, because until this point Robbie has given zero indication that he knows who Michael is. Why wouldn't he mention it? It's just weird.

Michael walks them into the house, giving a bit of a history of the place as he does so. It was a wreck until about thirty years ago when he stumbled across it. The farmhouse itself was so dilapidated it was easier to knock it down and not rebuild it. This building was the prize of the plot, an unusually large barn constructed solidly from local stone, which was in remarkably good condition. It oozed character. Michael bought the entire farm, and at that time he was starting out on his building and development business, so could access a lot of good workmen and local craftsmen to do the conversion. An architect friend did the plans and cleverly designed it as a kind of upside-down house, putting the bedrooms and utility rooms on the ground floor and bringing the kitchen and living spaces up here on the higher floor to take advantage of the views.

By this stage of the tour, they've walked to the end of the living room and to the rear wall of the barn – an extraordinary picture window running the entire length of the building, looking out on the valley and down to the main town. It's amazing.

"We'd normally eat on the balcony, but it's a bit cold for that. Still, at least we have the view."

Michael introduces Seline to his wife Tess and daughter Charlotte, who are just coming in with a variety of plates and bowls of food. Tess is about ten years younger than Michael, beautiful, with incredible bone structure and classic good looks. She's expansive and welcoming. Charlotte has inherited her parents' good genes, but possibly not their bonhomie. She's a couple of years younger than Seline, and is quiet and rather awkward.

Michael asks Seline about the school, how her lessons are going, whether she likes the job. She answers as enthusiastically as she can, given the fact that she feels she isn't doing that well. She talks instead about how great the facilities are.

"Oh, that's good. We helped out on that, didn't we, hon? Felt like art was a bit under-invested as a subject, so we were able to make a donation over the summer, smarten the rooms up, get some new equipment." Michael looks at Tess, who smiles at Seline and tops up her glass.

"I saw your art actually," Michael continues.

This throws Seline for a moment. How has he seen her artwork?

"Yes?"

"I was in for a governors' meeting, thought I'd take a look at the new print room, and came across some of your drawings. You've been working in there in the evenings?"

"I... er... yes, I have."

"I hope you don't mind me looking. They're good. Very good."

"Oh. Thank you."

Seline feels strange. Someone was in her room before, vandalising her drawings, and she felt violated, like her private world had been intruded upon. She's jolted into a terrible thought: was it Michael who ruined her drawings? But then she catches herself with how ridiculous the idea is. Why would this sophisticated man who has helped her so much and who is a friend of her parents do something like that? It's absurd.

They're not very far into lunch when Seline begins to

notice with rising dread how much Robbie is drinking. He started with a pre-dinner beer, and since then has been chugging the wine liberally. At first, he waited for his hosts to top his glass up – but when this didn't happen quickly enough for his liking, he's taken to filling his own glass, copiously and frequently. He started the afternoon quite shy and reserved, almost like an awkward teenager, but now he's in a drinking rhythm he's losing his inhibitions and gaining confidence, talking too much and too often. He's like a naughty boy showing off at the grown-ups' table. Seline wants to make a good impression here, and can feel herself becoming increasingly embarrassed and anxious. It's excruciating.

If the others notice Robbie's behaviour, they choose not to show it. Michael chats freely and easily and his relaxed manner helps to put Seline more at ease. He talks at great length and with real warmth about her parents. It's odd that her parents never mentioned him until she got the message from him about this job, because the warm way he talks about them you'd think they were still the closest of friends. He's full of stories about him and his dad at school and the mischief they used to get up to. She's always thought her dad was quite a straight and serious character, but the way Michael tells it they were a pair of proper tearaways – not how Seline has ever imagined her dad as a boy at all. It's quite eye-opening.

There's something else too. When Michael talks about her dad just after leaving school, he paints a slightly different picture than the one Seline has in her mind. Michael doesn't appear to be deliberately insulting, but something in how he talks about Seline's dad paints him as a bit of a failure. There's a hint that her dad didn't advance because of something he did wrong in the past. Sitting here, in this lovely house with this beautiful family, Seline can't help feeling the smallness of where she's come from and finds herself judging her dad a bit against Michael's achievements. She hates herself for it, but she can't help it, and feels suddenly sad. When Michael sees Seline's getting a bit uneasy he casually shifts the subject to something else. But Seline is rattled by it.

"Cheer up, it might never happen. Unless it already has!" Robbie's grinning inanely, pointing at Seline's serious face, performing for the room and thinking he's being more entertaining than he is. Seline feels so embarrassed that she wishes the room would swallow her up.

Tess tops up her glass of wine, then subtly takes the half-full bottle and moves it away from the table with some plates she's clearing. Oh God, everyone can see what a show Robbie is making of himself. When Tess comes back in with dessert, Charlotte – who has been strangely quiet through most of the meal – excuses herself and leaves the table. Seline feels somehow judged by her because of Robbie's awful behaviour, like his actions reflect poorly on her.

"Come on, lad. Let's smoke a cigar." Dinner is over and Michael gets up, walks towards the picture window. Robbie gets unsteadily to his feet and follows. The two of them step out onto the balcony and close the door. Robbie has taken his jacket off and left it on the back of his chair, so he stands out in the autumn twilight chill in just his shirt sleeves, hugging his arms. Maybe Michael is hoping the cold will sober him up.

Tess looks at Seline and gives a half smile. Seline can't read her expression – it could be sympathy, or pity, or judgement.

"Will you help me clear while I get some coffee?"

"Sure."

Tess heads for the kitchen and Seline begins to pile up the bowls and spoons. She looks out onto the balcony where Michael is puffing on a fat cigar. She can only see Robbie's back as he leans against the railings, cigar in his limp hand, his head dropped, not looking at the view. He has the uncomfortable posture of someone about to be sick over the side of a ship.

Seline heads into the kitchen. Unsurprisingly, it's beautiful – its sleek cream and chrome units and cool black marble counters bringing a modern contrast to the traditional stonework and heavy exposed wooden beams of the barn. She puts the pile of bowls on the work surface, then begins to load things into the enormous dishwasher.

As she goes back into the living room to get the last of the serving dishes, she catches a glimpse of something on the balcony. It's dark out there now, and she can't quite be sure of what she's seen or not – but she thinks she sees Michael slap Robbie, hard, across the face.

She stops dead in her tracks.

It's so quick it's over before she can take it in.

Robbie has stepped backwards so he's obscured by one of the large stone columns that splits the windows into sections. Michael stands casually where he was. He takes a long puff on his cigar. He turns slightly, spots Seline inside and smiles, raises his hand in greeting. He's utterly relaxed.

She must have imagined it. She must have.

As Tess and Seline come back from the kitchen with the

coffee and cups, Michael and Robbie are already sitting at the table.

"Ah, lovely!" Michael's jovial and relaxed, exactly as he was before he went out onto the balcony. Robbie on the other hand is very different – all his noisy swagger has gone and he sits quietly, staring down at the table, not making eye contact. Maybe something *did* happen outside with Michael. Or maybe the excess of alcohol has finally taken its toll and Robbie is crashing.

Michael pours coffee for everyone, including Robbie.

"Here you go, lad. That'll see you right."

They drink their coffee and after a while Michael announces that their taxi is here. Seline guesses he's quietly ordered one, knowing that Robbie is far too drunk to drive back. Robbie doesn't say anything, so she assumes he must have already known what's been arranged.

At the door to the barn, Seline thanks Michael and Tess.

"That's our pleasure," says Michael. "We wanted to make sure an old friend of the family is settling in okay. Let's do it again, soon."

"That would be lovely, thanks."

"And please remember me to your parents when you speak to them. Tell them Michael says hello."

"I will. Thanks."

IN THE TAXI back into town Robbie doesn't say anything. He just stares down at his lap. Seline doesn't say anything either. It's been a strange afternoon. She likes Michael very much, has warmed to him immediately, and finds him charming and interesting. She can't understand why her parents haven't spoken about him more. And she still can't work out what's gone on between Michael and Robbie.

Robbie looks up, stares out of his passenger window, his face utterly blank in the moonlight. He casually rubs his arm. Seline looks down and sees something on his wrist. She only sees it briefly before it gets covered up again by the sleeve of his jacket. A red mark.

It looks like a cigar burn.

# 16

When they get back to the flat, Robbie still doesn't say a word. He takes himself off to the bathroom and Seline goes into the kitchen, not bothering to turn the light on, sits at the kitchen table under the window in the rectangle of yellow light cast by the streetlights, waiting for him to come out. She doesn't even know what she's waiting for really. She's learnt the hard way not to ask him about stuff he doesn't want to talk about... and in any case, she doesn't really know what she'd ask him. There *isn't* anything to ask him. His behaviour today has been excruciatingly embarrassing. She can't bear how he was, can't bear thinking that those nice people might believe she finds this acceptable. Finds *him* acceptable.

No, she isn't waiting for him to come out of the bathroom. She'd rather he stayed in the bathroom all night than come in here and say anything to her.

She sits at the kitchen table in the half-light, in a kind of limbo.

Eventually, she hears the bathroom door creak open and

the scrape of the doorstop on the floor, and waits for him to come into the kitchen, but he doesn't. After a while, she goes out into the passage and looks into the bedroom. Robbie is in there, collapsed face down on the bed, snoring. The drink has completely got him in its grasp now and dragged him into a heavy sleep.

The whole flat is illuminated by the strange sodium glow of the streetlights. Robbie is asleep, and the flat seems asleep too. Seline stands in the doorway looking at him, and has the thought that she is also asleep. She has been in some sort of peculiar dream ever since arriving here, sleepwalking through her life, events happening around her, and *to* her, and her passively watching them play out, as if she has no control over them. She left Manchester because she felt life was passing her by, and now here she is, letting the events of her life play out once more as if she's watching a film of it all, like it has an inevitable engine of its own and she is merely a passenger.

What the hell is she doing?

Wake up. Wake up!

Seline goes to the kitchen, opens the drawer where she keeps the Bags for Life. She takes a few out and goes back into the bedroom. Quietly, she slides the drawer open and takes out her small pile of belongings, her blouses and underwear, her skirts and trousers, her stash of tooth-brushes. She puts them in a bag. She goes to the bathroom and collects up her toiletries, her deodorant and toothpaste and make-up remover. She goes to the living room and picks up a small pile of art books, puts them in another bag.

She's packed.

It's taken her less than two minutes. She'll walk down to the minicab office next to the Indian restaurant, get herself a taxi up the hill to her digs. She reaches into her pocket, takes out her key ring, removes the key to Robbie's flat and puts it on the coffee table. She turns to leave.

Robbie is in the doorway.

What happens next is a blur. He crosses the room with such determination she steps back in fear. But he doesn't touch her. He picks up the coffee table and sends it flying across the room, its corner leaving a sharp dent in the wood-chipped wall. He upends one of the armchairs, then stamps fiercely on one of its legs, splintering it off. He lashes out, kicking the door with such force his foot goes clean through its plywood panel. He picks up a plate and a cup from the floor and hurls them across the room, exploding a shower of porcelain shards over them both. One hits him just below his left eye, and blood slowly trickles down his cheek, but he takes no notice. He rips the curtains from the window, bringing the curtain pole down with a huge chunk of plaster, a cloud of dust billowing up from the plaster and the filthy curtains. He sweeps ornaments and photos from a shelf on the wall – then rips the shelf itself out of the wall and smashes it to the ground. He moves around the room in a violent frenzy. He doesn't stop until every piece of furniture is up-ended, everything that can be broken or smashed or ripped has been destroyed. Only when the place is utterly ruined does his fury subside.

He stands there panting. Seline hasn't moved an inch from where she flinched and stepped back, frozen in fear. He hasn't laid a finger on her.

He sighs deeply, then leans over and picks up something from the floor. Slowly and calmly, he walks over to Seline, stands close to her. He lifts the object he's holding so she can see it, glinting in the hazy yellow light bleeding in from the window.

It's her key to his flat.

He holds it by the tip, twists it down so it's horizontal and moves it slowly towards her, until its rounded end is touching her lips.

Slowly, he slides it into her mouth.

His lips are practically touching her. She can feel his breath on her face. Barely making contact, he wraps his hand gently around her throat. He leans into her and whispers.

"If you even *think* about leaving again, I'll fucking kill you."

With icy calm, he steps back and walks out of the room.

For the first time since he came into the room, Seline lets herself breathe.

She's terrified.

She absolutely, one hundred per cent believes he means it.

# PART II

## 17

S eline stares at a blur of mottled green and brown flashing past. The countryside is desolate and abandoned in this winter half-light, the twisted shapes of dark leafless trees like scratches on the barren landscape, out of focus behind the glass window streaked with tears of rain. The train trundles along, practically empty, stopping occasionally in remote towns here and there to pick up the odd handful of waterlogged travellers looking like bundles of wet clothes or corpses pulled from a river, happy to escape the rain and to be leaving the miserable countryside for the attractions of the city.

Her phone buzzes in her pocket. She takes it out and looks at the message.

where r u ?

Immediately after Robbie threatened to kill her and smashed up the flat, she hadn't been able to move, convinced that he might burst back into the room at any moment and attack her. But after a while she heard him snoring from the other end of the corridor. Not wanting to wake him, or to be anywhere near him, she moved a few of the upended things from the sofa and lay down, still fully clothed. There was no way she could sleep. The fear-induced adrenaline still coursed around her body and her mind raced with half-formed thoughts. And under everything else, her own voice, over and over: *What am I going to do? What am I going to do?*

In the morning she waited until she could hear him moving, then got up and called from the corridor in as relaxed a voice as she could manage.

"I'm going to school."

She took her coat from behind the door, went out and down the stairs, then on to the street. Instead of turning right to head up to school, she turned left and down a few doors to the minicab office, where a couple of drivers stood outside, leaning against their cars and smoking. She booked a cab and went directly to the station at Holts Hill, calling the school on the way to say she had a migraine and wouldn't be in that day. Then bought a ticket to Manchester and boarded a train ten minutes later. It's the first time Seline has gone home since starting her teaching job a few weeks ago. She remembers being nervous on that first train journey across – but nothing in her anxiety then could have prepared her for what has followed.

She texts her mum and dad to let them know she's got a day of free periods and is heading over. Just as she's sent the message, her phone vibrates again.

i m at the school. ure not here

SHE GETS off the train at Piccadilly Station and makes her way down the slippery platform. As she approaches the mechanical barriers, she sees her parents waiting on the other side. Her heart turns over. She had no idea how much she has missed them until this moment. She leans against the barrier as it opens, launches herself forward, dives into the outstretched arms. Her mother and father wrap her in an embrace. It feels like she has fallen from a great height and they have caught her.

Somehow she manages to engage in small talk and hold it together on the short drive home.

Home!

As they pull into the road and her house appears in front of her, she feels like someone dying of thirst emerging from the desert and discovering an oasis. Her whole plan was to get away from this place and step out into the world. Now she can't think of anywhere she'd rather be.

It's a cosy house, small but carefully looked after. It was a tight squeeze growing up; fine when they all moved here when she was five, but decidedly cramped in her teenage years, when everyone lived constantly on top of each other. But as she matured, Seline began to appreciate the closeness, the solid values her parents instilled in her, and this tightness of the family struck her as a strength when she compared it to some of her wilder, more chaotic school friends. Kids crave freedom, but they also need rules – and she certainly felt she got these from her hard-working, security guard father.

She feels a huge surge of relief as she gives in to the comforting lure of her bedroom, her safe haven. She spent so much time alone here. Seline's love of art seemed somehow to grow with her solitary nature. Did she lock herself away in her room to draw and paint? Or did she draw and paint to give herself something to do while she was alone in her room? Either way, art became increasingly important to her, and as she approached the end of school she became more certain it was something she wanted to pursue as a career. Although it was never spoken of in these terms, Seline had a sense that this passion of hers was at odds with the sensible, practical sacrifices her dad made in his job – a self-indulgence compared to the serious graft of his own work. As a trade-off, Seline chose an art course in her home city so she could live at home and save money. And after she graduated, she followed her degree with a year of teacher training, also in Manchester, so she could turn her passion for painting into something vocational – probably to appease what she imagines her father expects of her.

She feels her phone vibrate in her pocket again. She takes it out and, without checking the messages, turns it off.

LUNCH IS a massive roast with all the trimmings. A huge chicken, too big for the three of them, roast potatoes, carrots, peas, big fluffy Yorkshire puddings, parsnips... It's a vast hug of a dinner. She's spent the last twenty-four hours in a state of hyper-alertness, so it takes her a while to wind down and relearn how to be her unguarded self.

But at the same time, she can't be entirely unguarded. Naturally, her parents have a thousand questions about how she's getting on, how she likes the school, where she's living, how she's taking to teaching. She does her best to tell them, but each one of these questions has an answer that she can't fully disclose. How to tell them she feels she's failing at teaching, can't control the classes, has been warned by the

Head? How to mention she's been threatened by one of the pupils?

And biggest of all, how to begin to tell them about Robbie? Oh God, she can't tell them about Robbie!

She hates lying to her parents, can feel the emotion welling up in her, and doesn't want to worry them by seeming unhappy – so she decides to change the subject to something easier to talk about.

"Michael sends his regards to you both."

"Does he? How is Michael?" Her dad seems keen to hear about his old friend.

"He left a really lovely welcome card in my pigeonhole at work – and invited me round for lunch with his family. Isn't that nice?"

"Oh yes, lovely," says her mum. "More potatoes? Don't let them go to waste. Oh, I must show you later, those foxes have been in the garden again – dug a hole right under the fence at the back. You can smell them on the lawn in the mornings."

And like that, her mother has changed the subject.

Why has her mum reacted in such a weird way? Probably all to do with her lack of confidence in how Seline will do in her new job. If they're worried now, she can't imagine what they'll think when she tells them the full story.

Seline heads off to the toilet. She locks the door, sits on the edge of the bath and takes out her phone. Once she turns it on, it takes a while for it to find a signal. Then its starts to vibrate, over and over and over again. She can see she has an avalanche of messages from Robbie. She scans a few.

where the fuck r u ?

youd better anser me

???????????

Pick up bitch

don't make it any worse 4 urself than it
already is

WHAT THE FUCK?

She can feel the anxiety rising in her again. She didn't
consider what would happen next, only that she needed to
get away. But this barrage of angry messages cascading out of
her phone is alarming. There's something insane about the
number of texts he's sent in just a few hours. She scrolls
through the messages, trying to work out how many he's
written. Then her eye falls on one text in particular. She
opens it.

abdul at the minicabs says one of his guys
took u to the station. u gon to Manchester?

He knows where she is.

## 18

W hat if she stayed here?

What if she locked herself in here?

What if she just stayed here and didn't go back?

Seline's sitting on the bed of her childhood bedroom. More than childhood – she's lived in this room for almost the entirety of the twenty-three years of her life. She's never really left before, like most children do after school or university, so this is her first experience of coming home. She feels the oddness of it. You're a grown-up in the outside world, but coming back to your parents' house makes you a child again.

Until not that long ago she felt she was in danger of getting trapped here – but now, looking at the shelf that used to house all her cuddly toys, the walls with Sellotape marks where she stuck up her boy-band posters, it feels like sanctuary. To think she worried she was missing out on life! Well, she's seen life now, and she doesn't like the look of it. She was mad to leave. There are monsters out there.

She could. She could just stay.

The messages on her phone keep coming.

> When u back? Tell me what train u on and I
> can colect u from holts hill stn.

She turns off her phone again.

THE VOICE in her head won't stop its insistent, nagging questioning: *What am I going to do? What am I going to do?*

To distract herself, she kneels on the floor and feels under the bed, pulls out a mountain of objects wrapped in old bedsheets – her paintings. Though there are a lot of canvasses and sheets of paper here, this is a tiny fraction of the artwork she's been making in this room for the last fifteen years or so. The works under the bed are some of her earliest paintings and drawings. More paintings from her teens are squirrelled away in the attic above her. The work from her degree is out in the garage. Several artworks from all the stages of her life are hung on the walls downstairs, each one a signifier of the time she's spent in this room – like countdown marks scratched by a prisoner on a cell wall.

She carefully folds back the sheets and removes the paintings one by one, laying them out on the floor and the bed, twenty paintings or so arcing out in front of her, so she can get a proper overview of them all. Her younger self, speaking to her from the images. She tries to look at them dispassionately, from a distance. What would the twenty-three-year-old art teacher Seline think of these works if they came from one of her pupils? She attempts a critique.

Seline's certainly not vain – but she can see immediately that they show real promise. There's a technique in the composition, real competence and interest in the colour palette. Naïve, certainly, but there are signs of a proper craft emerging.

The subject matter is consistent throughout: solitary, dark-eyed, waif-like girls looking passively down or directly at the viewer, with blank, inscrutable expressions. There's something provocative in the gaze-out – the emotion isn't clear, but somehow the images challenge the viewer to act, or to feel something.

The rooms the girls occupy are pleasant ones. Plain, but represented in calming, restful colours. These are peaceful spaces. Each one has a window or a door, always with the window open or the door ajar, and with nothing clearly discernible in the shadows outside. The room itself feels safe, but the door or window might give access to something from beyond.

The girl could get out if she wanted to.

Or something else, something unknown, could get in.

Looking at them now, it's impossible not to connect the subjects to their creator. These are self-portraits. Not literal ones, but the girls in the pictures must be herself. And presumably those rooms in the paintings are *this* room.

Seline looks more carefully at the shadows outside some of the doors and windows. Is there something going on in them she hasn't recognised before? Something out there? A shape? A person? Perhaps these shadowy figures have always been there and she has never noticed them before? Though how would her younger self know *then* what she knows *now* – the malevolent forces that lurk in the shadows outside this room?

Or perhaps the grown-up her is seeing something in the shadows that isn't really there, her own knowledge of the horrible world she's encountered – making her see terrors in the shadows, like a person seeing monsters in an inkblot test.

Again, she tries to look at the pictures dispassionately, imagining they are works made by one of her pupils. What would she think if a child she was teaching painted something like this?

She'd think they had a secret.

What doesn't the grown-up Seline know about those shadows that this younger version of herself knows?

She's pulled out of her musings by chatter downstairs. At first she thinks it's just her parents talking in the hallway, but then she realises there's something off about her dad's voice. She opens her door and looks down the stairs. She can see her mum at the open front door, chatting to someone on the front step. Her mum turns round at the sound of Seline's bedroom door opening, and Seline is able to see past her to the man outside.

It's not her dad.

It's Robbie.


"Sorry I didn't get here sooner, sweetheart. I came as soon as I got your texts." He beams a warm, relaxed smile at her up the stairs, as if him being here is completely normal.

"Robbie was just telling me about you needing to get back. We'd have driven you over, luv. You didn't need to make him come all this way."

"Aw, it's no trouble, Mrs Henderson."

"Well, it's very good of you." Her mum smiles and pats Robbie lightly on the arm. Seline can tell immediately she's been won over by that charm he turns on so easily.

"I was just telling your mum you've remembered a lesson you've gotta prepare for tomorrow. Go on, sweetheart, grab your coat. Don't hang about."

Robbie looks at her expectantly, eyebrows raised.

She comes down the stairs in a daze. She was building up to telling her parents about Robbie, but now he's turned up and pulled the rug out from under any plans she had. Her mum has turned round and taken Seline's coat from the hook in the hallway. She has to say something, quickly, right now.

"Funny thing is, Mrs H., she asked me to pick her up, but forgot to send me the address, the daftie. Luckily, when I went up to her digs they had some of the post you forwarded her with this address on it."

Robbie waves a couple of envelopes he's just taken from his pocket. He's still smiling at Seline, relaxed as anything. He's clearly been running around town, trying to hunt her down. And now he's here.

"Have you not got time for a cup of tea before you go? Colin will be sorry to have missed you." Her mum is fawning over him. She's obviously excited Seline has a secret boyfriend she hasn't told them about. She has no idea of the real secret.

"Oh, out, is he? That's nice of you, but she's in a hurry, aren't you, treasure?

Seline's frozen to the spot. Robbie steps into the hallway and takes the coat from her mother. He wraps it around Seline's shoulders. He's still smiling, but he holds her by the elbow so hard she thinks his thumb is going to go right through her skin. It feels like he could crack the bone in his fist.

"Or maybe we should stay and have a cuppa. Give your

mum a chance to get to know me better? And your dad too. Will he be back soon?"

"I don't think so," says her mum. "I don't think he'll be back for a couple of hours yet."

"Oh, that's a shame," smiles Robbie. "Just us then. Cosy. What do you reckon, Seline?"

He squeezes her elbow harder.

"Let's go," Seline says in a low voice.

"Good idea." Robbie releases his grip on her elbow and she gives her mum a hasty hug before moving out through the open front door. She can tell her mum is thrown by the speed of her departure, but Seline knows she has to go, now, before Robbie does something terrible.


THEY'VE BEEN DRIVING for a half an hour or so in silence before Robbie speaks.

"She seems nice, your mum. Love her a lot, do you?"

"Yes."

"Yeah. Then it's probably a good idea we left when we did."

Her mind is racing. Now he hasn't just threatened her – she can feel his implicit threat towards her parents as well. How can she tell them what's going on? He's made it clear he's a danger to her parents too, if she tries to use them to get away. And she has no idea what he might do if she doesn't go back with him.

"I never really felt so close to my parents." He talks casually as he drives. "Not so much as I'd go running back to them with me tail between me legs if owt happened to me. My dad was a proper bastard really. He used to leather me pretty often, me and me brothers and sisters. Our ma never stopped him, 'cos she knew she'd get a bit as well."

He holds a balled fist in the air to signify the kind of treatment his father would hand out. Is he telling her this for sympathy, or to justify why he is like he is? She doesn't care. She imagines him being hit by his father and finds she likes the idea of him suffering.

"Only time I ever saw me dad be gentle was with his birds. He used to keep parakeets. Had a cage with them in the living room, over in the corner by the telly so they were out of the sun and the draft from the window. He'd stand in the kitchen cuttin them up bits of carrot and broccoli. Never made us kids a dinner, not once. He hung up all little toys for them and used to stand there, chirruping and talking to them. Every couple of weeks he'd get them out and give them a bath in a bowl of warm water. Change the shitty paper at the bottom of their cage."

All the while he's looking straight ahead as he drives. His face lights up as they pass another vehicle coming the other way, or thunder past the hard yellow glow of a streetlight. Otherwise he talks to her from the shadows of the car interior.

"Parakeets need exercise, so by rights you should have a big cage. But he only had a small one. He used to let them out to fly round the living room. God help you if you opened the living room door when they were out. He'd proper belt you. They'd flap about, not knowing what they were doing. They can get right silly once they're out. Overexcited to get a taste of freedom, I reckon. They can do summat stupid and end up hurting theirselves. So what you have to do is, you have to clip their wings. Clip their wings for their own good, so if they flap about and do summat silly they just fall safely to the ground."

She doesn't want to look at him, but she can see him out of the corner of her eye, his face dark, then briefly light, then dark again.

"I used to watch me old man do it, get the birds out and hold their tiny little bodies in his hands. You hold them on their backs, and you stretch out the wings, and then you cut them, carefully, with your scissors, all along the tips of the wings. It doesn't hurt if you do it right. You have to do it right, so you don't cause any permanent damage – but just enough so it stops them flying."

He talks slowly and precisely. She wants to shift in her seat, but she doesn't move. She doesn't want him to see her react.

"It can be a bit nasty if you're careless. So best not talk to anyone about any of this, there's a good girl. Let's hope we don't have to clip your wings again, eh, little bird?"

Neither of them speaks again for the rest of the journey back to Statheley Bridge.

# 19

"Who's your boyfriend, Miss?"

The catcalls go up from the class who have just entered the art room. Seline follows their eyeline to where they're looking and immediately understands why. Another bunch of flowers sits on her desk, wrapped in what looks like the pages of *The Sporting Life*. Somehow she manages to tame the unruly mob, gets them to sit down, start drawing something – studies of their own hands. That will shut them up and keep them still.

From Robbie, of course – the flowers. Ever since he brought her back from her parents' house last week, she's known he's not going to give her any room to breathe. This is the second time in three days he's been into the school to leave her flowers – his twisted way of letting her know she has nowhere to escape from him.

They're never nice flowers either. Maybe it's because Seline feels they're marking something awful – not his feelings for her, but a statement that he has his eye on her, that there's nowhere she can go without him being able to follow.

In any case, she looks at this sad bunch of wilting blooms, their browning stalks beginning to flop, their petals bruised and folded, and all she can think is that he must have stolen them off a roadside lamp post where they'd been left to mourn a fatal accident.

Seline still holds out a tiny hope that not everyone in the school has worked out she's been seeing Robbie, but she knows deep down she's fooling herself. He's around so often that any amount of effort she makes to keep it a secret is washed away under the weight of evidence. He's started bringing her to work every morning in his car, and picking her up at night, not letting her out of his sight. His car is in the staff car park so often he might as well be working here.

Annie thinks it's all very romantic. She's started making little secret faces with Seline when Robbie's about, or he gets mentioned by someone, or she sees the flowers. Scared to talk about things, Seline just nods and smiles back, playing dumb. Now she feels it's too late to talk to Annie about any of it. The truth is, she's let herself get trapped in this situation with Robbie and is terrified to tell anyone anything. She desperately wants to talk to Annie, but after Robbie's threats, she can't.

But not being able to talk about what's really going on makes Annie curious about her silence, and the more Seline tries to change the conversation, the more intrigued Annie becomes. It feels like Robbie is all Annie ever talks about. Every time his name comes up it's like a punch in the stomach. It makes Seline feel completely isolated from the people she works with.

To make matters worse, Robbie now has Seline going round at the end of every week collecting people's lottery money, nagging away to get their contributions. She knows she's annoying people, chasing them round for pocket change. It's demeaning. But Robbie's put her on the job and she can't refuse – she doesn't want to have any kind of confrontation with him, not while she works out how she's going to get away.

So when Annie corners her one day and tells her that they're arranging a staff drinks do down the pub in a couple of weeks and that she should come along... "And why not bring Robbie?"... all Seline feels she can do is nod and smile again and say yes, they'd love to come, she'll mention it to him. She knows she'll *have* to tell him now, in case someone else does and he's furious she didn't mention it herself. So everyone is going to see them out together – the happy couple.

The only time Seline gets alone is when she paints. She's managed to make Robbie believe this is something she needs to do to protect her job, so he allows her to stay at the school after the pupils and other teachers have left and paint in her art room. Seline uses this time to think about how she's going to escape.

But even when she paints she can't seem to get away from him. Her work is laden with anxiety. The images have female figures in them who look just like her, sad or melancholy looking, with dark, tired, heavy eyes, often in a room with a half-open door or window, and with a shadowy light outside the opening. She can't see what's there, in the shadows, but she can feel it isn't good. The pictures are loaded with a sense of menace once you notice this. She knows you don't have to be Freud to work out that it's *herself* trapped in the room... and that it's Robbie lurking outside, the faceless ever-present threat.

She feels she's just about holding it all together. But then one Thursday afternoon at final bell she gets called up to the Head's office.

"Sit down, Seline. How are you? How are you settling in?"

This is the first time Mrs Jessop has properly spoken to her since that awkward confrontation with the horrible green-haired Julie. Seline didn't feel at the time that the Head believed her. It has played on her mind ever since.

"I think I'm doing okay, thanks."

"Well, I'm sorry, but I can't agree." The abruptness of the Head is startling. "I hear rumours from other members of staff about a constant level of disruption coming from your classroom. You seem unfocused or distracted in many of our staff meetings. Your energies seem boundless when it comes to your own work, which I note is piling up in your class-room, or as far as collecting money for the staff room lottery is concerned. I do hear things, Seline – I may seem remote, but I do know what is going on."

Seline can feel her cheeks flushing. This is awful. It's all she can do to stop herself from bursting into tears.

"I can make concessions for the fact that this is your first job. And I note with some surprise that you have your supporters amongst the governors for some reason. But I made it clear to you at the start of term what was expected of you, and I expect to see some improvement, and fast. Please take this as an informal warning. Next time it will be a formal one."

ROBBIE'S CAR is in the car park. Seline gets in – and immediately falls apart. Huge raking sobs convulse her body. She can't catch her breath. She's a wheezing, snotty mess.

Robbie looks utterly lost with this. He's an expert when it comes to anger, but faced with grief, he's completely out of his depth. He sits there in silence, staring at her while she cries miserably, not saying or doing anything. After a couple of minutes, the best he can manage is, "Christ, what the fuck's wrong now?"

She tries to deflect his question; he's the last person she wants to talk to. But now he's asked, he insists she tell him. Seline manages to explain between gasps the gist of the conversation she's just had with the Head. How she's failing. When she mentions the prospect of a formal warning, he looks concerned. He leans towards her in the car, and for a moment she thinks he's going to give her a hug of comfort. But instead he grabs her firmly by the shoulders and shakes her so violently that she cracks the back of her head against her window.

"No way can you lose your job. No. Fucking. Way."

With each word he pushes her backwards again, so her head smacks against the glass. She can feel a burning pain on the back of her head. There are kids milling about in the playground and she prays no one notices what he's doing. She's ashamed of the mess she's got herself into.

"Do you understand? Say it: *I won't lose my job.*"

"I won't lose my job," she repeats flatly.

"You're fucking right you won't, dummy."

And with that, they drive off.

What she doesn't dare tell him, of course, is that the reason she's so distracted and in danger of losing her job is all his fault.

## 20

I n the days immediately after Robbie threatened to murder her, every fibre of her being, every nerve and sinew, neuron and synapse tingled with energy, on high alert. But the human body isn't designed to operate at that level of stress for more than short bursts of time. After days of thinking about the way in which he's fenced her in, threatened her if she talks to anyone, threatened to injure her family too if she talks to them, her fight-or-flight energy gives way to exhaustion, the absolute certain knowledge that she is trapped, with no chance of escape and no hope. And so she sleepwalks through her days at school, her nights at the flat, in a state of numbness – her mood a kind of squashed, flat nothing.

Her mum has rung her and left voicemails, but she never picks up the calls. She doesn't know how to call her back, or what she would say. She's sent a couple of short texts to stop her parents panicking, but other than that she avoids talking to them.

Back at the flat, Robbie continues to disappear at odd hours, summoned by the ping of one of his many phones. It's a relief when he leaves, because although the flat is horrible, at least she doesn't have to worry about what he's going to do next. He's never laid a finger on her again in anger – but that doesn't mean he won't. In fact, Seline is almost certain he might at any moment. If he comes back to the flat when she's in bed, she lies there, rigid, eyes closed, heart thumping in her chest, praying he'll just go to sleep.

One day she comes back from school to discover all her cases in the hallway. He's been up to her digs and collected all her belongings. He's cancelled the lease on her room with Mary and moved her into his flat full-time.

Deep down, Seline can't work out why he even wants her there, why he didn't just let her go when she tried to leave. He doesn't seem to get any particular pleasure from having her there. He's like someone who bought a dog because he likes the idea of having a dog, and has now discovered he doesn't want any of the inconvenience of looking after it.

One night he comes in drunk and starts burbling about his father again, about the lunch at Michael's, and about him threatening her. He grabs hold of her hand and looks like a wounded boy, like he could cry at any minute.

"It won't happen again. I promise."

Seline doesn't say anything, but waits for him to pass out on the sofa before she can pull her hand away, disgusted. She's not an idiot. His snivelling apology is just whining self-pity. *Of course* it will happen again. She's read enough about men like him to know they always say they're sorry, and they always say they'll never do it again – until they do. *She's* not the dog. *He's* the dog – a dangerous dog you must never take your eyes off, never look at directly or speak to in the wrong way, a dog that might attack, unpredictably, over some trivial slip, which might lock its jaws on and never let go.

Lying in bed, she worries again about what she's going to do. The obvious thing is to talk to someone, but she's too scared to. In an incredibly short space of time Robbie has managed to crush what little confidence she had. But this can't go on. This can't. She has to be brave. She has to talk to someone.

She'll talk to Annie. Annie is bright and confident. She'll know what to do.

The moment Seline seizes on the idea, she knows it's the right thing. She'll talk to Annie. Annie has always been nice to her. She'll find some way of raising the subject with Annie and she'll be able to tell what Annie really thinks of him. She'll think of some way of raising it with her. She just needs to find the right way to bring it up.

She looks at the clock by the side of the bed. 04:18. It's hours yet before she has to get up. She'll think of something, rehearse how she'll say it, how she'll talk to Annie about Robbie.


SELINE'S EATING a quick slice of toast before leaving for school when Robbie comes into the kitchen, up uncharacteristically early for some reason. She feels immediately guilty, like he'll be able to see from her face that she's planning to talk to someone about him. She's terrified that he'll be able to read her mind or know what she's up to, so covers it by talking about something else, anything else.

"Do you want some toast? I'm just leaving, but I have time to make some…?"

"Yeah. Go on then. And tea."

Robbie scratches himself inside his tatty dressing gown, sits at the table and begins to flick through messages on his phone. Seline fills the kettle, puts a slice of bread in the toaster and then waits. Waiting for the bread and the kettle, with Robbie just sitting there, becomes unbearable. It feels like he can hear what she's thinking. She needs to fill the silence with something else, something normal, so he won't know her thoughts.

"Have you got the lottery tickets?"

"Hmm?" He doesn't look up from his phone.

"The lottery tickets. For the school. I thought I could take them in, pin them to the noticeboard so people can see they haven't won. I thought it could be a new way of doing it."

"What?" He's staring at her now like she's a lunatic. She can feel herself getting more anxious, so she keeps rambling.

"I thought, instead of you having to text everyone the numbers, I could just collect the money and then, on Monday, I could put the tickets on the noticeboard so everyone could see what they've won. Or haven't won."

He laughs. "There aren't any tickets."

"There aren't any...?" She doesn't understand. Maybe he hasn't understood what she means. "The lottery tickets."

He stares at her flatly and she can see he's getting annoyed at having to repeat himself. He talks to her like she's an idiot.

"There. Aren't. Any. Tickets."

She still doesn't understand. He looks at her confused face and heaves a sigh.

"People give you the money for tickets. You give *me* the money for tickets. I keep the money. It's the lottery. No one's going to win it, so what's the point in buying tickets when no one's ever gonna win? I pocket the money and I just make the numbers up. Every now and then three numbers come up and I have to send in a tenner, but that's peanuts compared to what I've made in the last few years."

Seline lets it sink in. He's been stealing money from everyone in the school all this time, taking their money and keeping it himself. Except, of course, he hasn't been taking their money – *she* has. She flushes red, burning with shame. Robbie spots her blushing.

"That's right. You're in on it too, so you'd better not tell anyone or it'll be your arse on the line as well as mine. And what will all your precious friends think, when they know you've been robbing off them? Eh? Naughty girl..."

By the time Seline arrives at school she's already realised she can't talk to Annie, or to anybody. Robbie has driven a wedge between her and all of them. She's going to have to do something about this on her own. But what?

She stands in the playground trying to summon up the energy to go into the building. Perhaps she could just stay here all day, forever. She hears the first bell ring and walks heavily towards the main entrance with the other stragglers, all children, who are putting off the school day for as long as possible.

She goes into the staff room, watches a group of people chatting and laughing by the coffee station, but doesn't go over. She sits on one side, on her own, and pretends to look at things on her phone. Outside she can hear children moving around the school. Laughing. Screaming. Hundreds of happy, carefree voices.

But her focus isn't the school. It's Robbie. She needs a plan to get away from him, and in a way where he can't just come and drag her back in.

*What am I going to do? What am I going to do?*

Perhaps the answer is in that locked room.

## 21

It takes her about fifteen minutes to set things up. There's a bucket and a mop at the end of the hallway, behind the front door. She's moved the small hall table and the football trophy doorstop and the pile of shoes from the side of the passage to the end, so they sit heaped up against the front door as well. Seline figures if Robbie comes back, this collection of things will buy her a bit of time.

She's examined the locked door several times before and knows every detail of it so well that if she closes her eyes she can picture every knothole in the wood, every drip and scratch in the paintwork, the tarnished metal of the door handle, the rough edge on the gap underneath where someone has crudely sawn off a centimetre of the door at some point, maybe to clear a carpet that is no longer here. There's an old-fashioned heavy-duty mortise lock on the door with one of those keyholes that has a metal cover which swings on a pin at the top. She knows there's no way to get the door open without the key.

Seline closes all the other doors and then turns off the

light, so the windowless passageway falls into complete darkness. She stands for a few moments, eyes open but staring into nothingness, waiting for her eyes to adjust to the darkness. She listens out for movement on the stairs, but she can't hear anything other than her heart thumping in her chest. She's worked out from the layout of the flat that the locked room is on the corner of the building. She's looked up at it from the street and seen that there's some kind of covering at the window, curtains it looks like, or possibly a sheet hung up across a curtain pole, but she's hoping these won't be too thick and will let some natural light through.

Once she's waited for what she thinks is long enough, she feels her way along the passage to the locked room, kneels on the floor, pushes the lock cover to one side and presses her eye against the keyhole.

She can't see anything. It's either pitch black in there, or possibly the keyhole is covered on the inside as well. She closes her eye for a minute, then opens it and looks again.

Total darkness.

She goes to the kitchen and gets a chopstick left over from a Chinese takeaway. She comes back into the hallway and pokes the chopstick through the keyhole. She gets it in halfway without any obstruction. No, it's definitely not covered from the inside. It must be that the room is in total darkness. She takes the chopstick back into the kitchen – she doesn't want a single thing to seem out of place – and then comes back into the passageway, closing the kitchen door. She lets her vision adjust to the darkness again. Then she kneels on the floor and presses her face against the floor-boards, so she can get her eye as close to the gap under the door as possible. Still darkness.

She takes her phone out and switches the torch on,

beams the light under the door. She tries to look under the door, but she can't get her eye low enough to see into the room – the angle under the gap is all wrong. In any case, her eyes are now so close to the torch beam that she's dazzled and can't see anything properly. She turns the torch off and closes her eyes. Instead of darkness, now all she can see is a glowing red after-image, etched with shadows of blood vessels like eerie red tree roots. She waits for her vision to adjust again.

One last try. She closes her eyes so they won't be affected by the light, then turns on her phone torch again. Through her eyelids she can tell there's light in the passage. She points the torch upwards and rests the face of her phone on the floor. Then she feels down to the rough sawn gap under the door and begins to slide the torch end of her phone under. It's a tight squeeze against the rubber edge of her phone case, but it just fits. Once the phone is in about half-way, she opens her eyes. Then she pushes the keyhole cover to one side. She can immediately see there's now light in the room. She presses her eye to the keyhole.

Because the torch is pointing upwards rather than into the room, she can't see the back wall at all. Some of the light is spilling to the sides and Seline can make out shapes in the gloom. There's a table on one side with something on it – maybe some boxes. Something is near the table, a flat, shadowy expanse hovering in the air. Maybe this is the back of a chair. Over the other side of the room there are what look like more boxes, and something less square, more organic – this could possibly be a pile of sacks or bin bags.

She doesn't feel any the wiser about what is in the room. Maybe it *is* all of Robbie's dead brother's things, boxed and bagged up – but she can't understand why Robbie would be so defensive and secretive about the room if it was just that.

There's a noise. Not from the room. From outside.

The door to the street downstairs being opened.

It's Robbie. He's back!

Seline leaps up, lurches in the darkness to the passage light switch and clicks it on. Having been in the dark for so long it's dazzling. She grabs the mop and sloshes a bit of water on the floor. Then she rushes back to the locked door. She can hear footsteps coming up the stairs. She grabs the end of her mobile and starts to slide it out along the floor – but part of her phone case catches on the rough edge of the door.

It jams.

She can't get it out! She tugs again, but the rough wood just bites deeper into the rubber of the case. About ten centimetres of phone is poking out from under the door. When Robbie comes in he's bound to see it.

She can hear the steps – he's at the top, about to come in any second.

As she hears the door handle turning she makes a snap decision and pushes her phone further under the door of the locked room so it's no longer visible.

"What the fuck—?"

Robbie has tried to open the front door and found it wedged by the pile of shoes and the table. Seline grabs the mop in one hand and starts pulling the shoes away from the door with the other.

"Sorry, I didn't think you'd be back. I was just doing some cleaning."

He shoves the door again, sliding the table across the passage, and squeezes past her. Leaving the door open, he steps past where she's gathering up the shoes and is putting them back where they normally sit in a row on the other side of the passage.

"I forgot something."

Seline tries to stay calm and look normal, though she can feel her breathing is shallow and fast and her heart feels like it might explode. What if the thing he's forgotten is in that room? If he opens it he'll see her phone and know what she's been up to. Or what if someone rings her on it now, or sends a text message and it bleeps? He'll know it's there. Then God knows what he'll do.

Seline stands frozen as Robbie walks towards the locked door –

– and then past and into the kitchen. She stands transfixed for what feels like an eternity before he emerges back into the passageway, now holding a jacket that he must have left on the back of one of the kitchen chairs.

"Who the fuck does cleaning at half past nine at night?"

He picks up the football trophy still lying next to the front door.

"And stop moving my fucking trophy!" He waves it menacingly near her head. It looks just like the sort of thing murderers use to cave in their victims' skulls.

He walks past her and out of the flat door, slamming it behind him. She doesn't move as she hears him going down the stairs.

The door to the street opens and bangs shut.

She waits. Waits for about a minute. Silence. He's gone.

She rushes over to the locked door and crouches down. She can see the short edge of her phone. She tries to grab at it with her nails, but she can't get a grip on it. She can feel the panic rising up in her. Come on! Come on!

It's no good. She can't get hold of it.

She bounds into the kitchen, grabs the chopstick again, comes out and lies on the floor. If she can hook the stick around her phone she may be able to get it out. It's incredibly fiddly. She has to hold the chopstick precariously by the end and twist it against the floor, making sure she doesn't push the phone further out of reach into the room, or lose the chopstick in there too. Then, once she's moved the phone enough to get hold of it, she has to wiggle it back and forth until she can unhook the rubber case from the rough underside of the door.

Eventually she gets the phone out and turns the torch off – but she can see to her horror that a small section of case above the camera has been pulled off by the door. Seline spends a further fifteen minutes gently sliding the chopstick along and back under the door until she sees the missing bit of rubber roll out into the passageway.

Thank God.

She tidies away the mop and bucket, puts the chopstick back in the kitchen.

By the time she's finished getting everything back how it was and got to bed it's about 10.30pm. She's so wound up she can't sleep. She's still not asleep at 2am when Robbie comes in, though she pretends to be as she hears him clatter about in the bedroom, get undressed, get into bed, start snoring. She lies there awake, unable to shake her feeling of anxiety and dread, her mind racing with scenarios of what might have happened had she been discovered.

She hasn't learnt anything new about the room, but she's learnt something new about Robbie and herself. The more terrified she realises she is of him, the more determined she is to come up with a plan to get away.

## 22

The following day is Friday, the end of the school week – and the evening of the staff drinks. The plan is to meet at The Butchers Arms at 7pm. This gives them all a chance to get home, dump their bags and things, and get out. Seline has headed back to the flat to get scrubbed up before wandering down into town.

She's been dreading this outing ever since telling Robbie about it. She was hoping he'd say it sounded boring, that he didn't want to go – and even if he hadn't allowed Seline to go either, that would have been better than him coming along with her. But he *is* coming. It's bad enough that she's with Robbie in private, but to have to be seen out with him, seen by people, as a couple – it's just too painful.

But all day another thought has been taking shape in her mind: if people see her with Robbie, see how awful he is, see what he's really like, then maybe she *might* be able to talk to someone about him. Annie maybe. It wouldn't really matter if Annie thought badly about her, about the lottery money and stuff – so long as she could get away. Maybe tonight will give her a chance to think about it properly and talk to Annie, if it feels right.

When she gets home from school there is no sign of Robbie. She takes the briefest of showers in the musty bathroom and puts on her dressing gown quickly in case he comes back – she can't bear him seeing her naked now. She sorts through her clothes to find something nice, hoping it will make her feel better about herself. It's so long since she's been out anywhere, and most of these dressy things she hasn't worn once since coming to Statheley Bridge. She chooses something pretty but not too fancy and digs out the tatty ironing board from behind the wardrobe, flicking water from the kitchen tap onto her dress so the cheap travel iron won't burn it.

She sits in the chair with the best light nearest the living room window and does her make-up. There's still no sign of Robbie. She begins to hope that he may not come home, that she can enjoy getting dressed up and going out with her colleagues and have a night to herself for once – and maybe really get a chance to talk to Annie.

She goes back into the bedroom and opens her drawer to take out her small jewellery box. She hasn't worn anything except her small ear studs for weeks now. She's been depressed really, being with Robbie, and has kind of given up on herself. But now, getting nicely dressed is giving her self-esteem a boost. Looking through the box she finds the earrings she'd like to wear, a delicate amber pendant that will tone beautifully with the orange detail of the embroidery on her dress – or rather, she finds *one* of them. The other one doesn't seem to be in the box. Perhaps she's dropped it in the gloomy light.

She gets down on her knees to search, leans her face

against the side of the mattress and scrabbles her hand around in the shadows under the edge of the bed in case it has rolled out of sight.

She's got it! Just to the side of the bedside table. She pulls her arm back out and looks at her earring in her hand.

But it's not her earring.

This earring isn't an amber pendant. It's a crucifix. It isn't hers – she's never had earrings like this. And it can't have been there for long, because she spent an entire night cleaning in this filthy room the week she moved in, including hoovering under the bed.

She scrabbles under the bed again – and finds another earring, the pair to the crucifix.

Robbie has had another girl here.

She takes them back in the living room to look at them in the better light, to see if they give any clue as to their owner. They must have been taken off, put on the bedside table, knocked off somehow, by the bedding maybe, and fallen down the side of the bed and forgotten. She can't work out whether they're silver or cheap tat. She's staring at them closely to look for a hallmark – when Robbie comes in.

"Good, you're ready."

"Yes." She smiles at him. Behind her back, her hand closes in a tight fist around the crucifix earrings. She can feel the earring posts digging into her palm.

"What time's this pub thing?"

"Seven."

"What time is it now?"

"Quarter to."

"Right, let's get down there."

"Alright." Seline picks up her jacket from the arm of the chair.

"Chuck us my coat as well, yeah?"

Now what to do? Her hands are full. Seline is holding her jacket in one hand and the earrings in the other. She can't put her jacket down again as it'll look weird. She decides to put the earrings down on the table, as casually as she can, so she can pick up Robbie's coat. She hands it to him.

"Thanks. Don't you want those?" He's noticed the earrings she's put down.

"No, that's okay."

"Put them in. We've got time."

He has no idea the earrings aren't hers. Slowly, she picks them up, takes the clasps off, and one by one pushes the stranger's earrings through the holes in her lobes.

"They look nice. Come on."

Robbie heads for the door. It's the first time he's ever complimented her on something she's wearing, and it's his other girlfriend's earrings.

The fixed half-smile never leaves her lips. All she can think about is some other woman's earrings poking through the flesh of her ears. She follows him to the front door and out of the flat.

## 23

The Butchers Arms is surprisingly packed and very noisy. At first glance it looks like the entire town has turned out to ram itself into the quaint old pub.

Seline follows Robbie as he squeezes past tables towards the crowd at the bar. They stand there for a minute or so until a beefy, ruddy-faced man pivots towards them and muscles past holding three pints of beer, squeezed together like a bunch of flowers in his fat hands. Seline and Robbie step into the space he's vacated at the counter. After a few seconds it becomes clear that Robbie isn't going to offer to buy them drinks, so she asks him what he wants and makes the order – a pint of Best for him and a gin and tonic for herself. She pays and, steadying their glasses, they push back through to a more open area of the lounge. Seline looks around and sees Annie waving to her from a corner table where several of the teaching staff are gathered. Robbie spots them too and marches over, leaving Seline to follow in his wake.

. . .

THEY'VE NOW BEEN HERE LESS than an hour and the table is already loaded with dirty glasses and empty crisp packets. Everyone's in high spirits. Even Graham appears to have loosened up now he's had a couple of pints. Annie is bubbly and full of life, the perfect audience for everyone's stories. She has an infectious laugh with an involuntary snort which she tries to control but can't, so each time someone says something funny she laughs at what they've said, then snorts, then laughs at her own snort, and that sets everyone else off.

Though everyone's having a good time, Seline can't relax. Her guard is always up. It's as if the frivolity of the evening is a sheet of thin ice everyone is having fun skating around on, and Seline is waiting for the ice to crack, for the mood to change, for everyone to crash through to the shocking reality of the icy waters below.

The conversation has drifted onto people confessing the worst jobs they've ever had. Graham takes his turn and begins talking about a job he got in the early 2000s as a laboratory assistant for a company trying to develop home DNA testing. Family trees were all the rage, and someone smart and enterprising spotted you could cash in on the trend by using DNA samples to tell people all about their ancestry, if you could make them cheap and easy enough to use. It all sounded very exciting at his interview – but his job turned out to be spitting different amounts of saliva into plastic cups for months, and rubbing mountains of cotton buds round his mouth and up his nose for eight hours a day. Graham is quite dry as he tells his story. He emphasises the distasteful details, playing up to the crowd.

It's a good story which he tells well, and everyone is laughing.

Then Robbie launches into a story, clearly feeling himself to be an honorary member of the group.

"I must have been about fifteen, I reckon. Should have been at school really, but I don't need to tell you lot how boring *that* is..."

Robbie grins, eliciting laughs all round.

"I was bunking off, earning a few quid. My old man was never one for school either, so if anyone wrote home he'd just screw up the letters. I ended up on a building site, workin' for a local developer bloke I knew."

Seline assumes he must be talking about Michael, though Robbie doesn't mention him by name.

"I was labourin', hefting bloody great piles of gravel from one place to another, mainly with a shovel and wheelbarrow, proper back-breaking stuff. After two weeks I was ripped like a fucking bodybuilder. Every now and then a nice old boy let me drive the little dumper truck, which was a right laugh, until I pissed about too much and nearly stuck it in a ditch. It was the middle of winter, freezing cold, an' it rained non-stop for about a month. You couldn't wear waterproofs 'cos you'd sweat to death inside 'em, so you just had to carry on with your donkey jacket plastered to you like a drowned rat. When you got too drenched or couldn't feel yer fingers anymore, you'd all go and sit in front of a one-bar fire in a scabby Portakabin and watch the steam coming off your coat."

Robbie's a good storyteller. He's in his element, the star of his own show. Seline looks at her colleagues. None of them will have ever been near a building site. Robbie comes from a different, tougher life, and they can all play cultural tourists, looking through a window onto how another class lives, slumming it by proxy. They're charmed by him. But they don't have to go home with him and live it for real.

She's waiting for him to finish so she can take Annie aside and talk to her about her situation with Robbie, but she's scared she might miss her chance. He isn't going to finish any time soon. Besides, Annie is right next to Robbie. She's sitting at one side of the table and Robbie has squeezed himself in on the corner on a stool next to her. And she's clearly pretty sloshed. As she laughs at his story, she throws her head backwards, eyes closed, face to the sky, then leans forward and steadies herself by placing her hand on his arm or, a couple of times, on his thigh. Every time it happens Seline feels her chance to talk to Annie slipping further away.

Robbie carries on.

"One week I was put on foundations. Putting up a building is shit in winter when it's pissing down and you're sloshing about in the mud. But you can't just stop. You have to keep going. But foundations don't work in the wet. The concrete goes to shit, the mix is all wrong, so you gotta pump all the water out the trenches, keep 'em as dry as possible.

"Me and my mate Phil was in charge of the gennies powering all the pumps. We had a high water table and bad weather coming out the arse and we were runnin' them babies twenty-four seven. But it was light work, see? You'd go round, keep 'em topped up with diesel, then go and smoke in the warm. Tea and biccies most of the day while the other buggers were doin' the heavy shit out in all sorts."

Seline looks at everyone's faces, following Robbie's every word. He's got them in the palm of his hand.

"We gets to Thursday and the weather breaks. Me and

Phil don't have to run the pumps now, so we don't even have to top the gennies up. We're on standby, so we spend the day smoking and drinking tea.

"Come Friday Phil gets an idea. He says it ain't gonna rain all weekend and they pour the footings on Monday. They ain't gonna run the pumps again. What if we siphon the diesel off the gennies, sell it to his mate who does haulage, and we can make fifty quid each from it? Obviously, I'm in."

Everyone apart from Seline is loving this tale of petty thievery.

"So Phil and I knock off with everyone else, give it twenty minutes, then sneak back up. We knew the blokes on security – we sometimes had to check on the pumps at weekends so they didn't bat an eyelid when we went back in. We goes round all the gennies and started siphoning, filling the empty fuel cans again. Phil moved his car up to the other gate, so we loaded up and headed off. Gave the diesel to Phil's mate, we split the money and went to the pub."

Everyone's laughing at the audacity. No one seems to care that this is a story about a criminal fifteen-year-old.

"That's not the best bit," says Robbie. "I've had a good weekend on the genny-money and I wake up in the middle of Sunday night proper hung over and needing a piss. I look out the bathroom window – and it's raining. It's my job to check the weather the night before, but I've been too pissed an' haven't bothered. I fly round to Phil's in the dark, somehow get 'im up, and we shoot up the building site. The pumps haven't been on all night and the trenches are waterlogged. We're fucked. There's four big mixers full of concrete on their way and they can't be poured in this mess. The mix'll be goosed. We run around like nutters getting all the pumps on, hoping they'll last, 'cos we've nicked all the diesel and the gennies are running on fumes.

"Then Phil has an idea. There's a whole shed full of cement. Let's lob it in the trenches, Phil says, soak up the water. The mix'll still be fucked but we might just get away with it and we've got nothing better, so we leap on the dumpers and start unloading tons of cement into the trenches, skiddin' about in the mud and hoping we don't make a balls of it and drive in ourselves. Once you slip in them muddy trenches you can't get out again."

Robbie pauses for effect. Clearly he didn't slip into a trench and die, as he's here telling the story, but it's a dramatic moment nonetheless. He's the charismatic centre of the group. Seline can see why she was drawn to him in the first place, why she's now slipped into her own kind of muddy trench and can't get out.

"So what happened?"

"We just about finish as the sun's coming up. It's still raining, so we manage to wash most of the cement dust off us just as the crew start arriving. It's still so gloomy no one can see into the trenches anyway. They pour the footings, and no one's any the wiser. God knows what the mix was like, but the buildings haven't fallen down yet. That's the toughest day's work I ever done, and it wasn't even breakfast."

AT THE BAR, Seline is getting a round of drinks in. No one sees it. No one sees Robbie for what he is. To everyone else, he's a cheeky, charming tearaway, a rough diamond. She pictures him smashing up the flat with unrestrained violence, remembers his hand round her throat, the way he threatened her. Then she looks across the room to where he's sitting with her colleagues, laughing, affable, more a part of the group than she is. She can't tell anyone what he's really like. No one would believe her.

Annie appears at her elbow.

"Thought I'd help you with the round. Having a good time?"

"It's nice to get out and see everyone."

"It's great you brought Robbie. What a character! He's so funny, isn't he? A proper joker. He's a wrong 'un, but you've got to love him, haven't you?" Annie gives Seline a drunken wink and a conspiratorial elbow in the ribs.

Seline can't bear the pretence any longer. She must talk to someone, whatever the consequences. She has to say something now.

"Annie—"

But before she can continue, Annie interrupts her.

"Oh, those are pretty."

Annie's leaning towards her. For a moment Seline can't work out what she's talking about. Then she realises what Annie's looking at. The crucifix earrings. She prods at them drunkenly.

"You don't usually wear them, do you? They look really nice. You should wear them more often."

A confused look crosses Annie's face.

"Actually, I'm sure I used to have some a bit like that. Now I see how nice they look on you, I must dig them out."

Annie lets go of the earring, picks up a couple of drinks from the order and drifts back to the rest of the group.

Seline stands rigid at the bar. Is it really possible the

earrings she's wearing now are Annie's? How can she talk to Annie now? How can she take the risk?

The pub is a riot of noise and laughter and people enjoying being together. It's packed to the rafters. But she's never felt more alone.

When she gets back to the flat later, the first thing she does is throw the earrings in the rubbish.

F ootballs lie still in the playground. The corridors don't echo with screaming voices. The classrooms are darkened and silent. Everyone has left for the night. Only one room is still lit up: the art room. Seline is staying late in the empty school to work on her paintings – and to avoid going home to Robbie.

The theory is great, but it soon gives way to the reality of the situation when Robbie appears around the door.

"Alright? I've come to pick you up."

This is one of her prisons, and he's her jailer, come to transport her to her other prison.

She wipes her brush on her painting smock, takes it off. Slowly she puts the lid back on the tube of oil paint she was using, begins to clear up, moving her canvas and easel to one side.

For want of anything better to do, Robbie starts looking at her completed paintings leaning against the wall, leafing through them like a customer in a second-hand music shop flicking through record sleeves, not expecting to find anything of interest.

"You have been busy. Are they all just women in rooms?" His tone speaks volumes about a lack of engagement with what he's looking at. He probably thinks he's appearing polite and interested. Seline wishes he wouldn't bother feigning interest, would rather he just didn't look at all. She can't bear watching him now, his clumsy hands pawing at her private work.

Now she sees him with her paintings, she wonders whether it was Robbie who came into her room and vandalised her drawings that first week, damaging her work to make her feel vulnerable so he could feign sympathy and worm his way in with her. That's exactly the sort of unpleasant, calculating thing he'd do.

"Can you leave those alone, please?"

He stops moving the paintings about and gives her a cold, hard stare.

"You what?"

She's challenged him and he doesn't like it. She thinks better of it and tries to back down.

"It's just that they're new ones. The oil isn't dry."

"Oh right. I see. Like this, you mean?"

He puts his finger on the face of the figure in the painting he's holding, then drags it hard across the canvas. The paint smears so that the features of the girl get stretched into a grotesque smudge.

"Oh yeah. You're right."

He puts the painting down on the table and starts walking slowly towards her. She's certain he's about to hit her for talking back to him.

And then there's suddenly someone else in the classroom doorway. Michael.

"Knock, knock. I've just been in a governors' meeting. Thought I'd come and see if our star artist is still at work. Hello, Robbie."

"Mr Lockwood." Michael's presence has a sobering effect on Robbie. He keeps his head dropped, looks at one of the paintings with intense concentration, his gaze fixed.

"Ooooh, are these some new paintings? Mind if I take a look?"

He makes his way over to the canvasses as Robbie steps back deferentially. Michael begins to study the paintings one at a time, making a variety of approving noises to himself. After a few minutes he looks up from the work.

"Well, Robbie, you've got yourself a bit of a talent here, haven't you?"

"Oh yeah. Definitely," says Robbie, wiping the paint from his finger onto his trousers. Seline knows Robbie wouldn't know whether a painting was good or not even if it was hung in a gallery – but Michael's admiration of them has certainly stopped him in his tracks.

Michael turns to Seline. "They're wonderful, really wonderful. I particularly like this one."

He tilts back a few paintings to reveal one in the pile – a blank-faced mousy girl sitting on a bed, her legs pulled up to her chest and her arms wrapped around them in some kind of foetal self-comforting, her sad eyes looking directly at the viewer; or rather, her fixed, blank stare looking right *through* the viewer, into nothing. The walls of her room a cool mint green. A window high behind her with a sense of louring storm clouds in the shadows.

"Thanks."

"She looks so sad. Is she for sale?"

"Really? Um, yes, I suppose so."

"Oh good. I'd love to have her. Think about a fair price."

"Okay." Seline can't believe it. Oh my God. Her first ever sale!

"Well, I shouldn't keep you any longer." Michael steps back towards the door. "In any case, I've got a couple of errands I need to run."

He pauses in the doorway, a thought drifting across his face.

"Actually, have you got half an hour?"


THEY'RE in Michael's car, driving west up the hill and out of town. It's a smart, shiny new limo, plush with leather and dark wood detailing, a delicious new car smell. Michael drives smoothly and confidently while Seline looks out of the passenger window, admiring the countryside – not, for once, hanging on for dear life like she is when Robbie is behind the wheel.

"Okay in the back there, Robbie?"

Robbie is sprawled in the corner of the back seat like a sulky schoolboy.

"Fine."

"Like the car? They dropped it off this weekend. Just getting used to it, but it seems to drive very nicely."

"Sweet."

"Maybe you should get one yourself, Robbie. I saw yours in the car park. Lovely old car, but it looks a bit tired now, eh? What is it, petrol or diesel?"

"Petrol."

"That's a shame. You can run more cheaply on diesel if you know where to go."

"Hmmm."

After five minutes they come to a long, high wall made from plyboard wooden panels. Michael pulls to the side where the wall is broken by a gate, honks his horn. A security man emerges from a hut and peers from a distance into the car. When he recognises the driver he raises a hand in acknowledgement, walks back and opens the gate.

"IRONCLAD." Seline's reading the name emblazoned on the wooden panels. "I remember that logo from a jumper my dad wore when I was a little girl."

"It's the security company I own." Michael drives through the gate and onto a plot of open land.

"So Dad worked for you?"

"Kind of. For a bit." Michael pulls the car to a halt next to a couple of muddy four-by-fours parked in front of a Portakabin. He jumps out and goes to the rear of the car and pops the boot. When Seline and Robbie get out, Michael hands them both hard hats and hi-vis jackets and all three of them put on the safety gear. They turn and look out at the view.

"I know it's dark and you can't properly see it, but I thought you'd be interested anyway. This site is my next big project. We're developing it with the council. It's an arts centre."

The area of field they are looking at is massive. It's skirted by the same wooden fencing they came through and is lit by a series of vast floodlights on stands. The ground is level, and Seline can see it's a kind of natural step in the hill. Looking to one side, the land carries on up and gets lost in the darkness of the sky. Beyond the vast field they are looking over, the gradient drops away and down the valley to where the lights of Statheley Bridge twinkle below them. Even on this dull winter night she can tell it will be the most incredible view.

So Michael was kind of her dad's boss? Michael owned all this, and her dad was just a security guard for him. It all makes a lot of sense to Seline, her dad's disappointment and how that must have seeped into his moods when she was young. Once again, Seline isn't happy with herself, but she can't help comparing her dad's modest life to Michael's achievements.

"It's an ambitious timetable, but we aim to be open in a year. We've staked it all out and we'll start digging the foundations in the next few weeks. I'd walk you down onto the main footprint, but these muddy building sites can be lethal in the wet; isn't that right, Robbie?"

"Yeah, definitely."

"We've got to pump out some of the groundwater first. Can't lay foundations without doing that. Rule one, eh?"

Robbie shifts awkwardly and says nothing.

This can't be a coincidence, thinks Seline, this talk of foundations and water and pumps, that conversation about diesel in the car. Michael knows about Robbie's story. Someone in the pub must have heard Robbie talking and told Michael about it. And now here's Michael, acting normal but letting Robbie know that he knows. Robbie certainly looks awkward about it all. On one hand Seline's delighted to see Robbie with the wind knocked out of his sails. But then again, when life brings Robbie down a peg or two he doesn't like it and usually takes it out on her. She'll end up paying for his humiliation.

Michael deliberately ignores Robbie's discomfort and

carries on. "There's going to be a four-hundred-seat theatre space, two cinemas, a shop, a bistro, a bar – and a gallery."

"Wow. Sounds like it's going to be incredible."

"It is. There's lottery cash, regional grants and local council money, as well as a few private benefactors…"

Seline assumes Michael is one of those, though he modestly doesn't say.

"I'm running the build, and I'm also on the steering committee. We're very keen that this place is a cultural beacon for the area, bringing world-class theatre and cinema and art to our towns and villages. But we also want to support the local arts ecology, give opportunities to local creatives."

"That's amazing."

"I guess what I'm saying, Seline, is that there may well be an opportunity for the gallery to open with an exhibition by a talented local artist. Might you be interested?"

ON THE DRIVE back down the hill Seline can't really think straight, she's so excited. She questions him several times, but Michael is deadly serious – he wants to bring his arts centre people to see her work, wants to discuss how they could support Seline towards presenting the opening show in the gallery. She can't believe it. She almost has to pinch herself. It's not definite, of course, she knows that; it's just an idea right now. But it's so exciting. And the way Michael talks about it all makes her feel good about herself for the first time in ages – special, like the whole place is somehow all being built just for her. She liked him the first time she met him, but seeing him again she feels a real affinity with him.

"Your mum and dad would be pleased. You can give them a ring about it from the car if you want...?"

"No, that's fine, thanks. I'll wait until I get home." The last thing Seline wants is her parents on speakerphone with Robbie in the car.

Michael swings into the school, pulls his car up next to Robbie's and turns the engine off.

"It must be very dull for Robbie having to drive you everywhere. You should get yourself your own little car."

Seline doesn't say anything and tries not to react. She doesn't look round, but she knows Robbie won't like this suggestion, the idea that she might have her independence, that he won't be able to keep her under guard morning, noon and night. She can hear him shift a little in the seat behind her. Robbie doesn't say anything either.

"Isn't that right, Robbie? I know a great little garage in the next village. What say we scoot up there at the weekend and I introduce you to the owner, see if we can sort you out with a set of wheels? Then poor old Robbie won't have to play chauffeur all the time. Eh, Robbie? Sound like a plan?"

"Fine by me." Robbie's painted into a corner. He can't refuse. Seline thinks he'll probably find a way of bullying her out of it later. Robbie opens his door and starts to get out. Seline reaches for her door handle to get out as well. As she does so, Michael moves his hand so it sits very lightly on her arm. She stops. Michael turns towards Seline. His easy, casual manner has given way to a seriousness.

"I've wanted to properly meet you for a long time, Seline. Because of my relationship with your parents, and because of what we shared in the past, I feel a real investment in what happens to you. You have an extraordinary future ahead. I know it."

"Thank you."

"I know it must be hard being away from them. I want you to know that I'm here, in loco parentis as it were."

His eyes are locked on hers. He looks at her with real intensity. Something about it makes her feel very connected to him in this moment. Robbie is standing awkwardly outside the car, next to his open door. What if she didn't get out? What if she told Michael everything now, about her fear, about all of it? Asked for help?

"Come on. I'm starving." Robbie leans back into the car on Seline's side. He takes hold of her elbow. He's smiling, but he's squeezing her elbow hard, which Michael can't see – his usual threatening trick to let her know that she'd better do what he says.

"Well, goodnight then." Michael takes his hand off her arm. She can feel herself losing the connection with him, handed back to Robbie, like a trapeze artist thrown through the air to be caught by someone else.

"Yeah, goodnight. Thanks." Robbie pulls her from the car and marches to his own car. They get in and sit in silence.

Seline can see Michael, sitting in his car, just five feet away. Then Michael moves off and out of the carpark.

Robbie turns to her. "If you tell *anyone anything* about me, I'll kill you."

"Robbie, I—"

"Shhh." He interrupts her by placing a finger gently on her lips. She stops talking. Then he slowly curls his finger and slides his finger into her mouth. She can taste the oil paint. She sits rigidly as he moves his finger around her mouth, pressing down on her tongue, pushing back towards her throat so she nearly gags. Then he curls his middle finger and puts it in her mouth. Then his ring finger. Then his little finger, flattening his hand and stretching her mouth so wide she thinks her lips might split. He pushes his fingers deeper into her mouth, up to the knuckles of his hand.

She can feel herself choking now. She tries to move her head, but the back of it is pressed against her seat. She tries to writhe sideways, but he uses his thumb to grip her jaw while he forces his fingers in. His hand is filling her mouth and she can hardly breathe. She's terrified he's going to suffocate her here in the car. She gasps for air, her eyes watering. She's retching now as the tips of his fingers are near the back of her throat, but each time she thinks she's about to be sick, he eases the pressure a little and she recovers. Then he jams his fingers in again. She isn't sure how many times he does this, but it feels like it's been going on for minutes. Eventually he relaxes his hand a little so he isn't prodding her throat. But he keeps all four fingers in her mouth, holding her lower jaw. She catches her breath.

He leans in to her. Stares into her eyes.

"Understand?"

She nods urgently, keen he should know she's not a threat to him.

He slips his hand out of her mouth. She coughs from the pain of it, wipes the tears from her cheeks.

"Good girl."

He wipes her saliva on the thigh of his trousers and starts the car.

"Right. Dinner."

He hums to himself breezily as they drive off.

# 25

In the days that follow, Seline can feel Robbie watching her more carefully. To her surprise, he's still allowing her to stay after school to paint. She assumes it's because Michael was encouraging about her artwork. She can't work out what there is between Robbie and Michael, but Robbie doesn't seem to want to cross him. Sadly though, painting has lost most of its attraction now she's no longer able to fully lose herself in her work.

Around school she tries to keep herself to herself. Robbie has thoroughly terrified her about talking to other people, so she avoids having any sort of conversation if she can. But one morning at break Graham approaches her in the staff room.

"Are you doing anything later, straight after school?"

"Why?"

"I wondered if you'd like to go for a drink. I wanted to talk to you about something."

"Thanks, but I don't think I can—"

Graham interrupts her. "Please. It's important. It's about Robbie."

Though she knows it's a risky thing to do, something about the urgency with which he says this makes her think she should hear what he has to say. Robbie expects her to stay on for a couple of hours this evening to do some painting, so she could meet briefly without him knowing about it."

"Okay."

THE BUTCHERS IS ALREADY BEGINNING to fill up with the Friday night crowd. Seline and Graham have been here for about fifteen minutes and Graham is already onto his second pint. Something about him seems different to usual. Nervous. The table around his glass is covered in tiny balls of paper where he's picked away at a beer mat.

The door to the street opens and a group of noisy girls enter. The screeching laughter makes Graham turn round and he must spot what Seline sees immediately: the shock of green hair. It's a group of young girls, pupils from the school, including Graham's daughter Julie. Graham turns back to the table, avoids Seline's gaze and stares morosely at his pint. The noise of the giggling girls carries across the pub. It's impossible to ignore. Graham heaves a weary sigh and gets up, crosses over to where they're sitting.

Julie and her group are seated some way away, so Seline can't hear most of what's said between father and daughter. It's clear that Graham is trying to have a reasonable conversation, no doubt pointing out that Julie is fifteen and shouldn't be drinking in the pub. It doesn't take long though for things to get heated, and Julie's attitude is anything but reasonable. She's standing up now, getting louder. People at neighbouring tables are beginning to look round. Graham holds his hands out, palms downwards, and makes a 'calm down' gesture, but this only seems to inflame Julie further. Seline can hear snatches of what Julie's saying. There's a very loud "*oh fuck off*" which makes it clear Julie's going to turn this into a scene. Then Julie looks past Graham and stares straight at Seline.

"Oh sorry, am I interrupting a night out with your slut?"

Oh God. A few heads turn in Seline's direction. She stares at her drink, trying to be as invisible as possible.

There's more shouting from Julie, then the sound of chairs scraping across the floor and one being knocked over. A final few hurled insults and then some glasses being smashed, to the amusement and cheers of a few other drinkers. And they're gone. The general murmur of the pub resumes. Seline still doesn't look up. After a moment Graham returns to the table.

"Sorry about that."

Graham carries on the conversation as if nothing has happened, but he's clearly agitated. Ten minutes later he's on his third pint, and instead of avoiding what's just happened he begins to mention it, then talk about it more openly, and finally starts pouring his woes out about his miserable marriage and his daughter who hates him. Seline didn't know what to expect from this meeting, but it certainly wasn't this, being confessor to a sad, drunken man she barely knows. She is beginning to feel anxious about being here and knows she should get back to the school.

"Graham, I have to leave very soon."

As if it couldn't get any worse, Graham has come to sit next to her rather than opposite, has been grabbing at her hand whilst telling his miserable tale, and then, out of nowhere, makes an awkward lunge to kiss her. Seline pulls back in surprise, utterly stunned. Graham looks equally surprised, as if he had no idea the attempted kiss was going to happen until it happened. He leaps up, burbles some kind of awkward apology and goes round to sit on the opposite side of the table. He slumps, crumples into himself like a balloon slowly deflating. His face is grey. His sad eyes begin to glisten and then tears start to roll down his cheeks.

"I'm sorry, sorry, I'm sorry..." He chokes down sobs, a bubble of snot runs from his nose. He thumps his head with his fist. "Idiot. Idiot." It's awful, embarrassing. Seline prays that no one on the neighbouring tables will notice. Fortunately, people seem too absorbed in their own fun evenings to pay any attention to her miserable one.

Eventually, Graham gets control of himself. "I'm sorry. It wasn't meant to be like this."

"It's fine. Forget it." How can she forget it? This is what she'll remember now, every time she sees him at school. She reaches for her jacket, knowing it's time to leave.

"Look, I'm sorry, I'm just drunk and stupid. But I *need* to talk to you, and I don't want that, what I just did, to get in the way."

Seline's putting her jacket on. "I have to go."

"Look! About Robbie..." His voice is urgent.

She finishes putting on her jacket but doesn't stand up. She should hear this. Probably Graham trying to put her off Robbie so he can clear the field to make another awkward pass at her. She can give it another five minutes.

"I've been at this school a long time. I was here when Robbie was here as a pupil. I taught him. He was a proper troublemaker. Look, tell me to mind my own business, don't talk to me again, but I couldn't live with myself if I didn't talk to you about this. He isn't just some cheeky tearaway everyone thinks he is. He's a nasty, vicious little shit."

There's real vitriol in Graham's voice when he says this. He's upset. His voice has got louder. It feels like he's been sitting on saying this for too long and now he's releasing the pressure. It's like a dam bursting, gushing out.

"I've had plenty of students who mess about, who are cheeky or disruptive, who just muck about and be the class clown to cover up the fact they don't want to do the work, or don't understand it, or are just stupid. You learn to manage those kids so they don't get in the way of the good ones. But Robbie was different. He wasn't just a troublemaker – he was *trouble*. Proper nasty, evil little..."

His thought trails off as he remembers something. Seline can't listen to much more of this aimless chatter. She has her own very real problems with Robbie and doesn't need Graham's petty moaning about a few badly behaved boys.

"One lunchtime I found him in my classroom. Robbie was playing football, booting a small ball about and not caring where he was. When I came in, Robbie snatched the ball up. I reminded him that kids weren't allowed inside at lunchtime, certainly not inside a science lab. He made some snide remark and left. Once he'd gone I started clearing up the mess he'd made, knocked over stools and whatnot. Then I saw the fish – we kept fish and animals in the lab back then, for biology – the fish tank was full of pink water and the fish were floating on the water. He'd poured in an entire tub of potassium permanganate crystals. The little shit. Killed them all for some reason. I checked on the other tanks but they were fine.

"That's when I noticed the hamster cage. Door open. It was empty. He'd let the hamster out. I started looking for it, down on the floor, looking along the edges of the benches, into the corners, crawling along on my hands and knees thinking where it would hide, looking for any holes it might have got into. I put my hand in something wet, which I thought was water from the fish tank. Only it wasn't. It was blood. A little smear of blood.

"Then I realised. He hadn't been playing football with a ball. He'd been playing it with the hamster. Kicking it hard across the room. Kicking it and laughing. What sort of person does that? Thinks to do that? Enjoys torturing an animal?"

Seline has listened to the story impassively. She can see Graham looking at her, looking for some reaction. But she daren't react.

"You should steer clear of him. Really."

Again, she doesn't react.

"You don't believe me."

But she *does* believe him. Every word. It's all too horribly, upsettingly credible. That sounds completely like the Robbie she knows. Vicious and callous and cruel. She could tell Graham that now, that she believes every word he's saying – but what good would that do her? Graham's a defeated, snivelling wreck and he's no match for the kind of threat Robbie presents. He couldn't even deal with him as a schoolkid, so what would he do against him now?

She gets up and starts to leave.

"Seline..."

She can't stay. There's no point in Graham telling her anything else, confirming what she already knows – that the man she's living with is a violent, sociopathic monster. Graham's up and trying to follow her. But what can she say? She can't tell Graham she knows all this to be true. How would it help? What could he do? How can he help her with Robbie? He can't even confront his fifteen-year-old daughter without bursting into tears.

As she makes it to the door and out into the night she can hear Graham calling behind her.

"Be careful. He's not just trouble. He's dangerous."

---

## 26

True to his word, the following weekend Michael takes Seline to look for a car. Like last time, Michael and Seline sit in the front of Michael's limo, while Robbie is confined to the back seat, like the child of the family. His surly body language and petulant silence make it clear he's not happy with the arrangement, but he doesn't explicitly resist anything where Michael is concerned. If Seline stares ahead and doesn't look round, she can almost imagine he doesn't exist.

THE GARAGE IS A COMPLETELY unfamiliar environment to her. It's a relatively small place, just off a main road, with several cars packed together on the forecourt and on the grass verge in front, all glistening and shiny from a recent rain shower. This was clearly a fuel station at one point, with a covered area over the tarmac at the front of the building, but the pumps have all been removed and the signage changed to make it clear it is now a second-hand car dealership, including a tall, bright red tube-dancer writhing in a manic dance as it inflates and deflates.

The office itself is small and has a burnt dust smell from a bank of electric bar fires. The back of the office opens into a mechanics' workspace, with cars in various states of repair, on ground level or up on hydraulic lifts. Several men in blue overalls, smeared black with oil and grease, move between the vehicles and a large wall of tools on one side. A pair of legs poke out from beneath the nearest car, and a faceless mechanic reaches out and sightlessly lands his hand perfectly into a box of spanners, finding precisely what he's after by touch alone.

Michael goes through an adjoining office door, presumably to where he'll find his friend, the owner. Robbie drifts through into the garage, chatting to a mechanic he clearly knows from somewhere. Everyone knows everyone here. Seline sits in a tatty vinyl chair and keeps watching the mechanic under the car, his arm appearing and disappearing like a snake's tongue. She notices his bare arm, an extraordinarily intricate dragon tattoo with a burning jet of fire wrapping around his wrist, its scaly body entwining his forearm and disappearing at the elbow beneath his overalls. Other than this flash of beauty, it's a decidedly male environment.

Michael emerges with some keys and leads Seline back out front to a blue four-door hatchback. He opens the driver's door and pulls out the array of cardboard resting on the dashboard.

"Ignore the price."

Seline gets in behind the wheel. She instinctively flashes her eyes towards Robbie, assuming he'll want to come too. But Michael passes her the keys.

"Take her for a spin."

Michael closes the door, standing next to Robbie, who's now firmly excluded, on the forecourt outside.

SELINE DRIVES the car along the sweeping country roads. She tries to remember the last time she felt like this, in control, in charge of where she's heading and what she's doing, and alone – properly alone. Who knew that sitting behind the wheel of a cheap hatchback could feel so utterly liberating?

She turns a corner and finds herself facing a magnificent view, the road bordering onto a picturesque lake, and behind that an expanse of open ground dotted with trees that sweeps up into a hill crisscrossed with zigzagging dry stone walls. She spots a gravelled lay-by, clearly placed here for sightseers, and pulls over.

"Hi, Mum."

"Oh, hello, darling." Seline can detect the note of surprise in her mother's voice. With all this Robbie business, she hasn't been phoning home of late. But something about being out in the open and away from him makes her desperate to hear her mum.

"How are you?"

"I'm good, thanks. Sorry I haven't spoken to you for ages."

"That's okay, luv. I'm just glad you're okay. What have you been up to?"

Seline looks out of her window. "I'm just sitting looking at an absolutely amazing view. I'm test-driving a car and thought I'd stop to say hello."

"Oh, that's exciting. Have you seen anything you like? Can you afford it?"

"Yeah, I'm sure I can."

"Well, that's good. Perhaps that means we'll see a bit more of you."

Seline feels a wave of emotion come over her. She misses them so much. She hasn't let herself feel it, but now the weight of it washes over her. She feels like she could cry.

"God, I'd like that so much."

"Maybe you could come over next weekend?"

She remembers back to the last time she travelled home – and Robbie turning up uninvited, dragging her back. He's never let her go.

"Maybe. I'll see."

"Didn't you say a while back you wanted to come over and get some of your paintings?"

"Yeah…" She doesn't really know what to say. She knows Robbie won't let her go, but she can't say that. Her mum picks up on the reticence in her voice.

"Or we could come to you. Would you like your dad to come over and look at the car first? You don't know much about cars."

"No, really, it's okay. I've been taken to see it by Dad's friend Michael. He knows someone who owns a garage."

"Oh yes?" There's a silence. "Well, if you're sure."

"He's being really helpful." She's desperate to share her one bit of good news. "In fact, he's setting up an arts centre here and I may be getting an exhibition of my paintings."

A pause.

"Hang on." Her mother covers the mouthpiece of her phone. There's some talking. Seline can't make out what's being said. Then her mother comes back on the phone.

"Sorry, luv, there's someone at the door. I'll call you back in a bit and we'll work out whether you come to us or we come to you."

"Oh. Okay."

And Seline's left on her own again, looking out at the view.

"Well?" Michael's quizzical face greets her as she comes back into the forecourt office. "You like?"

"Yes, very much."

Robbie's still in the rear garage, out of earshot, so Seline feels safe to be enthusiastic.

"Excellent. I thought you would. I've spoken to Craig, and he's going to do you a good deal on it, and some cheap finance as well. Congratulations! Consider yourself an independent car owner."

Seline, Michael, Robbie and Craig, the garage owner, cram themselves into the small back office so Seline can complete the paperwork. As she's filling in the forms, her phone rings again. It's her mum.

"I've spoken to your dad. We'll come over at the weekend and bring your paintings."

"Mum, can I call you back? I'm just—"

Michael holds up a finger to get Seline's attention.

"If your parents are coming over here, tell them to come to lunch with me, Tess and Charlotte. I insist."

Seline returns to the call. "Did you hear that?"

A long pause. Her mum is mumbling something to her dad. Finally, she comes back on the phone.

"Alright. We'll see you next weekend." Her mum ends the call.

Seline thinks that was oddly abrupt. And the earlier

conversation was odd too. She'd have thought her mum would be more excited about her getting an exhibition. Maybe she just took her by surprise. Anyway, she'll be able to tell them all about it properly next weekend.

Michael's smiling broadly. "It will be wonderful to catch up after all this time."

SELINE DRIVES her and Robbie back to the flat in her new car. She can tell Robbie hates being in the passenger seat with her at the wheel, but he could hardly do anything about it with Michael there. Robbie spends the entire journey in silence, but once he and Seline are in the flat, he starts ranting, won't shut up about having to sit in the back of Michael's car and getting ordered about like a child. He seems completely oblivious to the irony that he couldn't be acting more like a child if he tried. He clearly feels belittled by the whole experience, even to the point of saying he should have hit Michael for pushing him about like that.

"And him lording it about over that fucking car!"

Robbie picks up her car keys from where they're sitting on the kitchen table. He jingles them intimidatingly close to her face.

"Don't think this car means you can swan off whenever you want to. You wanna go somewhere, you ask me."

He tosses the keys in the air and, giving her a hideous grin, puts them in his pocket.

## 27

"Can I have my car keys, please?"

Seline is standing in the kitchen. It's Sunday. She's dressed and ready to go and meet her parents and Michael's family in the pub as arranged. She has her coat and shoes on. Now she has to go through the humiliating ritual of begging Robbie for her car keys so she can get to the pub in time for their lunch.

Robbie's sitting at the kitchen table, flicking through the sports section of a tabloid. He doesn't look up.

"No. I'll drive us in a minute."

"Oh. You're coming?"

She tries to keep her voice as neutral as possible. They haven't discussed him coming before. He's just invited himself to lunch.

"Got a problem with that?"

"No. Not at all."

"Just as well."

Robbie continues to read his paper for a bit while Seline just stands there.

"Sit down for fuck's sake. I said we'll go in a minute."

Seline sits at the table.

"Oh, and take a look at this."

For a moment Seline thinks he means something in his newspaper. But then she realises he's taken his phone out and is scrolling through it, trying to find something. She waits until he finds what he's looking for.

"Here." He slides his phone across the table to her. She picks it up and looks at the screen.

It's her. Photos of her, naked. She remembers immediately when they're from. That first week at Robbie's flat, when he was charming and exciting and made her feel good about herself. Smiling. Looking defiantly at the camera. Breasts bare. Squatting on a ruffled bed. Kneeling on all fours. Sultry eyes. Wet-lipped. Looking brazenly over her shoulders, legs slightly apart. She scrolls through the photographs. She stops before she gets to the most explicit ones, the images of them having sex. The videos.

"If you don't tell Mummy and Daddy anything they don't need to hear, I won't show them anything they don't need to see. Understand?"

Seline nods. Robbie takes the phone off her.

"Excellent." He stands up. "Now then. Lunch. I could murder a roast."

SELINE SITS SILENTLY at the pub table, nervously toying with her glass. Her mother is opposite her, rabbiting away about something or other. Seline can't concentrate on what she's saying and has lost the thread of the conversation. She has been considering how to tell her parents everything about

Robbie, but his scene with the photographs has made that impossible.

She looks out of the pub window to where she knows her father is standing with Robbie, obscured by the open bonnet of her car, which they have been inspecting for the last fifteen minutes. What are they talking about? Are they ever coming back in?

Eventually Robbie and her dad return and sit at the table.

"At last." Her mum gives her dad a hard look. "Really, Colin. We've been here for ages. The girl has been over to take our order twice."

"Sorry."

Robbie leans over and takes Seline's mother's hand and kisses it with a comedic flourish. "Diana. Lovely to see you again."

"Hello, Robbie." She giggles girlishly.

"Not a bad little motor, is it, Colin?"

"No, not bad," replies Seline's dad unenthusiastically.

"Now then, drinks! Who wants what? Colin, I'm on a pint – will you join me?"

And this is how Robbie carries on: jovial, charming, the sort of charismatic behaviour Seline first noticed on day one in the staff room and hasn't seen much since. By now she knows it's all an act, nothing like how he really is behind closed doors. It's just a hollow display. Robbie's talking, telling his stories, and keeps smiling at Seline and putting his hands on her – on her shoulder, on her thigh. All wide-boy charm and touchy-feely. She knows what it all means. He's got her. He still has her in his control. She isn't going anywhere. She's been so concerned about how her parents will react when she finally tells them what's been going on, what they will think of her shacking up with this monster, she hadn't even considered this eventuality: that he might charm them and win them over. How will they be able to connect her stories of a brutal, aggressive, terrifying thug with this man in front of them, grinning and schmoozing and putting on a big show, as if he's the jovial host who's invited *them* to lunch?

Fortunately, Seline doesn't have to endure the sickening display for too long before Michael, Tess and Charlotte arrive.

From that point on, the lunch passes in a kind of blur. Michael is open, friendly and greets Colin and Diana warmly. He asks them a few things about what they've been up to and seems genuinely interested in spite of their curt answers. They all order roast dinners and, while they eat, Michael talks expansively about his own life. He dominates the conversation, but not in a bad way. If anything, he's making up for how unforthcoming her mum and dad are being. They seem decidedly off-colour. Seline can't help wondering if it's because their own lives seem small and uninteresting when contrasted with Michael's wealth and success. Or does her own terrible mood mean her perception of everything else is skewed?

The one upside to this is that whenever Michael talks, he's the most interesting person in the room and his presence has a clear effect on Robbie, who stops all his bravado and sits poking his dinner about in relative silence, stabbing away at a roast potato as if he bears it some sort of grudge.

Seline's on edge because she knows that whenever Robbie's made to look small in front of Michael, she'll pay for it when they get home. Robbie is clearly not enjoying the experience. And her mum and dad are smiling away inanely at what Michael is saying, but barely joining in with the conversation at all. To an observer, they'd look like a perfectly normal group of people enjoying a pleasant lunch together. But close up, Seline knows that she, Robbie and her parents are all massively on edge. The whole awful experience is rounded off when the bill arrives and there's an awkward exchange between Michael and Colin about who will pay, Colin finally pulling the bill away from Michael rather too forcefully and insisting the waitress take his credit card, and Michael smiling, leaning back in his chair and thanking Colin.

"Colin, really, you didn't need to do that. It's too kind. That means we *must* do it again soon, and I'm paying next time."

Next time? Seline can't imagine going through the stress of this again.

OUT IN THE CAR PARK, they say their stilted goodbyes, Michael shaking Colin's hand heartily, saying they mustn't leave it so long next time, then hugging Diana warmly, almost lifting her up, kissing her on the cheek. Then Michael gives Seline a long hug too, and a kiss on the cheek, while his wife and daughter look on from his limo. Michael smiles at Colin again and goes off to his car.

With Michael out of the way, Robbie pipes up, doing the same handshake and hug thing with her parents. They all say goodbye and then Colin and Diana head off to their own car, while Seline and Robbie head to hers.

"Seline?"

Seline turns round. Her dad has stopped in the middle of the car park. He beckons Seline to come to him. She trots over. When she gets to him he pulls her into a hug. It's the first time he's properly engaged with her all day. For a split second Seline closes her eyes, feels safe, and imagines what it would be like to be carried off by her dad, put into the back seat of their car, taken home to her childhood bedroom, to safety, to her old life.

Her dad hugs her tighter, presses his head against the side of her own, whispers into her ear.

"If anyone tries to hurt you, does anything to harm you – I'll kill them."

He lets her go, turns and walks back to his car. Seline stands there, in shock, waiting for him to turn back and look at her, but he doesn't. He opens the car door, gets in. He starts the engine, looking straight ahead, and drives off, out of the car park and onto the road, then past a hedge and out of sight.

They're gone.

Once again, it's just her, alone with Robbie.

# 28

Seline lies awake most of the night.

*If anyone tries to hurt you, does anything to harm you – I'll kill them.*

Her father's words go round and round in her head all night, while Robbie snores in the bed next to her. Seline's never once known her dad to be aggressive, or violent. He's never shouted at her, even when she's been bad. The two of them were incredibly close when she was young. She worshipped him. He seemed so strong and good and always knew everything about everything, and always told her the right thing to do. All her values she gets from him.

One day, when she was about ten, she and some friends found a five-pound note in the street. It was the most exciting thing imaginable. They went to the newsagent at the end of her road and bought bags and bags of penny sweets, then took them to the park and ate them. It was one of her happiest days ever. But when she came home and told her parents about it, she immediately knew from the look on her father's face that she'd made a mistake. Her father told her how disappointed he was in her. Think of the person who lost that money, what they might need it for, how they would be feeling now on discovering they had lost it. That taking it and spending it was stealing, plain and simple. All this in such a calm voice that it made her burning shame worse.

If he'd shouted, that would have been better. And somehow she felt in that moment that some fragile, fundamental thing in their relationship shifted, had broken, and that things were never the same again. Their closeness had gone. She had disappointed him.

So no, he was never angry or aggressive.

*If anyone tries to hurt you, does anything to harm you – I'll kill them.*

Has he somehow sensed her terror of Robbie? What he's like? Has he seen through Robbie's act, beneath the surface charm, seen Robbie for what he is: a nasty, violent, controlling bully?

And if her dad has seen through him, have other people seen through him too? Graham certainly has; those horrible things he told her about him torturing animals at school. Maybe everyone knows. Everyone knows about Robbie, and they all think Seline is an idiot, that she has made some terrible, stupid mistake.

SELINE MANAGES to get up quietly while Robbie is still asleep. She dresses for school and puts her coat on to leave. She pauses by the front door and looks at the small bowl where Robbie keeps his car keys – and her keys too. She doesn't know what to do, but her dad's words keep going round in her head. Should she talk to him? Should she just get in her car and drive over there? But what will Robbie do, to her and to her parents, if she does?

She leaves the flat. She gets in her car and sits in it for ten full minutes, paralysed with indecision. She can't decide now. She'll think it through, work out what the best course of action is as she drives. She starts the engine. Is this it? Is she really driving home now? The car moves off.

She reaches a junction in the road and turns – but it's towards the church. She pulls up in the staff car park and stops the engine. She isn't ready. But if she does get up the courage to go, she's prepared now. She makes the short walk into school, clutching her car keys in her tightly balled fist in her coat pocket, like a drowning person clinging to a lifeline.

Her distraction isn't helped by the fact that she starts the school day teaching the Year 10s. Ever since that first lesson, where Graham's daughter Julie so terrifyingly threatened to cut her ear off, Seline has felt she's barely maintained the illusion of being in control of the class – like someone hanging on to a runaway horse, only riding by dint of the fact that they haven't fallen off yet. These lessons teeter on the edge of chaos, with Julie acting as ringleader. It's just a matter of time before something really bad happens.

Despite frequent requests for them to be quiet and concentrate, the class never fully settle and their work is scrappy and superficial as a result. She needs quiet to think through what to do next, so in an effort to frighten them into focusing, Seline talks about the exams they'll have coming up at the end of term and a portfolio review she'll do of their work. They don't seem to care. She asks a few of them to stay behind after class to go through their work folders, and adds Julie to the list. Even though Seline is afraid of confronting her, she figures if she can get control of Julie, the others will back down.

"Is this gonna take long, 'cos I'm gasping for a fag?"

Seline's made Julie wait until last, in a deliberate effort to demonstrate authority. She half expected the girl to walk out, but she waited grumpily, and is now sitting across a desk from her teacher, face locked in a permanent scowl, her scrappy dog-eared art folder on the table between them. Seline opens it and begins to leaf through the scant pile of drawings and paintings, each one the output from an hour's lesson and looking like the product of five minutes' work and fifty-five minutes' idle chatter. Seline doesn't bother commenting, assuming Julie won't care what she says. She knows she should say something, but it just feels like too much wasted effort.

Then Seline turns to a page of pen drawings. These are abstract sketches: rows of lines in different thicknesses; shaded cubes and spheres; outlines of skulls; a drawing of a rose on a stem covered in thorns; stars; planets; butterflies; a bleeding heart. They're not brilliant, but they are clearly the product of some kind of effort. Julie spots this sheet of paper and snatches it away.

"Fuck off. That's not for here."

"What are those, Julie?"

"Nothing!"

"No, really, tell me. They're good."

Julie pauses, then puts the sheet down again.

"Just some drawings I done for myself."

"Wow."

"For tattoos. I wanna get a job in a tattoo parlour. They're rubbish."

"They're not. They're really not. They're excellent."

Seline can feel immediately they've made a connection she wasn't expecting.

"I'll tell you what I see, Julie. I see someone who can do excellent work when she puts her mind to it. We both know you mess about in class, but these look like you've properly taken time, concentrated, given yourself a chance and done something really excellent."

"It don't matter. My dad won't let me work in a tattoo parlour. He's a stuffy twat."

"Well, I bet you don't know that. I know your dad and I'm sure he wants you to do well and be happy."

"He's a prat. Him an' my mum. I hate them. They're always arguin' all the time 'cos she knobbed some rich arsehole, but all they do is shout at each other. She's a bitter old prune and he's too much of a pussy to do anything about anything. They haven't even got the balls to split up."

Too much information. Seline decides to ignore it.

"I don't know about any of that, Julie. All I do know is that you've got a talent here. And if you don't like thinking of my lessons as doing school work, think of them as practising to get even better at the thing you love doing."

Once Julie has left, Seline allows herself a moment to reflect on what's just happened. She has felt such a failure here, but maybe without Robbie dragging her down she could properly make a go of this. Those drawings weren't great, but they mattered to Julie and Seline has used them to make a connection. Maybe Julie will pay more attention in art. Maybe she'll actually get better at drawing. Maybe she'll even get to do what she wants to do, however unlikely that is. But undeniably Seline has just accomplished an actual bit of teaching.

The morning passes. Seline sits staring at her lunch,

puzzling through what to do next about Robbie. But her thoughts drift back to her conversation with Julie. Something about this encounter gives her courage. She didn't duck the problem. She met it head-on and feels all the better for it. That's what she needs to do with Robbie. Whatever the consequences, she can't carry on as she has been.

That's it. She's going to drive home right now and talk to her parents about everything.

She's just about to make a move when Mrs Jessop taps her on the shoulder.

"Can I have a word?"

Seline looks down at her plate of cottage pie, then up at the Head, who has clearly seen her food and knows it will get cold but doesn't sit down to talk to Seline.

"You can leave that. Someone will clear it away for you."

Seline gets up, follows Mrs Jessop through the busy canteen, threading their way between tables of boisterous kids. The Head doesn't stop to admonish anyone for unruly behaviour, just keeps walking briskly with single-minded determination. When they pass by a food fight without comment, Seline knows this must be serious.

They leave the canteen and walk down the corridor towards reception, Mrs Jessop marching ahead, Seline practically trotting to keep up. She thinks they must be going to the Head's office, but they pass the door and go out through the main entrance and into the playground. Then round the corner to the staff car park. Seline can't fathom what they might be doing here.

Then she sees it.

Her car, which she'd parked out of the way in one corner under a tree, has been attacked with paint. It looks like house paint, white gloss, thrown onto the windscreen and the bonnet. And then obscenities daubed crudely onto the doors, the side windows, the boot.

"SLAG." "WHORE." "BITCH."

None of the other cars have been touched. This is nasty. This is personal. It must be Robbie. He's got up, seen her car keys have gone and knows she's defied him. He's raced down here and done this.

"I don't know what's going on here, Seline, but we can't have this in the school. The children can see this from the playground. This can be seen from the road."

"I'm sorry." She doesn't even know what she's apologising for. Someone has done this to her, yet here she is apologising. She's lost so much of her confidence it automatically feels like she's messed up again, as if this is another black mark against her. She is on the verge of tears.

Mrs Jessop adopts a more sensitive tone, wanting to avoid a scene. She puts a hand awkwardly on Seline's shoulder.

"This is horrible. I'm sure this is horrible for you. I'll get someone to cover your lessons this afternoon. You take the rest of the day and deal with this. Okay?"

Seline gets into the car, tries to start the engine. The electrics come on but the engine won't turn over. She turns the wipers on and immediately realises her mistake, as thick wet gloss paint smears across the windscreen, the slow wipers labouring under the load. They'll never remove the paint. She can't drive it anyway, she realises, not with all that written on the sides. And why won't the engine start?

She gets out and goes to the front of the car to look. The bonnet is slightly open. She takes a tissue from her pocket and uses it to lift the bonnet, not wanting to get the paint on her hands. She knows nothing about engines, but can see that some of the components have been pulled loose.


"HELLO? IS THAT CRAIG?"

Seline phones the garage she got the car from. She can't think who else she'd call. She explains the situation, that her car can't be driven, probably needs towing, and likely once cleaned up will need respraying. Craig listens to the details without comment, as if cars daubed with gloss paint and their engines ripped apart are a regular occurrence. He says something mumbled to one of the mechanics and then comes back on the line and confirms someone can come down and pick up the car within the hour.

"And shall I send the bill to Mr Lockwood?"

Seline's confused. "Mr Lockwood...?"

"Michael."

She can hear a kind of leery smile in his voice. What is he insinuating? What does he think is going on?

"No. Let me know how much it is and I'll pay it."

"Fair enough."


SELINE TRACKS down Dave the security guard in his office. She explains that someone has vandalised her car. She's noticed the sides of the school building and the fences have security cameras on them. Would it be possible to review the tapes so that they can track down who has done this? She tries to be casual about it, but she knows it must be Robbie. If she has tape of him doing something criminal to her car, maybe she can go to the police and get him out of her life that way. Then she won't have to get her dad involved and her parents won't have to know all the horrible details. She'd love to keep them out of this if she can.

"Sorry, love, I can't."

"What do you mean? This is criminal damage. What kind of policy doesn't allow me to look at the security tapes?"

"No, I mean we can't look at the tapes because there aren't any tapes. Those cameras are just for show. They don't record anything. In terms of security, you're looking at it right here."

He gestures to himself.

"Maybe one of the other teachers saw something? Or one of the kids…?"

He trails off. This is hopeless. She leaves the security office and wanders back listlessly to the playground, just in time to see her car being towed away.

It must have been Robbie, destroying her car so she can't go anywhere in it. She had a brief feeling of independence and Robbie must have seen that. He had to take it away from her. Now it's gone.

## 29

M rs Jessop has told her to leave for the day, so Seline packs her stuff up and walks home. As she turns into her road she spots someone unmistakable hanging around outside the flat. Even in the winter gloom she can see it's Julie, her green hair poking out from underneath a hooded sweater. What the hell is Julie doing here? How does she even know where she lives?

Julie leans against the door of the flat, looking shiftily up and down the road. She's clearly waiting for something – or someone – and she's not going away. Seline doesn't know what to do next. Just as she's puzzling this all out she sees Robbie's car drive up the road, past the flat and round the back to where he parks it. Seline steps back and watches from a distance in the shadows behind some wheelie bins. Then he walks up the pavement towards where Julie is standing. What's going to happen next? Presumably he'll tell this random schoolgirl to shove off and that will be that.

Only that's not what happens. Robbie and Julie exchange a few words, they seem to remonstrate for a moment, Robbie opens the street door, looks around – and then the two of them go inside.

Seline remains squatting behind the bins, getting colder, her feet beginning to lose feeling, pulling her coat around her against the drizzle that is starting to fall. She crouches and watches the door. She can't stay here all night. It's freezing. But what can she do? She watches and waits.

And waits.

Eventually, after half an hour has passed, the door opens and Julie emerges. She turns out of the door and starts to walk up the street, towards where Seline is hiding. Seline hunches down further, presses her back against the brick wall of the flats on the corner and listens for Julie's footsteps, approaching, then passing, then receding into nothing.

She gives it another minute, then stands up. She has to think carefully about what she does next. She can't just confront Robbie, as he'll go ballistic. But she needs to know what Julie wanted and what the hell he's up to. She stamps her feet to get some of the feeling back and brushes the worst of the drizzle off her hair and coat, so she won't look quite so much like someone who's been standing in the freezing rain for the best part of an hour.

"I THOUGHT you were staying late at school?"

No 'hello.' No 'how was your day?' The atmosphere is so bad that even this enquiry comes over as a hostile accusation.

"No. I was going to but... well, it wasn't a great day so I came home."

She doesn't want to say too much yet about the car, thinking he might say something stupid, give away that it was him who did it. But he just looks at her. She can't tell what he's thinking.

"You look a bloody mess. Like a drowned rat."

"Well, I had to walk. It's raining."

He's not going to say anything. She tries to nudge the conversation forward.

"The garage has got my car."

"Oh yes?" He doesn't sound that interested. He'd normally go ballistic if she took the car without asking him.

"Did you see the keys had gone?"

She waits. Still he doesn't give anything away.

"What's up with it?" It's impossible to read his tone.

"It got vandalised. Someone threw paint on it. And ripped out bits of the engine."

He laughs. "Blimey!"

He's either covering up for the awful thing he's done, or it really wasn't him and he just finds her suffering funny. Either way, it further cements her view of him as a horrible, uncaring shit. She feels tears welling up inside her, but refuses to give him the pleasure of seeing her cry.

"Was that Julie I saw outside?"

"What?"

As soon as she says it, she knows this could go anywhere, could mean all sorts of trouble.

"Julie, the green-haired girl from school. I thought I saw her leaving as I was coming in."

"Oh right. Yeah. She was looking for you. I told her to fuck off. She's a fucking nutter. You should definitely stay away from her.'

Julie was here for half an hour, so obviously she knows he's lying. He clearly doesn't want her talking to Julie. Is he sleeping with her? She's seen how he flirts with those girls at school. Julie's only fifteen, but she wouldn't put anything past Robbie. Did they vandalise her car together, or did he get Julie to do it? She decides she'd be wise to leave it there. But to her surprise, it's Robbie who keeps the conversation going.

"You know your precious Michael Lockwood, and his perfect life and his perfect family? He's shagging Julie's mum."

Seline stares at him. Is he making this up? Can Michael really be the 'rich arsehole' Julie said her mother was having an affair with?

"Everyone in town knows it. He was shagging your mate's wife, your mate Graham, and she told your mate all about it, said she was going to leave him – and then Michael dumped her. But the thing is, he'd lent her loads of money to set up her business, and so she was into him for thousands. The poor buggers didn't have enough money to split up and get new houses. So they're stuck there, living with each other, hating the fucking bones of each other but with nowhere to go."

She's not sure whether to believe him. Michael's made Robbie feel small and stupid whenever they've been together, so now maybe Robbie is inventing some story, trying to make Michael look bad, to bring him down somehow in Seline's eyes.

"So, not quite such a hero, is he?" Robbie laughs.

The whole story seems unbelievably funny to Robbie. And though Seline half believes he might be making it up, there's something about it, about how Julie described her parents, about how broken and defeated Graham seems, that makes it all ring true.

"Maybe Julie knows Michael got you that car. Maybe she smashed it up. Kids, eh?"

Robbie leaves the room, sniggering like a stupid schoolboy.

Seline sits at the kitchen table in her dripping coat. She doesn't bother to take off her wet shoes or dry her hair. Either Robbie vandalised her car, or someone else did and he finds it hilarious. He's a shit either way. She sits contemplating the casual cruelty of Robbie's behaviour.

She hears him move around the flat, watch some television and eventually go to bed. He turns the lights off as he goes, so the flat is lit dimly by the ethereal glow of the streetlights and the neon of the takeaway below. He doesn't once look in the kitchen, to see how she is or say goodnight to her. Once she can hear him snoring she gets up and goes into the darkened hallway, finally takes her coat off, which is dry now, and hangs it on the pegs by the door. She goes into the bathroom, picking up the football trophy to open the door.

She sits on the toilet and starts to pee, trophy in hand, letting her mind wander. *Robbie is sprawled on the bed. He's no longer snoring. His head and body cast a large shadow across the bedding. The shadow extends to the edge of the bed and down onto the floor. The clock is ticking. But it isn't the clock – it's the* drip drip drip *of blood, falling from the edge of the bed to the floor where it puddles out across the tatty rug. The shadow isn't a shadow, but a dark pool of blood oozing from a massive gash on Robbie's forehead. His skull is oddly misshapen, concave, the sodium light glistening on the bloody circumference of a shadowy hole as black as night. Seline stands over the bed, the trophy raised above her head, blood running down her forearm, pooling at the bend of her elbow.*

She finishes peeing and flushes the toilet. She puts the

trophy back down on the floor to act as a doorstop. She goes into the bedroom and slips silently into bed next to the snoring Robbie, as close to the edge as she is able.

Could she kill him? And if she did, what then? Her life would be over. She'd be sent to prison. She'd be cut off from her family for good. But she feels like she's in a prison now anyway, cut off from everyone and everything.

This can't go on. Something has to change. It has to.

## 30

T he following morning Seline arrives at school and discovers a buzz of activity. Several police cars are parked in the staff car park and, to the excitement of the swarm of children in the playground, a couple of police vans are pulled up right next to the main entrance, occupying the place where kids usually play football before the assembly bell. The whole place is a din of noise.

Inside the school it isn't much better. A couple of uniformed officers are standing by reception, and one whole corridor has been blocked off – a mass of kids standing behind a makeshift barrier made from tables, staring at where two uniformed police officers and a dog are looking into a caretaker's store cupboard. For all the activity, it's the dog that seems most incongruous.

Seline briefly wonders whether this is in some way connected to what happened to her car, before dismissing the thought as preposterous. No one calls out the riot squad and police dogs over a bit of graffiti.

The staff room is buzzing with as much chatter as the

playground, but no one seems to know what is going on. Someone's heard a rumour about Class A drugs, but it's no more than speculation.

Seline's first thought is that this must somehow be connected to Robbie. She suspected he was into drugs. This must be him.

Anxiously, Seline heads down to teach her first lesson, but discovers that her classroom is in the area that has been cordoned off by the police. The school secretary stands flustered, surrounded by a mob of over-excited children, checking their names against a list on a clipboard and instructing them to go to different rooms around the school. She spots Seline and directs her to the school hall.

When she arrives, she finds that her class has been allocated a corner of the hall. She has no art equipment, and clearly no one has considered how she is supposed to conduct an art lesson. The other corners are occupied by maths, history and geography but the atmosphere remains giddy and it's clear no one is going to get any teaching done in this environment.

Seline's mind is racing, but she has to act like she doesn't suspect more than anyone else. With the portable whiteboard she's been given, Seline quickly improvises a game of Pictionary. She splits her class of Year 7s into two groups and then whispers words to them in turn, which they have to draw on the board for their teammates to guess. The kids take to it with gusto, and the excitable mood feeds into a sense of riotous fun. Bizarrely, it's one of the best lessons she's taught.

About twenty minutes into the lesson the school secretary approaches and leans into Seline almost conspiratorially.

"They want you in the Head's office," she whispers.

"After the lesson?"

"No. Now. I've been told to stay here with your class."


"SIT DOWN, SELINE."

She's in the Head's office. Mrs Jessop is there, along with two police officers – a man and a woman. It's awkward and cramped. Seline sits, but everyone else remains standing. The atmosphere is tense. Maybe this *is* about her car. But why has she been called out mid-lesson? This seems incredibly serious.

Mrs Jessop steps to the side and the male officer sits down on a chair which has been placed on the same side of the desk as Seline rather than behind it. It's a crass way of trying to make things seem less formal, but in this small room and with two people in uniform it just feels obvious and awkward.

"We're investigating the fact that drugs have been discovered on the school premises. We're doing a wider search of the school, but for now we've found evidence of drugs in one area, which includes the art rooms. We're aware that this is a busy building with lots of people moving through a number of different areas throughout the day, so we're not at this stage suggesting the drugs belong to anyone in particular. I want to be clear that at this moment we are just gathering evidence to build up a picture of what may have happened here."

This must be Robbie. It's Robbie, and they've linked her to him. She can feel her heart racing but tries to not look nervous. Maybe if they connect all this to Robbie they'll take him away and she'll be free. But how can she make that happen without getting wrapped up in it herself?

The male officer keeps looking at her for what seems like an age. Then he speaks.

"Our investigation so far is concentrated on one main area of the school which encompasses the art room."

Again, there's a pause. A pause it feels like they are hoping she will fill.

"Oh. Well, I don't know anything about that."

Can they really suspect her? They *must* suspect her, or why would she be in here, being spoken to like this?

"As I say," the male officer speaks hastily, "we're just at an investigative stage at this point. We're talking to a number of people, as I'm sure you can imagine, to help us understand what's going on and narrow down our enquiries."

Maybe they don't suspect her. Maybe it's just that she's new and they're trying to cancel her out as a suspect, like a big game of Guess Who. But if they stop looking into her they'll never make the connection to Robbie. She wants them to get to Robbie somehow.

"The first night I was in town, there was someone in the school."

"Who?" The male officer is interested. The female officer starts making notes in a notebook.

"I don't know. They were in the window. A light was on."

There's a silence. Seline can feel the information isn't landing the way she wants it to.

"It felt suspicious. He was acting suspiciously."

"He? Could you describe him?"

Seline can't say it was Robbie. She doesn't *know* for sure it was, though she strongly suspects it. But she can't name him. He'd kill her if she did. She explains it as truthfully as she can.

"I can't really. A man. He was silhouetted against the light. Then he turned the light off."

The male officer leans in. "Did you report this at the time?"

"Um, no."

"Why not?"

"Well, it didn't seem important. Not then."

The police officer purses his lips. "So they *weren't* acting suspiciously?"

"Yes. No. Well... not as such. It felt odd."

Seline sees the female officer out of the corner of her eye closing the notebook. She hasn't managed to set them onto Robbie and can't say more without putting herself in danger. She'll have to think about what she can do to make them suspect him.

"Thanks, Seline. That's helpful. We'll ask you more about that if we feel it's relevant."

She thinks the interview is over, but no one moves. Then the officer continues.

"One thing we are asking people to do is take a drug test, just to cancel them out of the enquiry. But only if they're comfortable, of course. As I say, we're not formally investigating anyone right now, just eliminating our lines of enquiry. We're asking several people."

"Er, yes, well, I mean, sure, I don't see why that would be a problem, if it helps..."

"Thanks." He stands up. "Claire here can take you down to do that."

He indicates the female officer, who steps forward and

gestures towards the door. It's all suddenly abrupt and businesslike now they've got what they want.

"Now? Oh, right..."

SELINE IS IN A TOILET CUBICLE, peeing into a small plastic cup, the door ajar so the female officer can see inside and confirm it's Seline's pee going into the tub. This whole situation escalated very fast, and Seline can see how all that nicey-nicey chat in the office was to get her to do something she didn't legally have to do. She feels foolish and manipulated. But in any case, her urine sample will prove that she isn't the person they're after. And meanwhile, they might start looking into Robbie.

She hands the officer her tub of pee and watches it bagged up. She washes her hands. Then she goes back to the school hall just in time for the end of her lesson. It all seems surreally normal. The blue team beat the red team by 14 points to 12. Everyone is still in high spirits as the bell rings for the end of class. She has a free period next, so heads up to the staff room to think about everything that's just happened.

It's only as she's sipping her coffee that she properly starts to think about how drugs might have got into her classroom. She thinks back to Robbie, coming in with all those bunches of flowers. She'd thought it was a convenient way for him to spy on her – but what if it was a cover for something else? Maybe that's why he was coming into school all the time – not to see her, but to deal his drugs.

She remembers back to her very first night here, the light in the classroom window, the man watching her. Recalling it gives her the same sense of flesh-crawling discomfort she gets being around Robbie now. He watched her from the window, then got in his car and followed her up the hill, propositioned her and tried to get her in his car. Right from her first day here he's been after her.

Then she remembers the magic mushrooms.

What if they can detect she took magic mushrooms in her pee? Oh my God! If they can, she will be a criminal. She'll lose her job. Robbie will have ruined things for her. Ruined everything. Everything he touches turns to shit.

Consumed with worry, she somehow makes it down to her next lesson in the hall in a daze, on automatic pilot. Before she can start, Dave the security guard approaches her and tells her she can't stay late at the school any longer to paint at night. Everyone has to be off-site thirty minutes after the last bell, kids and teachers. He's quite officious and curt with her, almost rude. She gets the feeling he's probably been put under pressure over this drugs thing and is annoyed with her because he's turned a blind eye to her hanging around late. Maybe he thinks the drugs are hers. Anyway, she suspects he's had a bollocking about his work, as he's now wearing his full security uniform, which she's never seen him in before. She recognises the logo on the uniform immediately. IRONCLAD. The same firm her dad used to work for. The firm Michael owns.

That means she has nowhere to hide out at night, no excuse not to go directly back to the flat – back to Robbie. But now she feels she knows something about him, something important – this stuff with the drugs. She won't talk to her dad just yet. Maybe she can keep her parents from ever having to know what a mess she's made of things. Maybe there's a way to use this drug stuff to get Robbie out of her life forever.

## 31

S eline sits in the school cafeteria, poking her lunch around a plate with no appetite. She's spent much of the morning on her phone, searching the internet to learn everything she can about drug tests. What she's managed to unearth seems to suggest that traces of the magic mushrooms shouldn't show up in her urine after a day, which is a relief. But she can't find any information about the massive dose she took, or the drugs Robbie might have given her after the overdose, so she can't be certain the police won't find something with their tests. She's not out of the woods.

The nagging thought that Robbie must be behind all this drugs business at the school won't go away, and the noise of it grows in her head until it drowns out everything else. She can't think straight. She's almost sure it must be him. But she has to be certain. If this all links to Robbie, he's bound to be arrested and she'll be free of him.

Annie sits down opposite her.

"God, it's like we're in an episode of *The Wire,* isn't it?"

She's smiling from ear to ear, clearly relishing all the excitement. She digs into her lasagne with gusto and shovels a big mouthful in, chewing away through her grin. "Have you heard anything juicy?"

Seline thinks about asking whether the police have interviewed Annie too, or asked for a urine sample, but thinks better of it. What if they haven't? How will it look that she's been singled out as a suspect?

"Not hungry?" Annie is looking at Seline's uneaten plate of food.

"Not really."

A thought dawns on Seline.

"Actually, I'm not feeling very well. Could you let the office know I've had to leave for the day?"


SHE'S STARING at the door of the locked room. She has come home to find out once and for all what he's up to. Her heart was pounding all the way as she ran back to the flat. But now she's standing here, she doesn't have a clue what to do. Robbie's usually out and about during the day, so she has the place to herself. But she can't get into that room without the key. She can't see anything through the keyhole or under the door. She isn't strong enough to break the door down – and even if she was, Robbie would know and he would kill her. She glances around, searching for any clue that might help her find a way inside without leaving a trace. But there's nothing. No answer. Every thought brings her back to the key.

She's been staring at the door for twenty minutes when she realises she needs to pee. She pushes the creaky bathroom door open and sits on the toilet. She looks around the filthy bathroom. She has given up on her efforts to clean it, and it has steadily fallen back into its grotty, mildewed state. Robbie never cleans it, of course. Her eye falls onto the doorstop. How come someone so utterly messy in every other detail of the flat is fastidious enough to keep the damp bathroom propped open with a football trophy?

She closes her eyes and remembers the times she's heard Robbie going into that room. His footsteps in the hallway. The creak of the bathroom door. The unlocking of the door. The locking of the door. The creak of the bathroom door. Why the bathroom? She stops peeing, flushes, and begins to search the bathroom for a hidden key. She moves all the medicines and junk from the cabinet, then carefully replaces them. She looks around and behind the toilet, then unscrews the cistern and fishes about in the water. She takes off the bath panel.

Nothing.

She closes her eyes and mentally goes through the routine again. The footsteps in the hallway. The creak of the bathroom door. The unlocking of the door. The locking of the door. The creak of the bathroom door.

And something else. What else?

The scrape. The scrape of the doorstop on the floor.

She picks up the trophy and looks at it. The tarnished metal figure of a football player, strangely adult for a trophy given to a child, his face contorted with effort, his mouth open in a yell, leaning forward with a leg extended and a football on the tip of his boot, riding a tackle or taking a winning shot on goal – his other leg bent, foot planted on a circular wooden plinth. An engraving on the front of the plinth reads:

*Statheley Bridge Pack, Runners-Up, Yorkshire Cub Scouts*
*Football, 2008.*

Seline runs her fingernail under the edge of the plaque but it doesn't move. She turns the trophy upside down. The base of the wood is covered with a disk of threadbare green felt circle. She picks at the edge of the felt but it is glued firm.

She takes the footballer figure in one hand and the wooden plinth in the other and twists.

The figure begins to unscrew.

She keeps unscrewing, an unusually thick-threaded screw, until the figure comes off. Once it's apart she can see the base is hollow and has something stuffed inside it: a rolled-up ball of toilet paper. She pulls it out and unrolls it.

It's the key.

She takes a deep breath, her mind racing, trying to steady her nerves. With trembling hands she slides the key into the lock. The room's door clicks open, revealing the dark space within. Tentatively, she slips inside and reaches for a light switch.

Shelves. Row upon row of shelves lined with bags of drugs, neatly stacked in organised piles. Pills she immediately recognises, some in medicine pots, others in small clear plastic bags. There's also what looks like stuff she's seen in TV shows, large packs of white powder which might be cocaine, brown stuff that might be heroin. The room has an odd smell which she had just thought was the dirtiness of the flat, vinegary and sweet. There's money too. Bundles of what looks like ten and twenty-pound notes held in elastic bands. Of course he isn't keeping his dead brother's stuff in here. Just some sob story he made up to keep her away from the room. He probably doesn't even have a dead brother.

She picks up one of the small bags of pills, ten or so in a little resealable plastic bag, like a mini version of the ones you get at the airport. She's stunned. She knew he was up to something shady, but she had no idea it was on this monumental scale. This isn't what she expected. This isn't just a bit of petty crime. This is like the sort of room you see in a photograph on the front page of a newspaper.

Seline's heart is thumping. He's not just some abusive bullying boyfriend. He'd kill her for this for sure. But there's enough evidence here to send Robbie to prison for a long time. She's got him! She takes her phone out of her pocket. Should she call the police? How can she, when they think she is a suspect? She doesn't know how she can tell the police about Robbie without implicating herself in all this. But there *has* to be a way.

She looks at her phone, trying to get up the courage, to focus on a clear plan. But before she can do anything, she's interrupted by a sound.

It's the flat door opening.

## 32

F rozen with fear, she hasn't moved a muscle, hasn't even breathed since she heard the sound of the front door. This isn't like the last time she tried to look in this room. Then she could hide what she was up to, delay his entry to the flat with a pile of stuff behind the door – and the locked room wasn't even open. This time she's inside the room, door wide open, light on. There's nowhere to hide, nothing to be done.

Then he's there, in the doorway, staring at her. He's only travelled six feet from the front door to the room itself, but he looks like he's just finished running a marathon: eyes ablaze, adrenaline pumping, tense, rigid. She notices his fingers clamped to the door frame, his knuckles white with the pressure.

"What have you done? What the fuck have you done?"

He bursts into the room and she feels certain he's going to hit her – but he pushes past her, goes to the shelves, starts scanning the drugs and the money.

"Have you touched anything? *Anything?*"

"No. No, I haven't."

She's waiting for the inevitable attack. This is it, the moment she's been dreading, the inescapable conclusion to their time together, that he's going to kill her. Suddenly she feels herself swung round with incredible force. He has hold of her shoulders and leans in close to her face.

"What the fuck have you done?"

But instead of hitting her, he slumps. The rigidity goes out of his body. She feels the tension in his arms relax. He lets her shoulders go, steps back and collapses into the battered swivel chair in front of one of the rows of shelves. He leans forward, head in hands, and mutters something inaudible to himself, then goes quiet.

He's silent and utterly still for what seems like a long time. Seline's heart slows, and as the panic clears she thinks about sneaking out of the room. But she worries if she moves that she'll pull him out of his dazed state, like a parent trying to sneak out of the room and waking a sleeping baby.

"You couldn't just do what you were told, could you?"

He looks up at her and she can see that his anger has given way to something else. It almost looks like sadness.

"When I left school..." He trails off. "I did some stupid things and got mixed up with the wrong people. Once you do something for them people there's no end to it. Things... spiral. I'm in a whole heap of shit and I can't get out of it."

He really does look desperate. "But all that money...?"

Robbie laughs derisively. "Do I look like I've got money? Look at me! Look at this shitty flat. Do you think if I had money I'd be living here, like this? It's not mine. None of it. It all belongs to someone else."

"Who?"

He stares at her. "You should have left it the fuck alone, Seline."

She can hear the anger rising in him again. She takes it all in. Scans the room. It makes sense.

"Was it you, at the school? The drugs?"

"Christ, you don't understand how big this is. They've got stuff everywhere. Everywhere."

She tries to make sense of it all, the enormity of what she finds herself embroiled in.

"You can't say anything."

He gets up slowly, walks over to her, extending his arms as he does so. For a moment she thinks he's going to hug her. But then he grabs her by the shoulders, digs his fingers in hard, smashes her back against the wall and leans into her menacingly.

"You tell no one about this. *No one.* If they know you know about this they'll kill you. And me. They'll kill us for sure."

LATER, lying in bed, Seline tries to think things through. If that *was* Robbie's money, that massive pile of cash, would he be wasting his time stealing a few quid for the lottery from a handful of teachers? He must be working for someone else, hiding their money, selling their drugs.

If that's true, then he's right about them both being in danger. She's used to Robbie's emotional manipulation by now, the way he plays the victim. But something about how he was in that room, the fact that he *didn't* hit her... He was different somehow, not the petty bully she knows.

He was scared. Really scared.

After he locked up the room again and they moved to the

kitchen, he spoke to her softly, made out like it's the two of them in it together. But later, when she went to the bathroom, she noticed the football trophy was no longer there. It may be the two of them together – but clearly he doesn't trust her at all now.

So she's in danger from the people he's working for. But she's a threat to Robbie as well. Now she's seen what he has in that room she's a danger to him. He'll never let her go. How can he? He's a rat in a trap. And a wild animal is at its most dangerous when it's cornered. This has gone beyond bullying now. Now he has a reason, a proper reason, to shut her up once and for all.

She lies there, wondering what to do next. Her fists are clutched with tension.

Inside one of them, she still holds a small bag of pills.

## 33

A t about 4am Seline gets up to use the toilet. The corridor is darker than usual, now the bathroom door is no longer held open by the trophy doorstop. She pushes the creaking door, goes in, waits thirty seconds and then flushes. She runs the tap for a few seconds then turns it off. She creaks the door open again and steps back into the corridor.

She listens.

Robbie is still snoring. Good. If the noise of the door and the toilet flush haven't woken him, she has a chance of pulling off the next bit of her plan.

She panics when she notices his car keys aren't in the dish where he usually leaves them. She's next to the coat hooks at the far end of the hallway. She slips her hand into Robbie's jacket pocket and feels for the keys. With relief, she finds them. She slips her feet into her shoes, unlocks the front door and edges out of the flat. She tiptoes gingerly down the stairs, opens the main door and steps out onto the street.

The bracing cold hits her. She's wearing only her dressing gown over a thin nightie. Fortunately, the street is completely deserted at this time. At least it isn't raining. She notices how anxious she is by her urgent, panicked breathing, the plumes of condensation she's puffing out in the cold air. She hurries down the road, careful not to slip on the pavement where an icy frost is already forming. At the corner, she turns behind the row of shops and onto the patch of undulating waste ground, often slippery with mud but now frozen hard.

She's had the same thought running through her mind for some time now: is that why Robbie usually drives like a lunatic, but sometimes drives really conservatively? Because he doesn't want to get pulled over with something dodgy in the car? Like that time he met that bloke in the pub carpark and drove back sedately all the way to his flat?

She gets to Robbie's car, puts the key into the passenger side door and opens it. The interior light doesn't come on, so she has to reach down into the darkness until she finds the recessed handle and opens the glove box. She slips her hand into her dressing gown pocket and takes out the bag of pills, rubs the bag hard between the folds of her robe and puts it into the glove box, digging under the things he has stuffed in there – logbook and old sweet wrappers and the like. If he looks in there casually he won't see them. They'll only be found by someone who's deliberately searching.

Once she's back in the flat she gives herself a minute to warm up and calm her breathing, then goes through the ritual of entering the bathroom and flushing the toilet again before sliding back into bed next to the still-snoring Robbie. The whole thing has taken her less than ten minutes.

. . .

SHE ARRIVES AT SCHOOL EARLY. Although she's slept only a couple of hours at best – fitful, anxious sleep that gave her no meaningful rest – she is alert, wired, her body tingling with adrenaline.

Through assembly, through morning lessons in the hall, through lunch, she rehearses the plan in her mind. Robbie trusts her now less than ever – he's bound to pick her up from school. The police are still here, examining the school site and conducting interviews and searches. She needs to find a way to leave early, so she's no longer in the school when Robbie gets here. He'll find that out and drive home alone. She needs to find a way to ensure the police search his car on the way out and find the drugs, without her in the car, and know that it's *him* who's responsible for what's going on at the school. They're bound to search the flat, find the room, and Robbie will be out of her life forever.

When she tells herself this series of events it sounds like one step leads naturally to another. She whispers it to herself, over and over, like a mantra. But she knows there are lots of holes in it, the biggest one being the police searching Robbie's car. Why would they choose him? How can she be sure they'll do that? In her first lesson, she decides she'll phone the police and give them a tip-off; but by break, she realises she'd have to get to a payphone somewhere so they can't trace her phone. But do payphones even still exist? And do they have voice recognition software? And they'd know *which* payphone the call came from, and they'll have CCTV of her using it... She keeps thinking, but she can't come up with a way of ensuring they'll search his car. She has the rest of the day to come up with something.

Her final lesson of the day is a free period, so she's gathered all her stuff together and can make a bolt for the gates forty minutes before the end of school; plenty of time to escape before Robbie arrives. She shoos the kids out of her classroom and is just putting her coat on when the school secretary pokes her head around the door.

"Mrs Jessop wants to see you in her office."

Why does the Head want to see her?

"Now?"

"Yes. You have a free period, don't you?"

"Fine."

Seline hurries out of her classroom clutching all her stuff. She elbows past groups of children dragging their feet slowly to their next lesson. If she hurries, she still has loads of time to see the Head and get away before Robbie gets here. She races round the corner and trips over a bag some kid is kicking along the corridor. She falls heavily, banging her elbow.

"Sorry, Miss."

The boy looks meek, putting on the doe eyes and trying to soften her up for the telling-off he knows is coming. But Seline's in too much of a hurry. She snatches up her bag and rushes off up the corridor.

She's been so busy thinking about getting out of school early that she hasn't given any thought to *why* the Head might want to see her. But as she turns the corner and sees the office door a thought suddenly hits her. What if the urine test is back? What if they've found drugs in her pee and they're about to arrest her? She thinks back to yesterday, getting effectively told she's a suspect for drugs and then immediately pretending to be ill and taking the afternoon off. How suspicious must that have looked? What an idiot she's been. They'll have rushed her test through for sure. She thinks about running off now, but as she's frozen with indecision the secretary catches up with her.

"You were in a hurry."

Seline has no choice but to go into the Head's office. She opens the door and steps in, fully expecting to see a crowd of police officers.

But there aren't any police in here. Mrs Jessop is sitting at her desk and in two chairs facing her are Graham and Julie.

"Thanks for joining us, Seline. Please take a seat."

She sits down in the empty chair next to Graham. What the hell is this about? Has this got something to do with why Julie came to the flat?

"Mr Harrison and Julie and I have just been having a chat about Julie's behaviour and we thought you could clear something up for us. Julie has come into school today with a tattoo, which is against school rules and cannot have been legally acquired given Julie's age."

"I see..." Seline doesn't really see. She's trying to work out where all this is heading.

"Julie says you told her to get it."

Seline looks at Julie. She sees her exposed forearm, which is sheathed in a layer of clingfilm wrapped over a sore-looking tattoo of a rose, with thorns and tiny drips of blood. It's one of the designs she saw a few days ago in Julie's portfolio.

"I didn't tell Julie to get a tattoo."

"You're a fucking liar!" Julie is rising up in her seat. Graham makes a grab at her and wrestles her back. Seline can see he's having to use all his effort against the sheer brute strength of the girl.

"I saw her drawings, which I thought were excellent, and

said so. She said she wanted to be a tattoo artist one day, and I encouraged her to keep practising. Practicing *drawing*, I mean. I most certainly didn't tell her she should *get* a tattoo."

Again, Julie goes for her and has to be restrained, but not before she has grabbed Seline by the arm, crushing her painful elbow where she fell in the corridor. Seline shouts out in pain.

"You fucking bitch. I'm glad I ripped up your shitty paintings. I'm glad I done your car, you fucking slag."

GIVEN JULIE'S MELTDOWN, the scene in the Head's office goes on longer than expected. The tattoo. The attack on a teacher. Vandalism. There's a long history of transgressions and this is the final straw. Julie is permanently excluded. Seline hardly has time to think about it, that she has now made a firm enemy of this feral girl. Graham tries to have a word with her as she leaves the office, offering an apology, saying he'll pay for her car, but Seline invents some excuse about a dentist appointment and rushes off.

Now she is racing down the corridor. It's just a few minutes before final bell and she still hopes she'll get out before Robbie arrives. But as she comes out of the main door and into the rain, her heart sinks. There's Robbie's car, parked up under a tree in the gloomy dusk winter light. He flashes his headlights and she reluctantly trudges over to it and gets in.

As they drive off, she spots a couple of police officers in hi-vis jackets near the gate. Earlier she was hoping they would stop and search Robbie. Now she prays silently that they'll let the car pass and move off to safety.

As they near the gate, one of the policemen peers into

the car past the wipers and the rain-spattered windscreen to
see who is driving. He looks at Seline in the passenger seat –
then beckons them to one side to stop. Seline was searching
earlier for some reason the police would stop Robbie's car.
Now she has the crushing realisation that the reason they'll
stop the car is *her,* the chief suspect in their investigation.

"Could you step out of the car, please, sir, madam?"

Seline and Robbie stand at the edge of the car park,
pulling their coats around them against the wind and rain as
two officers ask them questions and then begin to search the
car. Robbie is rude to them, goes on about harassment. He
has the air of someone who's had plenty of dealings with the
law and has none of the natural fear or respect most people
have for it. Seline on the other hand has never had anything
to do with the police – and is now about to be arrested for
the bag of drugs she herself placed in the glove
compartment.

She and Robbie aren't dressed for the weather, but the
police sport thick, warm waterproof jackets and take their
time. She watches the female officer come away from the
driver's side, walk around the car and lean in through the
passenger door. She starts searching under the seat, around
the seat and in the ashtray. It's as if time has stopped. Seline
can feel the panic rising in her, the moment her life is going
to change utterly and forever. Then she hears the click of the
glove compartment latch. This is it.

"Thank you, sir, madam. You can be on your way."

Robbie and Seline get back in the car and drive off in
silence. Seline can't understand what has just happened.
How has she had such a lucky escape? Robbie does his usual
aggressive drive through the town and into their road, but
instead of turning the car onto the waste ground where he

normally parks, he keeps driving – on, through town and up the hill towards open country. The only sound is the racing of the engine and the angry swish of the wiper blades. She has no idea where they're heading. They reach a stretch of road far away from any lights or houses and Robbie suddenly swings the car violently down a narrow dirt track between hedges. It's barely a road at all, and the car bumps uncomfortably across the hard muddy undulations. She feels the exhaust thump against a large ridge. Eventually the hedges open out onto a field of some sort, some rough crop-less farmland.

They come to a halt. Robbie turns the engine off. He twists in his seat towards her. She looks straight ahead but can see from the corner of her eye that he's looking daggers at her. Suddenly he thrusts his arm towards her, fist clenched. She winces and closes her eyes, waiting for the crunch of bone against bone when he punches her.

But the punch doesn't come.

She opens her eyes and can still see the fist, right in front of her face.

He slowly uncurls his fingers.

In the palm of his hand lies the small plastic bag of pills. "You're dead."

He lunges at her and grabs her by the throat. This isn't idle threatening anymore. He's trying to kill her. She can't breathe. The pain on her windpipe is excruciating. She desperately claws at his hands and his arms, trying to get him to let go, but he's far too strong. She lashes out at his face, but he tilts his head away. She flails around wildly, trying to grab hold of the car interior, to pull herself out of his reach. She presses against the rainy windscreen, clutches at the sun visor, and grabs the rear-view mirror, which comes away in her hand. She swings at his face again and he screams and lets go of her throat. She's hit him, still holding the mirror. He holds his eye with both hands and making a high-pitched squealing sound. The stalk of the mirror must have dug him in the eye.

Coughing and gasping, she somehow manages to unlatch her seat belt and open her passenger door. She starts to slide out, but he grabs hold of her coat with one hand, still covering his eye with the other. Somehow she swings her upper body out of the door and gets both hands up onto the roof, then heaves herself backwards with all her strength. She falls out of the car and onto her back on the hard, wet ground, partially pulling Robbie with her before he loses hold of her coat. She lies in the field, still gasping for air.

She's looking up and sees Robbie beginning to pull himself out through the open doorway of her side of the vehicle. She pulls her knees up so he can't grab her legs – then kicks the door closed with all her strength. There's a sickening thud as the door makes contact with Robbie's head. She hears him sigh and then go silent.

She gets to her feet and starts to run, across the field, away from the car, stumbling and falling in the darkness. The wind is stronger on the open ground and rain lashes her face. When she's about halfway across the field she hears Robbie calling.

"Seline! Seline!"

His voice is thin and echoing as it carries on the wind across the field. It's more of a howl than a call, plaintive, animalistic. She keeps running as his voice gets quieter and thinner, until it's lost entirely in the roar of the storm.

She keeps running.

## 34

"Thanks – for meeting me. I didn't know – who else to call..."

Seline sits in the car, sobbing. Her wet coat clings to her, and she can see a patch of blood where Robbie grabbed hold of it. The moment she begins talking tears start flowing, and she has become almost hysterical. Weeks of pressure, carrying the burden of this secret, the stress of living with Robbie, the fear of violence, the incredible loneliness and shame and misery of it all... The second she allows herself to concede any weakness to someone else she's cracked like a dam, the emotion flooding out uncontrollably.

"That's fine. It's okay." Michael hands her another tissue and she scrubs away at her wet eyes, her runny nose.

They're sitting in the gloom of Michael's car, in a lay-by just on the edge of town. It's raining heavily outside and the windows are streaked with rivulets of water. The glass is beginning to mist with condensation, as if they're enveloped in fog. Every now and then they are dazzled by headlights of other passing vehicles, or drowned out by the roar of large trucks which buffet the car and make it rock.

"Tell me what's happened. Slowly. Tell me everything."

Seline tells her story. It's a jumbled mess of incidents. The sense someone was in the school watching her. Robbie nearly running her down on the road, then trying to pick her up, then getting her to live with him. Then him threatening to kill her – really, genuinely meaning it. How terrified she's been, utterly terrified, for weeks. And this is *before* the drugs were found in the school and her knowing that they were put there by Robbie – drugs he's been keeping in the flat. How she's a suspect with the police, how she can't stay at school and paint anymore and has no place to escape from Robbie. How she finally got into the locked room and found proof, drugs, loads of drugs. And piles of money. How she tried to get some of the drugs into Robbie's car for the police to find, but Robbie found them instead and tried to kill her. Her hand goes instinctively to her neck, which feels bruised and painful. How she somehow got away from him, but he is still after her.

"He knows, you see. He knows I tried to get him caught by the police. He won't stop until he kills me."

She breaks down again, a quivering, sobbing mess. She can't seem to stop. And yet she's relieved. Part of the crying is the relief of tension, the fact that she has finally told someone about this, at last.

"I'm glad you've spoken to me." Michael puts a hand on her shoulder. It's comforting, a fatherly gesture.

"It sounds like it must have been awful for you. I can see how incredibly upset you are. I want you to know we're going to do something about it."

Seline starts to cry again. Thank God. Something is going to change.

"So here's what's going to happen: I don't want you to do anything for the moment. I've known Robbie for a long time, and that sort of violent... that violence... Look, I really don't think you're in any more danger."

Seline is confused. "But he tried to kill me..."

"I know, I *believe* you. Let me talk to him. I'll talk to him. He needs bringing to his senses. When you and he came to lunch that time... well... I slapped him. Did he ever mention that to you?"

"No."

She was sure Michael saw her – saw her watch him slap Robbie. But maybe he didn't.

"Why did you hit him?"

"He was being a drunken idiot." He seems to drift into another thought for a moment. "Yes. That boy needs bringing to his senses."

"And what about the police?"

"Don't talk to the police, not yet. You say they found drugs in your classroom? And you're living in that flat. Don't do anything just yet. Not until I've spoken to Robbie."

"Okay."

Her relief at having spoken to someone is immense. And yet it doesn't feel like it's dealt with. Talking to Robbie. Bringing him to his senses. Has Michael understood? She remembers something else.

"Did you burn him?"

"What?"

"With a cigar?"

Michael lets out a laugh. "God no! He did that himself, probably. Acting out in anger."

"Oh. Okay."

Michael and Robbie go a long way back. Does Michael completely believe her? As if he can read her thoughts, he takes hold of her hand.

"Listen. I've got this. I'll message him now. I'll drive you to a hotel for the night and you can wait for me there. You'll hear from me soon. I've got this."


So THAT'S what she does. Michael drives her to a hotel. She goes to her room and sits on the bed. Now what? She feels in a state of limbo. But at least she's spoken to someone. At least she has said something.

Seline suddenly feels very tired. She feels like she could sleep for a year. Without even taking her coat off, she lies down on the bed and pulls her knees up to her chest.

Michael will talk to Robbie and then – and then what?

Worry gives way to exhaustion. She drifts into sleep.

## 35

She's lying on her bed, dozing. It's a lovely summer's day and the warm sun streams in through her bedroom window. Her curtains are moving in a light breeze. She has been drawing for hours, her papers and coloured pencils and felt tip pens spread out across the floor with some of her other toys. She has got so tired. She wants to watch the television downstairs but Daddy is out at work and Mummy is busy and she will be in the way, so she has to stay in her room. She's a good girl. She stays in her room so she doesn't get in the way of Mummy's work. She can hear Mummy working somewhere in the house. She's tidying the house and putting all the things in the cupboards. She can hear the cupboards opening and closing while she dozes.

And then the noise of the cupboards opening and closing gets louder and it makes it hard for her to doze, and she starts to wake up, and she isn't in her bedroom; she's on a different bed, in a hotel room, and the noise she can hear is knocking, knocking at the room door.

Is it Michael? Is he back with news about Robbie?

She shakes herself properly awake and goes to the door. She isn't prepared for the shock of what she sees when she opens it.

It's two police officers.

"Seline? Can we come in?"

Seline lets the police in. They stand awkwardly in the hotel room, too small and incongruous for a group like this.

"Take a seat, Seline."

Is this it? Have they come to arrest her for the drugs at the school? Her test must have come back and they've decided she must be guilty. She moves to a chair by the desk at the side of the room and sits down – but the police officers remain standing. The man keeps looking at her while she settles. The woman scans her eyes round the room, then sits down opposite her. Seline expects this to be the moment she is arrested. But that isn't what happens.

"It's about Robert."

"Robert?" She has no idea who they're talking about. She doesn't know any Robert.

The officer adopts a soft tone. "Robbie."

She's on her own in a bland waiting room, on a hard plastic chair, like the chairs they have in the hall at school. She's been here for about twenty minutes, listening to the muffled noises in the corridors outside. She's still trying to process what the police told her. Robbie has been taken to hospital, the hospital she's in now. They can't tell her any more; they aren't sure exactly what happened. There has been an accident, a car accident, and Robbie has been taken to hospital. *Of course* he's had an accident; it was only a matter of time, the way he drives like a lunatic. An accident waiting to happen. Her name was in his phone as his next of kin. The doctors will be able to tell her more.

Next of kin. Is that what Robbie thinks she is?

Eventually the door opens and a white-coated female doctor comes in.

"Seline?"

She sits on a chair near Seline. She looks at her sympathetically. She's young, a junior doctor presumably, about the same age as herself. She's still in training and hasn't yet lost the human touch in her bedside manner. Even the way she says *Seline* oozes with sympathy. Next of kin. These people are all talking to her about Robbie like she cares what's happened to him, like they don't know what a terrible person he is, or how much she hates him.

"Let me fill you in on how Robert is doing."

Seline says what she knows, "He was in a car crash."

"No. Well, he was hit by a car, yes. He was a pedestrian."

"Hit by a car? He wasn't driving?"

"No. He was on foot."

Seline backtracks in her mind, resets what she's hearing.

"He's in intensive care. He's stable right now, but he's received serious injuries. He has a number of fractures in his left arm and left leg. His jaw is broken. We're worried about his sight in one eye. He has some fractured ribs and we're concerned about potential internal injuries. We'll know more once we're in theatre. We don't know about spinal damage, but we've immobilised him until we can check properly. He was lucky—"

She stops. She's tripped herself up with the word *lucky*. He doesn't sound very lucky. The doctor gathers herself, picks up where she left off.

"It seems he was thrown clear by the impact rather than

going under the car, which means we're dealing principally with impact trauma rather than crushing injuries. He also has a fracture to his skull and we're monitoring whether this has caused any bruising or bleeding on the brain. His outsides have taken a knock but we're checking to see how his insides are doing too."

Seline realises the doctor has paused for her to take all of this in. She wonders how other people who are next of kin react. All she can think to say is, "I see."

The doctor battles on. "We've medicated him for the pain. He was unconscious when he came in and he hasn't so far regained consciousness. That's not uncommon for these sorts of injuries. As I say, he'll be going to theatre soon and it's likely he'll need more than one operation – probably several. It's too early to talk about what sort of recovery he might make. That'll depend on the extent of his injuries and his response to treatment. But he's going to be in hospital for some time."

Again, Seline doesn't really know what to say, so she elects to say nothing.

"He's going down to theatre soon. He'll then go up to ICU. He won't be allowed visitors there. Rather than wait here right now, you might do better to go home and pack some of his things and bring them in tomorrow."

"Okay. Thanks."

SELINE CALLS a cab from reception and heads back to Robbie's flat. She finds the small suitcase and unzips it on the bed. She moves around the bedroom, the bathroom and the living room packing items. Once she's done, she zips the case back up and wheels it down the corridor to the door.

Except the things in the case aren't Robbie's. They're hers. She takes out her keys and slides the flat key off the ring. She places the key in the bowl by the front door. Then she exits the flat, pulling the door shut behind her. She walks down the stairs and steps out onto the pavement.

She's left him.

She's free.

# PART III

## 36

Annie was great. She phoned Seline out of the blue and asked if she wanted to stay for a few days. She'd heard all about Robbie's accident. She drove into town, picked her up, cracked open a bottle of wine and showed her the spare room. She didn't bombard her with questions. Seline was going to hide away, embarrassed, but was tempted out by the smell of cooking and had a relaxing dinner with Annie and her flatmate. As they were chatting, she couldn't help noticing Annie was wearing some crucifix earrings.

"Yeah, I noticed yours the other day, so I dug mine out."

It's a relief to know that the earrings she found at Robbie's flat weren't Annie's, that she really can trust Annie as a friend. She doesn't spend much time wondering whose those other earrings were. It doesn't matter now.

Things feel even better the following day when she wakes up and remembers she's no longer in Robbie's flat. It's one of those delightfully bright, crisp winter days and the gloom of the recent weather is replaced by a clean, brilliant light that feels almost like spring. A new start. Annie runs her down to school and Seline teaches her morning lessons in a relaxed but focused manner, a whole weight of stress lifted from her shoulders. Even so, she occasionally gets little jolts of fear or anxiety, spikes of panic that make her catch her breath, as if she's forgotten something important, like that time she was halfway to the airport and realised she'd left her passport at home.

It's Robbie. He's the nagging thought in her head. Every now and then she remembers Robbie and has to remind herself he's in hospital, and not about to just show up. That she doesn't have to go back to his flat when the day ends.

It's a massive relief as well that she didn't have to drag her parents into it. She can't imagine how she would have explained it all. Even so, she still wonders why her dad spoke to her like that, about protecting her from anyone who did her any harm. Did he suspect more about Robbie than he ever let on? Maybe she needs to find some way to ask him.

"Hi, Mum."

"Sweetheart, how are you? Are you okay? Is anything wrong?"

"No, I'm fine." Seline laughs reassuringly. "What makes you say that?"

"Well, we haven't heard from you in a while. And you don't usually call in the mornings. Aren't you at school?"

"Yes. I'm on a free period. Is Dad about?"

"He's asleep. They've messed with his rota and put him on nights again. He just went up. I can see whether he's still awake. He'll be sorry to miss you."

"No, don't worry. Just send him my love and tell him I'm okay."

Seline has a brief chat with her mum, avoiding all the

stuff about Robbie. She's not telling the full story, but at the same time she no longer feels like she's keeping an awful secret from them. It feels good to reconnect, and she promises she'll make more of an effort to keep in touch from now on.

At break she heads to the staff room and finds a note in her pigeonhole.

*I heard the news about Robbie. I'm guessing you need somewhere else to live – I may be able to help you with that. Hope it's okay if I pick you up after school. Michael.*

She expects him to be in his limo, but when he arrives in the staff car park at the end of the afternoon, Michael is driving her repaired car.

"I was passing the garage earlier and saw they'd finished respraying it. I said I could drop it off for you."

"Thanks."

"I know it's your car, but are you okay if I drive?"

"Sure." Seline gets in and Michael pulls out of the school. "Where are we going?"

Michael explains that he's been working on another development, a residential estate. It's high-end stuff and they've been selling units off-plan. It isn't occupied yet, but they've fitted out a couple of the houses as show properties. Seline can stay in one of them until she finds herself somewhere more permanent.

"That would be amazing. Thank you so much."

As they drive out of town Seline peers through the window and can't help thinking about Robbie. Robbie on the pavement. Robbie flying through the air. Robbie by the side of the road, his body broken and bleeding. She finds herself coming back to the same thought – did Michael have anything to do with it? It seems so coincidental, her pouring out all her troubles to Michael and then Robbie immediately getting taken out of the picture. But it hardly seems credible... *Michael*?

"About Robbie..."

"I hear he's in a bad way. I know you told me all that stuff about him, but even so, it must have been a shock for you. Are you okay?"

Everyone seems to think she should feel worse than she does. She actually feels nothing other than relief. Perhaps *she* is the monster?

"I'm fine. You know it was a hit and run?"

"The police will be on it now. I'm sure they'll find out who did it."

Seline looks at him. "Was it you?"

Michael laughs. But not the laugh of someone who is amused. It's a shocked laugh.

"No. It wasn't me. After everything you told me I wish I could take credit. But I didn't run Robbie down, no."

She's inclined to believe him. "Okay. I'm sorry I asked. Do you think it was an accident?"

"Who knows?"

"I was wondering whether maybe my dad did it."

"Colin?" Michael sounds genuinely surprised. "I don't think so. What on earth makes you think that?"

"That day at the pub, when we were all there, when he met Robbie... he told me if anyone tried to hurt me he'd kill them."

"Really? *Colin*?"

"Yes. I know, it doesn't sound like him at all. Only, the thing is – I completely believed he meant it."

"Colin...? Huh." Michael ponders this for a while. "Even so, it's not very likely. If Robbie was dealing drugs, he probably had some dodgier enemies than your dad."

"I guess..."

The car pulls into a new-build estate and Michael parks next to a smart semi-detached house. Until this moment Seline can't shake a nagging worry: *why* has Michael been driving her car? Is his own car out of action because it's been involved in an accident – an accident with Robbie? But she's relieved to see Michael's limo parked here. As she gets out, she glances surreptitiously at the car, the rear that's facing her and the front as they walk towards the house. No damage. *Of course* he didn't run Robbie over. The idea of it is crazy now she thinks it through.

She goes in and explores the house. It's absurdly big, five bedrooms on three floors, with three bathrooms, a state-of-the-art kitchen, a games and cinema room. It's all been fitted out to an incredibly high standard. In forty-eight hours she has gone from a scrotty flat over a takeaway to a luxury house. And she's on her own. She's free.

SHE WATCHES from the doorway as Michael's car pulls away. She heads back into the kitchen. He's even arranged a little hamper of food for her, and a bottle of wine, put some milk and stuff in the fridge. She chops some vegetables, cooks herself some pasta. Once she's eaten, she realises how tired she is. She heads upstairs, cleans her teeth, slips into bed.

But she can't sleep. She imagines Robbie, lying in his hospital bed, waking after an operation, the pain he's in, not being able to move, angry with her for abandoning him, plotting his revenge. She goes to the window and pulls back the heavy curtain. The streets on the estate have lamp posts but none of them are lit. The weak moon shines a dull light onto the buildings around her; the flat, lifeless shapes of buildings and silhouetted mounds of earth and the curious twisted forms of diggers and cranes, like ancient fossilised monsters. There's no movement; no one anywhere, for miles.

She scampers tentatively downstairs and checks the lock on the front door, the back door, the ground-floor windows. She goes back up to her room and pushes a chair against her door. She gets back into her bed and tries, in vain, to sleep.

## 37

She looks at herself in the mirror. Seriously, does anyone ever look normal in a changing room? She's convinced all the mirrors are distorting, probably designed to make you look slimmer or something so you'll buy the clothes. Or maybe it's like that thing when you hear your voice recorded and think it sounds nothing like you. Maybe she really does look like this.

She goes out to the main part of the shop, to another mirror where she can step back a bit and get a proper look. Actually, it's not too bad – a chic little black dress that fits her better than she thought it did. It's quite expensive – does she like it enough?

"You look great in that." There's a woman flicking through a rail of sale items who has stopped to look at Seline. She's rocking a stroller with one hand, in which a toddler is sleeping in a contorted heap, like a bonfire night guy. She has a kind face.

"You think?"

"Yeah. It really suits you."

"Thanks."

Seline pays for the dress and the assistant folds it and puts it in a bag. It's been ages since she's been out. The last time was that awful evening in The Butchers. But a couple of days ago, much to her surprise, she got a text from Michael's daughter Charlotte, asking her if she fancied a night out with her and a few mates. She hadn't thought Charlotte liked her when they'd met. But maybe it was Robbie Charlotte didn't like. Either way, she's sure Michael must have put her up to the invitation because of all the Robbie business. She wasn't going to go, but then she thought about it and decided if she's going to make a fresh start she has to put some effort in.

As she leaves the shop she sees Robbie's car across the road.

She squats down behind a car parked on this side of the street and hides. Then she inches up and cautiously looks over to see if Robbie is in the car. It's empty. She nervously scans up and down the road – if he's not in the car he might have got out and be coming towards her! The street is pretty empty and it doesn't take her long to decide he's nowhere in view.

She looks back at the car. It's royal blue. She realises that Robbie's car is a darker shade of blue than this. Also, Robbie's car has a patch of filler on the front wing where it got dented and needs respraying. This car isn't marked. It isn't Robbie's car.

"Hello? I'm calling for an update on Robert Swales. I'm Seline Henderson. I'm his next of kin."

The hospital must think it's bizarre she hasn't phoned before, hasn't been in to visit him. The accident was three days ago. She has a sudden thought – what if he's dead?

Though presumably they would have called her if that was the case. After a couple of minutes, another nurse comes back on and gives some basic information: he's still in ICU, he's stable, he's off the ventilator, he'll be having another operation tomorrow morning. The nurse says Seline'll need to speak to his doctor to get more details. Seline thanks her and hangs up. But she doesn't want more detail. He's still in hospital; that's all she needs to know. She isn't going to run into him suddenly on the high street or in the pub. He isn't driving around. He isn't going to make a surprise appearance at school.

Fusion is bright and brash and noisy. Seline has never been much of a one for clubs, even at university, but she can tell that this isn't a good one. The building looked more like a bank from the outside and its conversion inside is slightly odd. The room is a weird shape, and the dance floor is a series of smaller connected areas between ornate curling metal pillars. There isn't much differentiation between the dance floor itself and the sticky-carpeted border that runs around its edge, so dancers bump awkwardly against drinkers. It's the only club in town, and the clientele is a strange mix of young people with nothing better to do and groups in their thirties and forties, here because the pubs have shut and it's the only place to get a late drink.

Charlotte and her friends are much more fun than Seline expected. They're all a couple of years younger than her, and are increasingly loud and giggly as their pub crawl drunkenness beds in, but they're welcoming and fun and Seline feels able to let her hair down. Charlotte asks a few questions about Robbie, but Seline manages to deflect them and changes the subject. She paces herself and doesn't do shots every time the other girls do, so she is merry but certainly not as sloshed as some of them.

While her other friends are up and dancing, Charlotte is particularly drunk now and has become maudlin. She's removed her painful high heels and they sit between them on the corner table, where they're minding the other girls' jackets and talking about Charlotte's dad, about whether Charlotte will go to university having taken a couple of years off, and about Seline's work and her painting, and the possibility of Seline doing an exhibition at the new arts centre. Charlotte starts by being complimentary and enthusiastic, but now the conversation has taken a funny turn. It doesn't help that they're having to shout at each other to be heard over the bad nineties' music.

"Oh yeah, he's *so* supportive of what you're doing. He's never been like that with me," slurs Charlotte.

"He cares what you do though, right? He's your dad!"

"Not really, no." Charlotte's face clouds over as she recollects. "I thought I might like to be an actor. He never asked me anything about it. And once when I was fifteen I had the lead role in a school play. He never even came to see it. So I gave that up. D'you know what he was doing for most of last weekend? Hanging your painting up in our living room."

Charlotte stares at her drink. She looks like she could cry. Seline doesn't know what to say. It's awkward.

"I'm sorry."

"What?"

"I'M SORRY."

It doesn't sound particularly sympathetic, yelled over a thumping dance track.

Charlotte gets up and downs her drink. "I'm going to the

loo." She straps her shoes back on clumsily, grabs her bag and totters off unsteadily towards the toilets. Seline is left pondering how the evening took a wrong turn. After a while, sitting there on her own goes from lonely to embarrassed, to awkward. Charlotte has been gone for about fifteen minutes. The other girls are still out on the dance floor and Seline can see Charlotte isn't with them. Maybe she's not just upset, but unwell. She downed enough of those sickly sweet sambuca shots to make anyone ill.

Eventually one of the group, a girl called Marie, comes over to the table for a swig of her drink. Seline takes her chance. "Can you watch the coats? I'm off to check on Charlotte."


THE LADIES' loos are surprisingly quiet when Seline goes in. A couple of the cubicle doors are locked. She calls Charlotte's name but doesn't get an answer. Careful not to touch the floor, she crouches down and looks under a cubicle door. She recognises Charlotte's shoes. She taps tentatively on the cubicle door. "Charlotte? Charlotte, it's me, Seline."

There's no answer. She thinks about leaving, but then worries Charlotte may be really drunk in there and she can't just go. She enters the cubicle next door and climbs up onto the toilet seat to look over the wall. The sight that confronts her makes her audibly gasp. Charlotte is sitting on the closed seat of the lavatory. She has her dress hitched up to her waist. She's shooting up, injecting herself in the thigh. Seline's gasp makes Charlotte look up. She's utterly horrified to be seen and pulls her dress down to hide what she's been doing. But it's too late. Seline has seen everything.

·   ·   ·

SHE RUNS BACK into the club, detouring briefly to grab her bag and jacket, before pushing her way past the crowds of people and out into the cold night. The chill is bracing, and combined with the surprise of what she's just seen she feels immediately sober. Her phone is ringing in her bag – Charlotte presumably, wanting to make sure she doesn't tell anyone what she's witnessed. She doesn't even bother taking her phone out – she has no intention of answering. It stops ringing. Starts ringing again.

She trots down the hill towards the taxi rank, keen to get away as fast as possible. Charlotte's a junkie. That's why she has been funny with her all night, why she was odd the time she and Robbie came round for dinner, why she's been asking about Robbie – she has history with Robbie; he's probably the one getting her the drugs. There's nowhere she can go, nothing she can do, no one she can meet that Robbie hasn't tainted.

"Seline!"

It's Charlotte, chasing behind her down the road. She's at the taxi rank now. People are looking at Charlotte shouting her name; she can't just run away. She doesn't want to talk about anything in earshot of other people, so she stops, walks back up to Charlotte, pulls her off to the side of the pavement into an empty shop doorway.

"Seline—"

"I don't want to know. Keep away from me."

"Look—"

"I don't want to know!"

"LISTEN!" Charlotte is unexpectedly forceful. It stops Seline in her tracks. "I'm diabetic."

"What?"

"I'm a diabetic. What you saw was insulin. Look!"

Charlotte pulls open her clutch bag and shows Seline the contents, her vials of stuff and needles, glucose tablets and the like.

"I don't tell people. I know it's stupid, but I've always been the one who's different, who misses out, who leaves dinner early to avoid all the questions over pudding. On a night out I just want to be like everyone else. I was stupid. I shouldn't have had all those shots."

"I'm sorry. I thought... Forget it. I'm an idiot. Are you okay?"

"Sorry for the shock."

Seline laughs, hugs her. It's been a terrible misunderstanding, a weird night – but the whole thing feels somehow bonding.

Seline's phone rings again. She stops hugging Charlotte. Clearly it's not Charlotte ringing. So who is phoning her insistently at one in the morning? It can only be the hospital with news about Robbie. He gets in everywhere, creeps into everything and spoils it, like tainted water seeping through a crack. Reluctantly she opens her bag and takes her phone out.

It's her mum.

"Seline?" She sounds awful. "Oh God, Seline. It's your dad..."

---

## 38

She's swinging the car around the country lanes like a lunatic. She couldn't stand how Robbie drove, but now here she is, driving just like him. It doesn't even make sense really – getting home to Manchester any faster won't achieve anything. It won't change anything.

He's dead.

Her dad is dead. And getting back to Manchester won't change that.

Yet she keeps driving like a mad thing, accelerating and breaking too hard, overtaking on blind corners. It's the guilt maybe. The guilt of feeling that she was away, wasn't there with him, hasn't spoken to him properly for ages. And now she can't. He's gone.

She takes a corner much too fast, and the car slides sideways and loses proper grip on the tarmac. The rear flicks out and swings round, pitching the car into a spin. She skates across the other lane, but thankfully there's nothing coming the other way. She's also lucky that the road widens here and there's a lay-by on the other side. She comes to a halt facing the wrong way, miraculously unscathed.

She releases her vice-like grip on the steering wheel and takes a breath, then bursts into tears. She hasn't cried since the call from her mother last night. She's been in a state of shock, too drunk to drive immediately, too agitated to think. She leapt into the car at dawn and started her breakneck drive home – and this moment now, facing the wrong way in a lay-by having nearly killed herself, is the first time she's let herself feel anything. Now the tears have started she wonders if they will ever stop.

THE NEXT FEW days pass in a haze of sad conversations with neighbours and friends, endless sympathetic cups of tea and biscuits, and the surreal process of funeral admin. Her mum is a complete mess, which in some ways is helpful to Seline, because it means she has to be the sensible one, has to hold it together, has the structure of practicality to act as a safety net.

It's still not wholly clear what happened to her dad. Some kind of freak accident at work. It seems there was a chemical spillage in the place he was working security, but witness statements are a bit vague and the security cameras don't cover the area where he was injured. Seline overhears bits of the occasional phone call to her mother, and catches the tail end of a visit from the police, but it's the one area her mum doesn't seem to want her involved. Maybe her mum knows more and is trying to spare Seline the gory details.

. . .

SELINE STEPS OUT of the black sedan and helps her weeping mother onto the path. Everything is eerily silent except for her shoes making a soft tap against the rain-dampened cobblestones leading to the chapel's entrance. It's cold, and a light drizzle falls from the leaden sky, as if the weather knows it's a funeral and has pitched itself to match the lumpen mood of the gathering mourners. The air smells of wet earth. Various people she doesn't know come up to her mother and give embarrassed smiles, grim nods of sympathy, hushed whispers of condolence, touch her arm lightly. None of it stops her mother crying or gives any comfort. Nothing is worse, when you are upset, than people being nice to you. Seline stands there awkwardly, smiling a thin smile at the strangers. She's glad it is raining; she doesn't have to take her coat off. She feels self-conscious, wearing the black dress she bought to go clubbing.

The mourners shake their wet umbrellas closed, flapping like soggy crows, then go inside. Seline and her mother follow, the heavy silence surrounding them like a cocoon. She finds her seat near the front and sits on the creaking wooden pew. Before too long, the funeral procession starts, the undertaker's men carrying the coffin on their shoulders up the central aisle of the chapel like some cruel and twisted parody of a bride arriving at a wedding.

As they lower the coffin, Seline is surprised to see that one of the pallbearers is Michael. He must have travelled over to pay his respects to his old friend. His eyes meet Seline's and he gives a sympathetic smile. Seline is grateful for the support. Her mother sees him too but remains inconsolable – if anything, she is crying more hysterically now the coffin is in view. Scattered sniffs and snuffles of the congregation puncture the peace of the chapel like a doctor's waiting room.

The service starts. The vicar's words wash over her. She closes her eyes, trying to summon memories of her father, trying to connect what is being said with the man she knew, but her thoughts jump about and won't stay still. The eulogy ticks off a chronology of events – birthdays, holidays, anniversaries – like flicking through photos on a mobile phone. But it all feels surreal, as if she's watching scenes from someone else's life, a character in a story that doesn't quite belong to her.

When it's her turn to speak, Seline rises from her seat. Her legs feel unsteady, as if they belong to someone else. Her voice wobbles as she recounts stories of her father's warmth, his unwavering support through her life. But the words hang in the air as they echo around the hollow room, unable to properly describe the person she knew, or to bridge the chasm between her past and present self.

STANDING by the rain-smeared window back at the house, she gazes out at the garden where she played football with her dad and tries to bring it into focus. They don't even feel like her memories anymore; more like scenes she's watching in a film.

In contrast to her sense of detachment, her mother's grief has been palpable throughout the day, a heavy cloud that seems to grow thicker as the hours pass. The weight of the day's events lingers in the air, and a knot of unease tightens in her chest. Seline's concern deepens as she can hear distant voices coming from the kitchen, the tones hushed but charged with tension. As she approaches the closed kitchen door, the sound of her mother's sobs grows more distinct, and then suddenly there's the jagged shattering of glass against the floor. A couple of the remaining mourners stand, seizing on the possibility they might finally do something useful. Seline pushes open the kitchen door.

Her mother stands by the counter, no longer crying, her hands trembling. Broken fragments of a glass bowl glisten on the linoleum at her feet. And opposite her stands Michael, his posture tense, his eyes locked onto Seline's mother.

No one moves.

## 39

W hat with the intensity of it all, she was bound to crack at some point.

That's how her mother explained it, the two of them kneeling on the kitchen floor, carefully clearing the fragments of glass and wrapping them inside a newspaper to put in the bin.

Michael had been full of apologies. The last thing he wanted to do was to upset her, he said. Her mum swatted his apologies away as he left, and didn't want to be drawn on the incident later. But Seline could understand it all – the raw emotion of the day, her dad no longer here and then his best friend from the past showing up, bringing all those memories flooding back.

Once everyone has gone and it's just the two of them, the house feels painfully empty. Nonetheless it's a relief not to have to maintain the rictus smile of the last few hours, the public performance of grief, like exhibits in some bizarre museum. They sit at the kitchen table and chat for a while before her mum says how tired she is and goes upstairs to bed. Seline's the same too – utterly exhausted and emotionally drained.

The following morning as the two say goodbye with a long hug at the doorstep, Seline promises to drive back over next weekend. Neither mentions the inevitable clearing out they'll have to do, the raking through papers, the digging it all up again. Let's get through this ordeal before starting on the next.

She drives back sensibly. Seline's looking forward to getting back to work. It will be a welcome distraction. Throwing herself into teaching and into her painting will help as she tries to come to terms with her father's death and move on with her life. Her life, which was supposed to have an exciting new start in Statheley Bridge, and which has had only disruption and pain ever since she came here.

She arrives at her place on the housing estate and changes into something suitable for school. They're not expecting her back until tomorrow, but she feels she'll just mope about and get sad if she stays at home all day – better to teach this afternoon's lessons and keep herself occupied. In any case, Michael arranged with her to drive out after school to a space she could use as a new studio, and she thinks that will be good for her as well.

Picking up her car keys from the kitchen, she spots something out of the window.

It's Robbie's car.

Not an illusion this time, not her mind playing tricks. The same colour, the damaged front wing. No mistake.

She sits on the kitchen floor with her back against the units, so she can't be seen through the window, and calls the hospital. After a minute or so, someone confirms what she already knew: Robbie's out. Against doctor's orders, he has discharged himself.

There's a knock at the door. Nothing. Then another. Nothing. Then the sound of the letterbox being pushed open.

"Seline?"

It's Robbie. She doesn't answer.

"Seline, I know you're in there..." He's more pleading than threatening. Even so, she's terrified. He's come for her. She crawls across the kitchen floor and looks up the hallway. His distorted form leans against the front door, the twisted shapes of him wavering in the rippled glass.

He hammers heavily on the door. "I fucking know you're in there! I'm not going away!"

The hammering stops. There's a silence. Then he calls through the letter box again, more gently this time.

"Look, I'm sorry. I need to talk to you. You don't even need to open the door if you don't want. Please."

Something about his tone feels different. She crawls out and up the hallway. She speaks to him through the front door.

"Step back."

"What?"

"Take a step back. Down the path."

His shadow moves away, clearing the door. She hears him take a few steps away. Seline kneels up and pulls open the letter box so she can get a look at him.

He looks terrible. The patterned glass of the door was distorting him. But even without the glass, he looks broken and fragmented, a fractured anagram of his former self. He's leaning over with one hand on the garden wall and the other supported heavily on a metal walking stick he must have taken from the hospital. God knows how he drove, how he even got into or out of a car. His face shows signs of bruising, grey and purple and yellow. There's a patch over one eye, which could be from the accident or when she hit him with the rear-view mirror. He looks somehow puffier and thinner at the same time. And so old! He has none of his natural charm and shininess. He's like an abandoned building; all the gaiety has left and the rooms of him are empty. All his lights have gone out.

She's suddenly no longer scared of him, tottering unsteadily at the end of the path, like a small breeze might knock him over or blow him away altogether. She opens the door.

"I need money. Have you got any? I didn't know who else to ask."

She's contemptuous. "What about your money at the flat?"

"It's gone. They've taken it. Taken everything. I'm leaving town, but I can't go without money. I'm not coming back. I have to go now, before they finish me off."

She's not terrified. *He's* the one who's terrified.

"Did you have girls at the flat? Other girls?"

"What? Why?"

"I found earrings that weren't mine." For some reason, with everything that's happened, she wants to know the truth of all of it. Whether he was lying to her about everything.

"No. Never. Well, sometimes they'd come round to score drugs. Like that Julie. They'd use in the flat rather than at home. Crash out on the sofa or the bed while they were high. That's all."

She can see how the crucifix earrings might have been

part of Julie's goth style. Or maybe Robbie is just lying so she'll give him money. It doesn't really matter now.

"I haven't got much. I can give you something."

"Right. Good." Robbie pauses. "And something else. Watch yourself."

"Me? What do you mean?"

"You're in danger an' all. I might have told him you know about the drugs. The ones at the flat. If he knows, you're in danger. Sorry."

"Told who?"

"Mr Lockwood. Michael."

*"Michael?"*

"Yes. Michael. Michael! Who d'you think I was dealin' drugs for?"

Seline tries to take in what he's saying. But it doesn't make sense. None of it makes sense.

"You're saying all that was Michael? The drugs? The money? The drugs at the school?"

"No. Not at the school. That was me, dealing a bit on the side, with some of the kids. There, or they'd come to the flat. Mr Lockwood didn't know about the school."

"He did. I told him! I told him about the drugs at the school, that it was you."

She can see Robbie working it out, that Seline is the one who has given him away, who's the reason he's been half-killed. Yet he decides not to challenge her on it.

"If he knows that, knows you know about my room, and the school, then you need to watch yourself."

"But that doesn't make any sense."

"Look at me!" Robbie's shouting now. He waves his arm to indicate himself, nearly falls over. "Look at what he's done to me! This is because of the school. He wants me dead. I'm a threat to 'im. You are too, knowing. He'll want you dead too."

"He won't." She can't believe Robbie is still trying to manipulate her. She shouts back at him. "I'm not like you. He likes me! He's looking out for me! He protected *me* from *you*!"

Robbie laughs derisively.

"It was him. It was all him. Right from when he heard I met you. Him who made me move you in, him who made me keep you with me when I didn't want you, right from the very first week, so I could keep an eye on you, report back on you to him."

Her head's spinning. "But *why*? What does he want to know about me?"

"I don't know! He's mad. He had me run down. He put a cigar out on me! He's fucking insane!" He waves his scarred hand at her, loses his balance and falls heavily on the path. For all of his injuries, it's somehow this cigar burn that seems to break him. He sits there snuffling. Then he looks up at her with sad eyes.

"I'm sorry. Sorry I done all those things to you, what I was like. It was him. He made me. He made me…"

Seline's never seen Robbie like this. She doesn't understand what's going on.

But she believes him.

Michael. It was all Michael.

# PART IV

## 40

Seline spends the day in the house. She needs to think it all through. Robbie never liked her at all. The whole time she was living with him, that was Michael making him keep her there? No wonder Robbie couldn't stand her.

But why? She can't work out what possible reason Michael would have to do this. In any case, she's decided not to go to school today so she can avoid Michael while she tries to get her thoughts straight.

There's no movement on the estate all day. Nothing. She's utterly alone.

It starts to get dark. Her phone rings. It's Michael. He must have gone to the school to pick her up and discovered she's not there. She lets it ring without answering. The ringing stops, and she expects him to ring again, but he doesn't. She waits for the ping to tell her he's left a voicemail, but there is no ping.

The dusk falls to proper darkness, but she doesn't put the lights on. Then she sees some kind of movement outside, a flicker of something. It's a car's headlights, turning into the estate, picking its way along the streets, past the unfinished buildings, turning into her road, stopping outside her house. She ducks down so she can't be seen. The engine stops and she hears the slamming of a car door. Then steps on the path. Then a knock.

If Robbie was telling the truth about Michael, then she's only a danger to him if she knows what he's been up to. In a split second she realises she's safer if he doesn't know what she knows, if he thinks she's utterly ignorant of what happened earlier with Robbie. She needs to play dumb.

"Oh hello." She rubs her eyes, like she's just woken up. "I'm sorry – I was asleep."

She flicks the hall light on. She tries for a breezy tone of voice.

"Do you want to come in?"

Michael follows her up the hallway and into the kitchen.

"When you weren't at school I figured all the stress of the last few days must have caught up with you. You have to take it easy on yourself, give yourself time."

"I'm sure you're right."

"You should take a few more days off school. I can talk to them if you'd like. Take some nice walks. Spend some time with your mum. Paint."

"That sounds good." She smiles.

"Talking of painting, I've managed to find you a studio. Tell me if I'm speaking out of turn, but I do think it would be good for you to have something to focus on, something constructive. I know it's a cliché, but life does go on, and you shouldn't feel guilty about doing something for yourself, for your future. That arts centre exhibition is yours if you want it, if you still feel you can get a show together in time."

"What you say makes sense." She gives a thin, neutral smile.

"I could show you now, if you feel up to it?"

He's smiling openly at her. She knows it might look suspicious if she refuses.

"Sure. Why not?"

THE CAR'S interior is suffused with a dim, ambient glow from the dials on the dashboard. It's raining again, and the rhythmic swish of windshield wipers matches the rhythm of her racing heart. She tries to control her breathing. In. Out. In. Out. She doesn't want Michael to see she's anxious.

She looks out at the blurred landscape beyond the window, her hands clenched in her lap. Once in a while she steals a look at Michael. His face is in darkness, his profile half-shrouded in the gloom, apart from occasional flashes as they pass a streetlight. His face gives nothing away as he stares at the road ahead, apparently lost in his thoughts, his fingers tapping rhythmically on the steering wheel in time to the wipers. His calm demeanour contrasts sharply with her jittery nerves.

Seline shifts uncomfortably in her seat. She can't shake the memory of Robbie's urgent voice, warning her she's in danger. The shadows dance across the warm car interior, the soft hum of the engine takes on an eerie resonance.

They're in town now and pull up outside a large office building, its brooding, monolithic structure towering over them, its windows reflecting the deepening darkness. Michael parks the car and steps out onto the damp pavement. He holds the door open for her, his smile warm but his eyes betraying an intensity that sends another wave of apprehension through her. Her breath forms misty tendrils in the chill air.

They enter the building, and the hushed echo of their footsteps reverberates in the empty marbled lobby. Seline's heart races as they step into the lift. The ascent is silent, the only sound the soft ding of the floors passing by.

At the tenth floor, the doors slide open to reveal a vast expanse. The open-plan layout is suffused with a haunting stillness, rows of empty desks lined up like sentinels in the half-light. They step out silently onto the plush carpet. Seline resists the urge to step back into the safety of the lift, to run from the void that stretches out in front of her.

Michael's voice cuts through her thoughts. "Welcome to your new art studio, Seline."

He flicks on the fluorescent lights, the tubes flickering and tinkling until the entire floor is illuminated in a stark, cold, brilliant light. She forces a smile as he gestures towards the corner of the space and explains the neat arrangement of canvases and paints.

"I've taken the liberty of moving your supplies here. I hope you don't mind."

She takes it all in. The space is amazing. Under other circumstances she would feel nothing but gratitude and excitement. Her own studio. Her own exhibition! But any sense of gratitude is tainted by a growing sense of trepidation. Even the art supplies he's brought are like props in some sort of strange game, Michael manipulating and controlling her destiny. A knot of uncertainty tightens within her.

Clearly he expects her to start work. Trying to appear relaxed, Seline explores the supplies. As the minutes stretch out silently, Seline works to focus on arranging her materials. The rhythmic sound of a paintbrush dipping into a jar and the soft swish of bristles against canvas provide an illusion of normality. Michael, meanwhile, moves around the space, occasionally peering out of the large windows at the dark town below. The emptiness of the space amplifies the hollow feeling in her chest.

When Michael finally announces his departure, Seline's pulse quickens, her fingers trembling as she offers a weak smile.

"You'll be safe here, Seline. Take your time and create something beautiful."

She turns back to the canvas. She listens intently to the sound of his retreating footsteps. As the lift door closes behind him, she feels an incredible sense of relief.

And yet somehow, being alone gives her a different sense of unease. The vastness of the office engulfs her. Is this a sanctuary or a trap? The brushes and paints that once gave her such creative freedom now feel like anchors pulling her under. The canvases used to be so inviting, but now they feel like ominous mirrors, reflecting her uncertainty back at her.

Her thoughts cloud and darken like a storm in her mind. Is Robbie right? Is she truly in danger from Michael, or is it just paranoia?

As the minutes pass her unease grows.

She knows she can't keep glancing over her shoulder forever.

# 41

Seline can't concentrate properly to paint – or rather, she can't clear her mind enough to stop her muddle of thoughts getting in the way. It's absurd! Robbie seemed so convincing, but the more she thinks about it, the less credible the whole thing seems to her. Michael, out to kill her? It can't be true.

While she's trying to puzzle all this out, she's casually flicking through a pile of completed paintings. The girls; the rooms; the doors; the windows. The shadows. What exactly is going on in these paintings? Why is there always something lurking, something wrong, in the shadows, just out of sight? What does her unconscious mind know that her conscious mind doesn't?

"SELINE?"

It's her mum. She answered on the first ring. Clearly she can't sleep either.

"Why have you phoned, luv? Not that I mind. Something wrong?"

"I want to ask you something. Something about Michael."

There's a long pause. Seline deliberately doesn't say anything else. Finally, her mum speaks. "Go on...?"

"What was going on, in the kitchen, when you dropped that bowl?"

"Nothing. What do you mean?"

"I could hear you. You were crying."

"Well, it was your dad's funeral, luv. Of course I was crying."

Seline presses on. "It wasn't that kind of crying. You were upset. Not about Dad. About something else. You were angry."

"I don't know what you mean, Seline. I was upset, and I dropped a bowl, and it made me more upset. I don't know why." Her tone is belligerent. Seline has touched a nerve.

"I don't believe you."

"What?" Her mum sounds genuinely hurt. "Why are you being like this? Has something happened?"

"If you won't tell me, I'll ask Michael."

"Don't!"

Seline has no idea what she's fishing for, but whatever it is, her mum is worried. There *is* something to find out about.

"Tell me then!"

Her mother heaves a long, world-weary sigh.

"Alright. Alright... So, I've told you how I met your dad."

"In a shop."

"I was working on Saturdays in a clothes shop and he came in and looked around at stuff for ages. I thought he was a shoplifter, hanging about for a chance to steal something. Eventually he came up and asked me for some help to buy something for his sister's birthday. Said she was about my size. He had me trying on all sorts for ages before he bought a cheap little top. He was sweet, so when he asked me to go for a drink I said I would. Months later I found out he'd seen me through the shop window weeks back and had been trying to get up the nerve to talk to me. He didn't even have a sister!"

Seline smiles. God, she misses her dad. Will it always feel this raw, remembering him?

"Typical Colin! So, we went for a drink. It was a funny little pub, and we played darts and I was hopeless and he took the mickey in a way that made me laugh."

She pauses.

"That was when I met Michael."

Her tone shifts when she says the name. The smile has gone out of her voice.

"Michael was Colin's best mate from school. He seemed nice, but he was always around. Me and Colin started going out, but Michael was never far away. I could tell he liked me. I never said anything because I didn't want to upset your dad. But Michael wouldn't back off, started hanging around more, making snide little jokes at your dad's expense. Not anything you could pull him up on exactly – he was clever like that – but I could tell he was trying to make me go off Colin, trying to let me know he was still there. Then one day Colin caught Michael kind of making a pass at me. They had words and fell out. Their friendship drifted and they stopped seeing each other as much, then at all. All this was before you were born, before we were married."

"So was Michael still jealous, d'you think? Or was that the end of it?"

"It wasn't the end of it. He never let on that he was jealous, he never caused any obvious trouble. But he was always kind of around. They'd been best friends from school, you see, and their lives overlapped. Your dad worked hard, set up his own security company. He was a real grafter. But money was tight, we had a mortgage to pay and you came along. We struggled on for years, living hand to mouth. It was hard. So one day, when someone from a big security firm popped up and offered to buy his company, he took the chance. It was a bit of a lump sum and he'd still have a job. So he sold."

"To IRONCLAD?" Seline remembers the name. "Michael's company?"

"That's right. Michael owned the company, though Colin didn't know it at the time. He'd done well for himself after school, Michael. Better than Colin, as Colin saw it. Word was he'd done some shady deals and made a lot of money. Anyway, when he bought your dad's company Michael kind of became your dad's boss."

Her mum sighs. Seline is beginning to regret putting her through this, but now she's started, her mum seems to want to get the whole story out in one go, like ripping a plaster off a wound. She gets more animated, angry even.

"Your dad is as honest as the day is long! He was. It stuck in his throat to be working for Michael. He's a criminal. He's up to no good. Your dad never said anything to me. Never. He would never want to upset me. But I knew – knew he thought things were going on in places where he worked, where he had to turn a blind eye. He was a proud man. Too proud to let Michael being his boss get to him, or to show it anyway – too bloody proud to just leave, like he should have done, as if that would look like losing."

Seline thinks about her lovely, honest dad getting dragged into criminal stuff he didn't want to do. Maybe that's why he was so strict with her when she was younger – that awful incident with the five-pound note. Maybe he was so weird about it because he felt so bad about his own values being compromised.

Her mum continues. "He started getting lots of antisocial shifts and I'm sure stuff was going on he couldn't tell me about. Dodgy stuff. He wasn't the same man after that. I think it broke his heart."

Her mum snuffles at the other end of the line. Seline doesn't know what to say. She realises she has made a mistake, should have talked to her dad when she had the chance... and spoken to her mum about this when they were together, not on the phone!

"I'm sorry, Mum. Let's talk about it another time. I'm coming back at the weekend to help sort Dad's stuff. Let's talk about it then maybe."

"I should have spoken to you about it, luv. When he turned up again. I didn't want to rake it all up. Even though I never said it to your dad, I knew what was going on. Michael hated losing to him, losing me to your dad. He wasn't even interested in me, not really. It was about losing. And he wouldn't let it go. He *never* let it go. He wanted to ruin your dad. And in a way, he did."

"Is this why you didn't want me to take this job? Told me I could come home? It wasn't that you thought I couldn't do it... it was because you didn't want me coming here, meeting Michael?"

"Truth is, I was worried about him. Worried for you."

"But he isn't doing bad things to me. He's helping me."

"But why, luv? *Why?* Outside he's all charming and polite. But he's bitter and twisted. That's why I was worried about you meeting him, luv. He's been around for years. Waiting. I mean – what does he want with you?"

## 42

She doesn't know what to do. If Michael does have some kind of dark plan in mind for her, then she's like a rat in a trap. He's arranged where she works, where she lives and where she paints. He's controlled everything. He seemed so kind, so helpful, and all the while, he's been painting her into a corner.

And yet she can't get her brain to lock it into place. In spite of what Robbie told her, what her mum has said, would he really do all this over a woman who rejected him thirty years ago? It's crazy.

She decides she needs to unpick the web she's caught in. She calls the school to tell them she's not ready to come back yet. That gives her the day to get organised. She heads into town and registers herself at all the estate agents who deal with rental properties. She'll also need to find somewhere to do her painting, but for now she decides she'll move all her art supplies and canvases back over to Manchester when she goes at the weekend. She'll never fit it all in her car, so she calls a van hire company to arrange something for the end of the week.

"Sure, love. No problem. What size?"

She realises she has no idea what van she needs. She can't get something too small as she wants to move everything in one journey. But she's never driven anything larger than a small hatchback and she won't feel confident with anything enormous. She needs to measure up.

THE LIFT DOORS open and she steps out into the empty office. She picks her way through the formal rows of silent desks and vacant chairs. Daylight streams in through the large windows, casting elongated shadows across the room. The soft hum of distant traffic echoes through the space, the reminder of the bustling world beyond making her feel somehow more alone. The expanse seems less eerie than it did at night, but there's still something unsettling about it. She wants to be out of here as quickly as possible.

She begins to move the paintings towards the edge of the room, leaning them against the walls so she can measure the largest one and work out the minimum size of van she needs. She works fast, lining them up with gaps in between so as not to damage the edges of the canvas. It takes her some minutes, but finally she has all the works laid out in a row. Even though she is only supposed to be doing this to measure up, she can't help standing back and looking at the body of work she has produced. She hasn't taken the time to look at them in this way until now. This is what it might look like if she were able to put on the exhibition at Michael's arts centre.

"They're good."

She's been so absorbed in admiring her paintings she hasn't heard the ping of the lift at the other end of the office. She spins round in surprise and sees him – Michael.

"Christ! You scared me." She's told him she's scared. She didn't want to do that.

"Sorry. I saw your car parked downstairs. I thought I'd come and say hello."

He just happened to see her car? That seems unlikely. Is he following her? She realises everything she's thought about him could have a suspicious undertone, now she's looking for it. Or maybe she's reading too much into things...

He's wandered over to look at the paintings. He's standing very close to her. She wants to move, but she daren't. After what seems like an eternity he speaks.

"They're amazing. They're going to make the most extraordinary exhibition."

"Thanks." She won't tell him yet there's no way she's doing his exhibition. One thing at a time.

He turns towards her. "You're looking for somewhere else to live?"

He says it lightly, casually, but it's a question full of meaning. He knows what she's planning.

"Sorry. An associate we rent property through told me. He called me just after you'd been in, actually, to see if I had anything suitable to let."

She knows she has to pitch this right so he doesn't think she suspects anything about him.

"Well, you've done so much for me," she says as airily as she can, "and that house was a real help after what happened with Robbie. But it was only temporary. Now's as good a time as any to start getting on with things."

She finally feels she can move away from him, freeing

herself from the claustrophobia of having him so close. She goes over to the art supplies, fiddles with some brushes and pretends to tidy them, trying to look casual.

"Yes. Good idea. You have to keep looking forward. It's what your dad would have wanted."

"Please don't talk about my dad!" She meant to sound like she didn't want to talk about something upsetting. Instead, the moment she says it, she knows she sounds angry.

"Sorry. I don't mean to upset you. All I mean is, I want to do whatever I can to help the daughter of an old friend."

Seline hears herself scoff. Now she's lost her cool, she can't seem to stop showing how she feels, like a bad poker player giving away her hand. He regards her quizzically.

"Is this about the scene I had with your mother at your parents' house? I want you to know, whatever she told you about us, and whatever your father did, I always thought of him as—"

"'*Us?*' You'd have liked that, wouldn't you?"

Michael stands and looks at her. She's seething with anger – probably all the pent-up Robbie stuff and the grief about her dad all coming out at once. He just keeps looking, almost expressionless. She feels a bit of her fury subside and it's like he is reading her. As she calms down a little, he finally blinks, gives a sigh.

"I may be speaking out of turn here, Seline, but there are some things you need to know, things you may find out about your dad now he's gone. Whatever you hear, he was a good man. And he loved you, whatever trouble he got himself into."

"What do you mean? What trouble?"

Michael puts his hand on the back of an office chair,

wheels it towards himself and sits down. Seline remains standing at a distance, arms crossed, guarded.

"Before you were born, and when you were young, your dad ran a security company fitting burglar alarms on houses and shops. I started to hear things. That he was making extra keys for places, or keeping copies of codes, and they were getting into the wrong people's hands."

"That's rubbish!" She remembers her shame over the stolen five-pound note. Her dad was honest. The most honest man she's ever met. He'd never do anything like this, like what Michael is describing.

"I tried to talk to him about it once," he continues, "but he denied everything. I knew if I pushed the point we wouldn't get anywhere. But from that time on he became more distant with me and we kind of drifted apart. Anyway, I thought that was that."

He stops. Looks down at his feet, adjusts the cuff of his shirt awkwardly. It's the first time she's ever seen him look remotely nervous or uncomfortable.

"Then I got a call out of the blue, from your mum. This was years later, when you were seven. He and I had gone our separate ways by then, but I always kept an eye on what he was up to. I don't know, maybe Diana always suspected he was up to something a bit dodgy – but anyway, she called me, without your dad knowing, asking for my help. I'd known your mum back when she and Colin met, and we'd always got on. So I said I'd meet her."

This isn't the story her mum told her. But if her dad *was* doing something criminal, something Michael knew about, then it would make sense her parents wouldn't want her going anywhere near him. They wouldn't want Michael telling her stuff, telling the story he's telling now. She doesn't for a moment believe her mum has been lying to her – but anyway, she decides to keep listening.

"Your mum and I tried to work out where we could meet, where we knew we wouldn't be seen together – Diana didn't want your dad to know she was talking to me. She helped him manage his work diary, and knew when he'd be out on jobs, so we agreed I should come to your house while he was out. I knew if I spoke to him about it again he'd ignore me, and I didn't want him to get in trouble. So I bought his company up, absorbed it into one of my own, and took over the contracts. He got well paid for it and I put a stop to what he was up to, kept him out of trouble. I tried to keep it quiet that I owned the company, but months later he found out."

Michael pauses. There's more.

"This was in the summer holidays and you were at home. So to keep you occupied, I stopped off at a newsagent on the way and brought round a load of drawing books and pens. You never saw me arrive, but your mum gave you the books and pens and you stayed in your room."

Seline feels her legs go weak. Her drawing, her love of drawing – that came from then? Just a stupid way of keeping a little girl busy in her room? Her love of drawing and painting comes from Michael?

"Diana was really worried about Colin. We kept meeting, trying to work out what to do about him. Even though time had passed, it was like being back in the old days. We bonded over... well, over a mutual love of your dad, I suppose. You mustn't blame your mum."

Blame her mum? For what? Seline tries to piece together what Michael is saying, to fill in the gaps. The penny drops.

"Are you saying you had an *affair*?"

"It was nothing, really. Just for a few months. I'd come

over, and you'd be in your room, drawing and painting and...
I guess I was a comfort to her. We both knew it was wrong,
and we stopped it. Your dad never knew."

Now she doesn't know what to believe. But something
about it feels all too credible. The detail of it. Those art
books. Those coloured pens and pencils.

"Though I never saw you, I thought of you. Sometimes
we'd sit in the kitchen while you were in your room, and I'd
see your paintings and drawings on the door of the fridge. So
in a funny way, I feel like I've been a part of your life, and
you've been a part of mine, for a very long time."

THE DUSK HAS FALLEN, but Seline sits in the gloom, not
switching on the office lights. Michael went half an hour ago,
but she has stayed here, trying to take it all in. Though she's
been warned about Michael, everything he says sounds so
credible. Does he seem like a criminal, a drug dealer,
someone who had Robbie hurt, and who's intent on hurting
her – who made it his mission to ruin her dad's life? Or does
he seem like someone who loved her parents, who knew her
as a child and who has been reaching out to help her?

She thinks she already knows the answer. It's here in this
room. It's in her paintings.

She gets up from her chair, turns on the light, goes over
to the wall of canvasses.

Room after room of solitary girls. The girls are her. The
rooms all have doors or windows, and outside are shadows.
Something is outside those rooms, in those shadows.

It's Michael.

Michael and her mother, moving about the house, whispering their secrets, while she is in this room, drawing and

painting. Michael introduced art to her with his gifts of pads and pens. She didn't know it, but she believes it. Her love of art links back to him. But more than that. He's *in* her art. Behind every door and every window, lurking in all the shadows.

The dark man. Michael. It's always been Michael.

## 43

Seline's kneeling on the floor of her old bedroom in Manchester. On the bed in front of her are several piles of papers – all her dad's official documents that need sorting through. She assumed it wouldn't be too taxing a job, other than the emotional strain. But it's taken her three hours so far just sorting these piles, and after the first hour's rummaging it became clear the absurdly long list of things that require official notice: the mortgage company, gas and electric and water bills, bank accounts and credit cards, savings accounts and pensions, stuff to do with his car... Tracking it all down is like detective work. Fortunately, her dad kept hard copies of most things. But in recent years he'd increasingly done stuff using his phone, and now Seline has sorted as much as she can with the paperwork, she's going to go on to the emails on that. Luckily, for someone who worked in security, his personal security was pretty lax, and he used the same PIN code for the burglar alarm, his cash card and his phone – quaintly, the same one as her mum, which is how she knew.

Though it's upsetting going through her dad's things, Seline is also grateful for the distraction. Increasingly, she's confused by what she hears about Michael, and what she hears *from* Michael. She knows she needs to talk to her mum about it all, but she doesn't know how to bring it up. She can hear her mum downstairs in the kitchen, clattering crockery and pans, probably emptying the dishwasher. Are these the sorts of distant noises she heard as a little girl, locked in this bedroom, while her mother and Michael were elsewhere in the house? She really wants to ask her mum about the affair Michael described, to ask her if it's true. But she's too worried that it *is* true. Does she really want to be certain? And in any case, she doesn't want to rake it all up for her mum again, now, when she's still so upset about Dad. The past is the past.

Seline uses the names of various banks and building societies and utility companies as search terms for the emails on her dad's phone, forwarding anything remotely relevant to her own email address. Then she does the same with the text messages. Once she's finished, she's about to put the phone down when something catches her eye in her dad's most recent texts: Michael's name.

She knows she's not supposed to be looking for anything else, that reading her dad's messages would be an invasion of his privacy, even though he's dead – but this feels too important to ignore. She clicks on the message.

It's an incredibly brief exchange.

> Colin: I need to see you.

> Michael: Sure. Tomorrow. 2pm. Here:

And then there's a link to a location. Seline clicks on it, and it brings up a field somewhere near Statheley Bridge, which she works out must be the site for the arts centre. She checks the date of the messages against her phone and finds they were sent the day after they all met for that pub lunch.

THEY'RE SITTING at the kitchen table eating cottage pie. Her mum has hardly touched hers, and Seline isn't hungry either. She pokes some peas around her plate before finally mustering up the courage to talk.

"I saw Michael yesterday. I didn't want to. He just turned up."

"Oh. Well, I'm glad you're okay."

"He told me you and he had an affair when I was seven. Is that true?"

Her mother stares fixedly at her plate, like some petrified statue. Seline waits. A single tear falls from her mother's face and lands silently on the table.

"*Is* it true?"

"No!" Her mother looks up. "It's not true. Not like that. Not how he means it."

Oh God. She isn't completely denying it. There's more.

"What do you mean? What *is* it like?" This feels weird, picking on her poor mum, taking the side of some strange man she's only just met. And yet she can't help feeling her mum has lied to her, kept something from her.

"When you were seven, Michael got in touch with me."

"He said you contacted him."

"*He* contacted *me*. He came to see me and span me some yarn about your dad being in trouble at work. I knew it wasn't true, I knew if anything it was Michael who'd be causing the trouble, but he persuaded me. He used to turn up when he knew your dad was at work and he'd chip, chip, chip away at me. I don't even know how it happened – you've met him; you know what he's like. He's so charming and persuasive you lose your way with what you're really feeling."

Her mum is trying to explain the dangerous appeal of a charming man who's anything but charming underneath. She thinks Seline doesn't understand. She has no idea Seline knows only too well from Robbie about getting drawn into something stupid with someone terrifying and utterly wrong.

"So you *did* have an affair with him?"

"If you want to call it that. I didn't know what I was doing. He got your dad out of the way, then moved in on me. I felt lost, like I wasn't in control of myself. I hated it. I bitterly regret it. I was stupidly weak. It was less than a month. One day I managed to stop it. I stopped it."

Now Seline knows for sure, she doesn't know what to say. Maybe the uncertainty was better. This feels awful. Bleak and awful. Everything she ever thought she knew about her parents and about herself feels like it's crumbling around her.

"So sending me to my room to do my drawings... that was so you could keep me out of the way? The reason I'm so shy – that's all so you could have an affair?"

Her mum starts clearing the table, trying to make it all seem more normal. She talks while she scrapes food from one plate onto the other.

"Please, sweetheart, don't. Don't you think I feel bad enough about it without this?"

Seline clears the salt and pepper from the table. But she

can't just play house like nothing has happened. Something massive has happened. She puts the things down and turns to her mum.

"Did Dad know? About you and Michael?"

"No. I never told him. I never told anybody, not for years. It all seemed like it was in the past. But then Michael turned up again, got in touch with you, got you that job, and it brought it all up again. Why had he shown up again? What did he want with you?"

Seline watches her mother's hands nervously toying with the dirty cutlery.

"Your dad could see I was worried about something. At first he thought it was just me upset because you'd moved away. But as the days went by he realised it was something more. So in the end I told him."

"What did he say?"

"He was angry, and he was upset." She can see her mum is getting tearful, but she pushes on. "But then he told me he forgave me. He knew what Michael was like as well as I did."

Seline thinks about this. "So why did he turn up again, do you think? Michael? Why did he get in touch with me? Get me that job?"

"That's what worried us. He couldn't get back at your dad through me. We were worried he'd try to get back at us through you."

"When did you tell Dad? About you and Michael?"

"Not long before we came over for that lunch, that time at the pub. That's why we came over." Her mum gives her a sad smile. "He wanted to make sure you were alright."

"After that lunch, Dad told me if anyone did anything to hurt me, he'd kill them."

Her mum pauses at the sink, still holding the plates. She

puts them down on the work surface, nods her head slowly. "Yes, I believe he would have done."

"I told Michael Dad said that. I thought Dad was talking about... about someone else. But maybe he meant Michael."

The two of them stand in silence for a while, thinking it through.

"Did you know Dad went to see him? Michael. After we had that lunch."

"No. Did he? He didn't tell me that. What did he go to see him about?"

"I don't know. It must have been about me."

Then her mum looks at her. She's stopped crying. She looks... icy.

"Seline. Do you think Michael could have had something to do with your dad's accident?"

Clearly her mum thinks he may have done. And Seline knows what Michael did to Robbie, though she can't tell her mum that or it will terrify her. But yes, he absolutely could have had something to do with her dad's accident. As if she can read her thoughts, her mum puts her hand decisively on Seline's arm.

"Don't go back. Stay here. Stay here and don't go back."

"I can't just hide here forever. And in any case, if he was going to do something to me, he would already have done it."

Her mum grips her arm. She looks panicked.

"You still don't get it! You still don't get what he is. He's so much worse than you think!"

Her mum is crying again now, becoming hysterical. Seline goes to comfort her, but her mum leaps forward, knocking the plates from the work surface as she does so, and grabs Seline so hard by the shoulders that it hurts her, makes her give a little cry of pain. The plates smash on the tiled floor. Food and cutlery and shards of porcelain explode across the kitchen.

"I saw a programme years later, on TV – a documentary, about psychopaths. About how charming they are."

Seline's shocked. "You think Michael's a psychopath?" Whatever a psychopath is, Michael doesn't seem like one at all; he seems so believable, so persuasive. But maybe that's what they are. Maybe that's the point.

"I remember they described a patient – how likeable he was, how charming and charismatic and confident, but also how controlling and manipulative and cruel he was, cold and detached and just... evil. And I thought, 'That's Michael'."

Seline tries to free herself. But her mum doesn't let go. She clamps her shoulders and stares intently at her with wild, panicked eyes.

"You can't go back. You can't! He's dangerous. He's mad!"

## 44

———————

Seline's driving out to get some shopping, having spent the night at her mum's. They talked until early in the morning, and then she couldn't sleep properly, so she's feeling pretty spaced out. She's driving extra cautiously to compensate for feeling so wired.

It's been the most taxing couple of days. Having spent weeks and months thinking Robbie was ruining her life, she now knows Robbie wasn't her real issue at all. He was just a symptom of a much bigger problem, and Michael has been behind everything all along. Michael, who has moved her around like a pawn, with her job and her home. Michael, who smashed his car into Robbie, or had someone else drive into him, leaving him for dead. Michael, who she now firmly believes must have been involved in her dad's death. It's too coincidental that her dad finally confronts Michael and then he 'mysteriously' has an accident, in a warehouse where Michael's cronies run the security, and where the security camera footage of the accident has somehow gone missing...

Seline sat with her mother until she finally fell asleep,

then tried to get a little sleep herself, feeling strangely closer to her mum now the truth is out, and trying to form a plan... a plan of what to do next. She can't go to the police; she doesn't have any evidence. And the results of that urine test still haven't come back, so if anything, they suspect *her* still for the drugs at the school.

But she's made a decision. She's not going back to Statheley Bridge. She'll just leave her things at the house – they're only clothes; she can get other clothes. She's not going back to the school either. She's going to ask for compassionate leave and come up with a longer plan for where she goes next. She's going to unpick every scrap of her life that Michael has touched, free herself once and for all of his interference.

Her foggy head races with other ideas. She imagines driving back there, waiting outside Michael's house, running him down like he ran down Robbie – smashing his bones, breaking him, destroying him. A mess of thoughts that aren't properly coherent, but which involve various ways she can get revenge for herself, for her dad.

She rounds the corner at the bridge and goes to slow down for the queue of traffic at the lights up ahead. Only the car doesn't slow down. She presses the brake pedal harder, but it does nothing. She stamps on it repeatedly in alarm. She's doing about forty miles an hour and she's about to slam into the cars ahead. At the last second she instinctively turns the wheel hard to avoid the collision. The car mounts the pavement, thumping the kerb as it does and unbalancing the car. In her panic she's steered too hard, and in an instant the car is across the pavement and into the thin metal fencing at the edge of the road. The force stretches the wire chain-link, before a section comes away altogether. The wing of the car hits a post with a sickening crunch, and the car swings round to the side, pirouetting further away from the road and towards the river. There's a teasing moment where it looks like things will be okay, before the car loses balance and topples off the edge of the pavement, through the split fence and down towards the yawning water.

The impact is brutal. Her head smashes into the steering wheel, then violently into the side window. She's dazed by the force of it and almost blacks out, before she comes to again and works out what's happened – that her car is in the river. Though every part of her aches from being buffeted against the hard surfaces of the interior, her real problem is that the car is filling with water and sinking fast. Before she knows it, the water is over her head and she's still strapped in. She's going to drown if she can't get the seat belt undone.

The river is muddy and it gets instantly dark as the water presses in around her. She unclips the seat belt and forces herself out of her seat. It feels like the car has tipped nose down, though it's hard to tell, but she pushes herself into the backseat and finds her head has emerged from the water into a trapped pocket of air. She gasps another breath.

She takes stock of the situation. She can feel she's still sinking. This air-pocket is small and if the car spins again she'll lose it. Panic fuels her urgency. If she's going to survive this she needs to get out now. She takes one more breath then ducks her head back under the water so she can reach the passenger door. She feels along the side of the door, unsighted because of all the silt in the water. She can't find it! She can't find the handle! Just as she thinks she'll have to give up and go back for more air, her hand lands on the recess in the door and she curls her fingers behind the handle and pulls. The door opens and she feels the pressure of the water as she pushes the heavy door open. She pulls herself through the gap and out of the car, disoriented, and tries to work out which way is up in the darkness. Her natural buoyancy seems to pull her in one direction, so she trusts that and begins to swim. Immediately, she sees light and kicks with every ounce of energy. In just a matter of seconds her head breaks the surface and she gasps in a breath of air.

Her wet clothes cling to her heavily and threaten to pull her under again. Struggling against the water's resistance she uses all her effort to swim to the side. People are standing there – they must have seen her car go off the road and stopped. Someone puts out an arm and she takes the hand. Then other people are grabbing her and hauling her up the muddy bank.

She's safe.

## 45

Seline is sitting in the back of an ambulance with a silver blanket wrapped around her shoulders. She's coming to the end of an assessment by the paramedics. She doesn't have any major injuries or broken bones, though there's a throbbing lump on her forehead and a cut that might need some stitches. There's a worry that she might have swallowed water and been exposed to all manner of bacteria, viruses, or parasites. They're quite near an industrial park here, so it's possible there might be chemicals in the water. They've given her a precautionary eye wash. They've also taken her wet clothes and swaddled her in blankets in case she has hypothermia or shock. She feels like one of those people you see on the news after a natural disaster. They tell her she's had a lucky escape. She doesn't feel very lucky.

They want her to go with them to the hospital. But she doesn't want to. Her head is full of images of Robbie in the hospital, wired up to machines. She knows she can't go to hospital. She feels okay and wants to get home. They make it clear they're not happy, but it's her choice. They want her to contact someone immediately if she experiences any breathing issues, vomiting or diarrhoea from the water, or headaches, blackouts or unusual sleepiness from the bump on the head. And she shouldn't be alone. Will she be with anyone.

"Yes, my mum."

One of the paramedics goes to phone Seline's mother, as her bag and phone are lost in the submerged car. Outside the ambulance, she can see several police vehicles and someone controlling the single-lane traffic, as they've coned off the side of the road where the fence no longer protects people from the water. A couple of policemen are hanging around outside the ambulance, waiting to get the all-clear from the paramedics before they can interview her.

"Hello. Seline, isn't it?"

She's now out of the ambulance and sitting in the back of a police car. Someone has brought her a cup of tea from a nearby house. Out of the window she can see a couple of police officers interviewing other drivers and a woman who stands at the gate of her front garden. Maybe it was her who provided the tea. The whole thing has caused quite a commotion.

"Seline, yes."

"I'm Officer Jackson. We know you've just been through a pretty scary situation, and we're here to help understand what's happened. Obviously we'd like to hear your account. We're not jumping to conclusions, and we're not assigning blame at this point. Our main priority is to gather all the facts so we can piece together what occurred."

"Sure."

"Because we're looking into the matter, we have to follow certain procedures. This includes what's known as a police caution. This is a formal reminder that you do not have to say anything. But it may harm your defence if you do not mention when questioned something which you later rely on in court. Anything you do say may be given in evidence. Is that clear?"

"Am I under arrest?"

"No, you're not under arrest. The caution is just to let you know your rights and responsibilities, and it's for your protection while we work out what happened. Okay?"

"I guess. Sure."

Seline explains that she was driving along just fine when her breaks suddenly failed and didn't work at all. She tried to avoid crashing but drove off the road and ended up in the river.

"Did you have any indication before the crash that the brakes were failing?"

"No. None at all."

"It's quite unusual for brakes to just fail. Was the car in a good state of repair?"

"Yes. I only recently got it back from the garage."

"For brake issues?"

"No, for – other issues. Nothing to do with the brakes."

Seline notices the policeman exchange a look with the other officer before writing something in his notebook.


LATER, back at home, her worried mum buzzes in and out of her bedroom with tea and soup and toast, fussing around her to make sure she is okay. She tucks her in bed like a little girl and tells her she should sleep.

But Seline can't sleep. She tries to think her way through what happened. She has no doubts whatsoever that the police don't believe her. They think she must have been driving dangerously, that it's her fault she crashed rather than because her brakes failed. Hopefully they'll realise she's telling the truth when they recover the car. She voluntarily did a breathalyser test for them, so they know she wasn't drunk.

She lies in bed with her mum's laptop and searches the internet. She understands why the police don't believe her: as far as she can tell, the brakes don't fail in that way on a modern car. *Of course* they suspect the driver. But she *knows* what happened and that it wasn't her driving at fault.

Was this just a freak accident?

Or could it be Michael? *He* arranged the car, *he* knew the garage, *he* had driven the car to her that day after it had been resprayed. Could they have somehow rigged her brakes when they repaired it? Or Michael? And why now?

Thinking about it, if Michael's whole plan was to use Seline somehow to get back at her dad, then he doesn't need her around now her dad is dead. And if Robbie was telling the truth, if all those drugs were Michael's and Seline knows about them, then she's a danger to Michael. He'll want her dead. Even so, meddling with the brakes is like something out of a third-rate crime film. If he wants her out of the way, he could do it much more efficiently. It doesn't make sense.

Every time Seline thinks about Michael, with every new bit of information about him, that makes her more convinced he's a terrible person. What was it her mum said? *Dangerous, a madman, an evil psychopath.*

And yet there's something else. Something just as disturbing she dare hardly admit it to herself. The awful thing is – she likes him. She's drawn to him. It's more than just what her mother was saying, the charisma of the psychopath. She has an affinity with him. She feels connected to him. But why?

She has a nagging feeling about something she can't quite put her finger on. Something she's seen. She gets out of bed and kneels on the floor next to the pile of her dad's paperwork. She rearranges the various sections until she finds the one she's been thinking about. She rifles through the pension documents until she comes to the earliest one. It's his pension from IRONCLAD security. Both Michael and her mum said he joined IRONCLAD when she was about seven. But this first document is dated a year before she was born.

"ARE YOU OKAY, luv? Did the television wake you up? Sorry."

Her mum is in the living room, watching the TV on an almost-silent volume setting. She reaches for the remote control.

"Forget about that."

"Do you feel okay? Do you need something?"

"I need you to explain this." Seline comes in from where she's standing in the doorway. She holds out the pension information. She hands it to her mother, who stares at it for some time without saying anything."

"Is that why you didn't tell Dad about you and Michael? Is it why you lied to me about when you had an affair with him? Because it went on so long? From years earlier? From before I was born?"

Her mum looks up from the paperwork and meets Seline's eyes. She looks ashen. She doesn't say anything. Seline stares back at her with a steely gaze.

"Is it possible that *Michael* is my father?"

## 46

"Thanks for seeing me."

A week has passed and she's sitting where she never thought she'd be again: in The Butchers Arms in Statheley Bridge, at a small corner table, facing Michael.

"Of course! I'm very pleased to see you. I'm so glad you're okay. Your accident sounded terrible."

"Well, it was certainly a bit of a shock."

She's trying to keep it light. She doesn't want him to know that she's nervous, that she's certain he's the person behind the accident, responsible for her nearly dying. But they're in a public place. She's safe, at least for the moment.

"You said the brakes failed? Do they know why exactly?"

Is he fishing, trying to find out if she knows whether the car was tampered with?

"They don't know. They pulled the car out of the river and I think the police mechanics or whoever must be working on it now. They won't tell me much. They think it was my driving that caused it, not something wrong with the car."

"Oh right. That must be difficult for you."

"Well, it's not very nice to feel like you're a suspect for something."

She drinks her drink, chugs it down, emptying the glass. This must look like nervousness to him, but she hopes he'll think it's nervousness about being suspected by the police – not because of why she's here with him now. The more she thought about him all week, the clearer it's become to her that Michael isn't just going to give up after one attempt. He's going to keep coming after her, like he did with her dad and with Robbie. She has to take matters into her own hands. She toys with her empty glass, hoping Michael will notice it – which he does.

"Can I get you another one of those?"

"Oh yes, please. Gin and tonic, thanks."

She watches him get up and go to the bar. It's busy, even though it's quite early in the evening, as it usually is on a Friday. She knows he'll take quite a while getting served.

After a couple of minutes, she watches him step back to let someone pass, a stocky man she's never seen before in a leather jacket with closely cropped receding hair, carrying two pints of lager. They exchange a couple of words. It's a fleeting moment, but she catches a small look between the man and Michael, enough for her to feel confident they know each other. But then that's hardly surprising – there can't be many people in this town that Michael doesn't know.

"Here you are." It's a couple of minutes later and he's back at the table, places her drink on the grubby beermat in front of her.

"Thanks."

He sits down, and notices the empty table in front of his stool. "Where's my pint?"

"The boy cleared it. I hadn't realised you were still drinking it."

"It was two-thirds full." He looks momentarily furious. Then he calms. "Never mind."

"That's my fault. Let me get you another one." She's getting up out of her chair.

"Really, don't worry about it."

"Well, if you're sure." She sits. "I can't stay long anyway."

"So," he fixes her with his gaze, "you wanted to see me?"

"Oh, not about anything in particular. I just thought I'd been away for a few days and it would be good to catch up. Just to let you know I'm doing okay. I'm still painting. I should still be on track for that exhibition."

"Oh good. That's good." He gives her an implacable smile. Whatever he's thinking, she knows she'll never be able to read it on his face. Now she really is feeling nervous. She drinks her drink as fast as she can without making it look obvious that she's trying to get away.

"Anyway, that was it, really..." She picks up her bag, begins to get up.

He rises from his stool as well. "Can I give you a lift somewhere?"

"Oh no, thanks, I'm fine. I've borrowed my mum's car. I don't need a lift."

"Well, let me walk you out. I'm heading off myself anyway."

"Okay."

Seline walks ahead, zig-zagging between the busy tables and noisy drinkers, Michael following behind. As they head towards the exit, their path takes them near the table where the stocky crop-haired man from earlier is sitting with his friend. He's taken off his leather jacket and is facing away from them, towards the bar. As he takes a sip of his beer, Seline notices his dragon tattoo that wraps around his arm with a jet of fire at his hand. She's seen it before, on the arm of the mechanic at the garage where she got her car. Where her car was repaired. Where her brakes must have been tampered with by this friend of Michael's. She looks away as quickly as possible, hoping Michael hasn't noticed what she's seen.

It's cold in the car park and beginning to drizzle, but Seline doesn't mind. The cold gives her a reason to shiver, masking her nerves – and her lack of coat means she has an excuse to keep their goodbye a brief one. But it's empty out here, and away from crowds of other people, she suddenly feels very vulnerable.

"Well…"

"Yes. You look after yourself." He leans over towards her and she has a sudden flash of panic that he's going to attack her – but instead he kisses her tenderly on the cheek. "I'll see you soon."

He walks over to his car. She trots over to her mum's hatchback and gets into the driver's seat, putting her bag on the seat beside her. She doesn't start the engine or put the lights on. She squints into the dark and watches as Michael's car headlights come on, and then the windscreen wipers. She can't see him, shadowed as he is inside the car. What is he waiting for? He's probably just demisting the windows, but him still being here unsettles her nonetheless. Finally, his car rolls forward, turns towards the car park exit and into the road. She cranes her neck and watches the red taillights of his car recede up the road and disappear behind the crest of the hill.

Finally she relaxes a little, though she's still a jumble of nerves, tingling with adrenaline as if she's just stepped off a roller-coaster ride. Carefully she lifts her bag from the passenger seat onto her lap and opens it. Pulling the sleeve of her cardigan down over her hand, she lifts out the object she placed in it ten minutes ago. Michael's empty pint glass.

---

## 47

She steps out of the rain into the porch and looks back down the path at the road behind her. There aren't any car lights and no one seems to be walking on the street. She's pretty confident she hasn't been followed. She presses the doorbell and waits. She can hear the chime inside, like an ice cream van version of Greensleeves. After a few moments the door opens.

"Hello. Come in."

Graham ushers her into the hallway and closes the door behind her.

"Come into the kitchen. You're soaked. Can I get you a towel?"

"Yes, please."

He shows her to the kitchen and then steps out to get a towel.

Seline removes her wet coat and folds it over a chair before she sits at the kitchen table. She looks around the room. It feels cold and sterile. The walls are painted in a kind of off-white apple green, which she can imagine might have looked fresh and clean on a paint chart, but its actual effect is to reflect back the light as a kind of sickly green hue. The house is completely quiet apart from the faint hum of the refrigerator and the occasional tick as raindrops fall from her coat onto the tiled floor below.

Seline recalls what Robbie told her about Graham and his wife, her affair with Michael. And the way Graham described his relationship when they went for that drink. This certainly doesn't feel like a happy family home. She lets her gaze wander to the cupboards – plain, functional and dull. A lone potted plant sits on the windowsill, its leaves drooping with dried browning edges. It's depressing. Seline notices a couple of clean wine glasses on the counter near the fridge and hopes these aren't for her benefit.

Graham returns with a towel and Seline stands, leans forward and rubs her hair to remove the excess moisture. "Thanks."

"I was very sorry to hear about your dad, Seline. How are you doing?"

"I'm okay, thanks." His sympathy about this barely scratches the surface of the things she's dealing with. He knows nothing about her car accident, and obviously nothing about her mum and Michael.

"And I'm guessing things are a bit better now Robbie isn't on the scene? I can't say I felt that upset when I heard what happened to him. He had something like that coming his way his whole life."

She gives a faint smile but says nothing. He has no idea about her whole new world of pain.

"Victoria's out with her girlfriends tonight and Julie will be at a friend's house somewhere."

"Right."

"Would you like a drink? Tea or coffee, or a glass of—"

"No, I'm good, thanks. I can't stay long."

She sees Graham slump a little, though he tries to mask his disappointment with an overly upbeat tone.

"So! You said you needed some help...?"

"Some advice, yes." Seline pushes a strand of damp hair behind her ear. Now she's about to start this conversation she's aware how odd it might seem.

"When we went for that staff night out and people were talking about old jobs, you mentioned something about working in a DNA lab...?"

"That's right. Twenty years or so ago. Why?"

When she asked her mum whether Michael is her dad or not, her mum had just broken down in tears and told her she didn't know. It was possible, given the dates. She hoped he wasn't, and she'd tried to put the terrible thought out of her mind. It was possible, though she didn't know one way or the other.

"I know this'll sound weird, but is it possible to test someone's DNA from an object? From their saliva? From a cup or glass, say?"

Graham stares at the table. He's clearly trying to work out why she'd want to know that. There's a story here and he's not getting all of it. To her relief, he elects not to ask.

"I assume you mean, would the science of those home DNA testing kits work if you used saliva taken from an object rather than from a cheek swab they supplied?"

Seline nods. "That's right."

He leans back, allowing the scientist in him to take over.

"In theory, yes. The home kits have very clear instructions about how to use those cotton-wool bud swabs, how many times you have to rub them on the inside of your cheek, how to avoid contamination of the sample, how to package the sample and so forth. But a lot of that is overkill. You don't need to get that much DNA to run the test. They just make the instructions idiot-proof for people who have never done something like that before."

He starts to warm to his subject, enjoying this little teaching moment.

"Think of the police. They're testing samples all the time in connection with crimes, much smaller samples, things people never knew they were leaving behind, on clothes or sheets or under victims' fingernails. Of course, you might have a contamination problem with a cup or a glass. Was it clean before the sample went on it? Can you be sure there's only one sample there? Was the sample deposited in a place with little other DNA around, or in a busy environment with multiple people who might have drunk from it, or touched it, or coughed or sneezed on it, or yawned near it, or sung near it? But even then, with multiple samples, you can still find some things out, if the DNA you're after is there."

"I see." Seline's thinking of the beer glass she took from the pub. How many other people had drunk from it before Michael? How many others were around, shouting and laughing, spraying their invisible clouds of spittle and DNA around the busy pub? She should have been more careful.

Graham continues. "But in reality, your problem isn't a scientific one. It's an ethical one."

"Ethical? What do you mean?"

"You can test most things if you've got DNA on them. When I worked at that lab, people sent all sorts of items. Used tampons, hair, fingernails, chewing gum. Someone once posted in a set of dentures!"

"And would there be enough DNA on that – on some-one's chewing gum?" Seline asks hopefully.

"Definitely. But we didn't process any of them. We could have, and we'd have got results... but no ethical lab is going to test material without the correct identification and paper-work. Samples have to be given with consent. If we processed these sorts of things from the general public, we'd have lost our licence like *that*." He clicks his fingers. The sound hangs in the air like a nail being hammered into the coffin of her plan.

"I see."

"I guess you could... *if* you knew someone on the inside of a lab... and *if* they were prepared to risk their job for you for some reason. Shame you didn't ask me this question twenty years ago!"

"Right." Seline's down-hearted – there's clearly no way her plan can work.

"I don't want to pry, Seline... but do you need help? Can I help at all?"


SELINE SITS IN HER CAR, looking at the passenger seat where she has spread out several DNA home testing kits – their labels and envelopes, their plastic vials and little clear bags with cotton buds. It's nice of Graham to offer help – but he doesn't have the first clue what kind of dangerous mess she's involved in. She needs to know for certain if Michael is her father, but there's no way she can possibly find that out without him knowing. The idea of her finding someone inside a DNA testing lab is absurdly far-fetched. Graham was her last and only hope.

She flicks on the windscreen wipers and drives off, trying to think what she can do next. But nothing comes to mind.

As she turns the corner she slows the car by the side of the road, pulls to a stop. She presses the button so her window slides down. She reaches to her left, then leans out of her window into the light rain towards the pavement litter bin. She listens to the echo of broken glass as she tosses in Michael's useless pint glass she took from the pub.

She winds up her window and drives off.

## 48

S eline doesn't know how long she has been waiting here in the dark. She's pulled the chair away from her dressing table and now sits in the window of the show-home Michael has loaned her. She's staring through the rain-streaked glass to the entrance of the estate, to see if anyone turns in from the road. It's been raining hard for days now, almost non-stop it seems, and the unlandscaped gardens and tracks from the heavy plant equipment have all filled up with water. The choppy ground around the houses looks like a war zone. It's stormy outside. Heavy sheeting has been pulled across some of the vehicles to protect building supplies from the elements, but the wind has teased some of the rigging loose. The tarpaulin claps against itself with loud wet slaps she can hear from up here.

It feels eerie, lurking here in the shadows – but safer than turning the lights on, where someone would be able to see her inside while she wouldn't be able to see them.

Someone. She means Michael.

She's thought it all through and believes she finally under-stands how his mind – his warped mind – works. He wanted to be with her mum but lost out to his childhood friend, her dad. He can't stand not winning. And since then he's made it his mission to ruin her dad's life: seducing his wife, control-ling his job, and then trying to take control of his daughter. But when her dad finally stood up to him, Michael killed him.

So if his plan with Seline was to get back at her dad, he no longer needs Seline in the equation. More than that, Seline knows too much about him – he needs her out of the way. And he's not going to go away, ever. Someone who maintains a mad revenge scheme like this for over twenty years isn't just going to back off. He's undoubtedly going to kill her.

Sure enough, she sees a vehicle's lights refracted in the raindrops on the window. As it approaches, the various tiny lights coalesce, and the form of a car emerges in the gloom. She recognises it as Michael's. He picks his way through the pools of water pock-marking the roads and comes to a halt outside her house. He turns the engine off. He sits there in darkness.

Does he even know she's in the house? She waits for a minute and tries to puzzle out what he's doing, but there's no movement from the car. Eventually, she takes out her phone and, holding it under the corner of the duvet to mask the light, she calls his number.

She finally sees his shadowy figure inside the car, illumi-nated by the glow of her incoming call.

"Seline."

"I think you should come in."

A pause. "Alright."

. . .

SHE OPENS the door for him and ushers him inside, but he's careful to let her go first. As always, he oozes confidence and authority, but she's certain he doesn't want her out of his sights, or behind him where she might take him by surprise. He turns on the lights in the darkened hallway, and then the kitchen lights as they enter. Yes, he's suspicious. She sees him glance casually towards the passage, where her packed suitcases and other belongings are piled up.

"Going somewhere?"

"I was getting ready to leave."

"But you haven't left." A very faint smile plays across his lips. It's a statement, not a question. Even so, she knows he must wonder why she hasn't just gone.

"No, I haven't."

This is the most dangerous moment of all – the two of them alone in this house, miles from anyone. She can feel him looking at her. He could do anything. She needs to push on with her plan before he executes one of his own.

"I thought we should talk," she says, as steadily as she can.

He takes a seat at the kitchen table. She can't stand how relaxed he looks. Her own heart is pounding in her chest so loud she feels certain he'll be able to hear it, but she fights to hold onto an appearance of calm. She sits down too, but is careful to keep the table between them. She looks at the array of fancy objects – the carved wooden fruit bowl, the ornate linen runner, the heavy salt and pepper grinders, the artfully arranged cookbooks, the glass vase full of polished pebbles – all designed to give the appearance of luxury, elegance and comfort. They look incongruous and out of place in the context of this bizarre and menacing encounter.

She attempts a casual tone. "I heard back from the police, by the way, about my accident."

"Oh yes?" He leans forward slightly.

She consults a set of notes she's made on her phone. "They say the brakes stopped working because of a 'failure of the master brake cylinder seal'. They said it was 'highly unusual for a car this age'. They apologised for any suggestion that it was a driving error on my part. I asked them how it could have happened and if it was possible if someone had tampered with the car, but they said they wouldn't be able to confirm that."

"Why did you ask that?"

"Because I thought it might be what had happened."

"Right."

"I know, you see. I know it was you. That your mechanic friend did it."

He thinks about this for a fraction of a moment.

"Is that right?" He doesn't give anything away in his tone of voice.

Now she's started, she must keep going.

"I know it was you who did that to Robbie; you or someone who works for you. I know it was you who killed my dad, or had him killed, and your security firm got rid of the footage from the security cameras. I know what you did to my mum. You know I know all this."

Michael looks puzzled, but he doesn't respond. Is he trying to look puzzled as a way of denying her accusations? Or is he genuinely puzzled why she's telling him everything she knows?

"And I know *why* you did it all... Getting me that job, luring me over here, spending all that money on the art department, messing with me. You were obsessed with my dad, getting revenge on him. Beating him. And messing with his daughter was a sick way to do it. But there's something you don't know."

She opens the drawer in the kitchen table and takes out one of her DNA test kits.

"I wasn't his daughter. I'm *your* daughter. *You're* my father."

Michael looks surprised. It's not his usual guarded style. She's caught him off-guard.

"What makes you think that?"

"Think about it. Think about you and my mother, when that was, before I was born. It's possible, isn't it? It's possible. And think about us. You and me. In spite of whatever else is going on, or what you might have done, we have a connection, don't we? I feel it. You must feel it too."

She's still finding it impossible to read Michael's face. What is he thinking? He looks at the kit for a long time before he finally speaks.

"I'm not going to say anything about those things you've accused me of. But for the sake of argument, let's say they're true. What now?"

"Well, before you do anything else, anything you might regret, don't you want to know? Don't you want to know if I'm your daughter?"


HE's GONE. She's alone again, in the kitchen, looking at the objects on the table: the fruit bowl, the linen runner, the salt and pepper grinders, the cookbooks, the vase of pebbles – and the DNA kit.

He said hardly anything, but the fact that he did the test, the fact that she's still alive, means he's interested to know if

Seline is his daughter. It was a curiously intimate act. They operated in a silence charged with a strange, unspoken connection, resonating with an understanding that this could change everything. Her fingers trembled slightly as she carefully opened the kit with a soft rustle of paper. Their movements were measured and deliberate. The swabs moved gently against the inside of their cheeks, then into their small pots, then into the sealed envelopes, echoing each other's actions as if to confirm already the link between them. And then repeating the same actions, like a bizarre dance, the backup samples taken to be doubly sure of the results upon which so much depends.

And if she *is* his daughter, that changes everything. Why would he kill her then? She's the object of ultimate triumph over her 'dad' Colin, who will have spent twenty years bringing up a child who isn't his – his enemy's child. Michael's child. Seline. Seline herself will be Michael's ultimate victory.

She looks at the kit. Now she has to send the samples off and wait, wait for the results to come back. She hopes they'll tell her what she desperately needs them to tell her.

If she's going to stay alive, she has to hope the man who was planning to kill her is her real father.

## 49

"Oh wow, hello!"

"Oh hi, hi!"

They're in Fusion. Seline has just bumped into Charlotte.

Charlotte hugs her. She shouts over the music. "I didn't think you liked clubs!"

"Well, I'm back in town and fancied a night out."

"Who are you here with?"

"No one. I'm really glad I ran into you." Seline hugs Charlotte again. "Shall we get a drink?"

It's been two days since Seline and Michael did the DNA test. It has kept Michael away from her so far, but she knows it's only a matter of time before she gets the results back, and if she *isn't* Michael's daughter she needs a back-up plan.

"Two gin and tonics, please. Doubles."

It doesn't make any difference to her whether Michael is her father or not. *Colin* is her dad as far as she's concerned, whatever some DNA test says. It actually makes her flesh crawl to think that the man who killed her dad could be her biological father. It's too awful to contemplate. But every time she tries to push it out of her mind, it creeps back in.

And anyway, she *needs* to think about it in case the tests are negative, and Michael isn't her father, and he comes after her again. She has to make a plan.

"Cheers!"

Seline and Charlotte chink glasses. What if Michael *is* her dad? Charlotte will be her sister. Will they tell her? How will that make her feel, a girl who is jealous of Seline already, even before she discovers they're siblings?

"Another? Two more, please."

Seline and Charlotte head over to a corner of the club and find the table where Charlotte's mates have dumped their coats. They down their drinks and go onto the dance floor.

The room pulses with energy, the kaleidoscope of neon cutting through the darkness. Strobe lights flash with a mesmeric beat, casting shadows that dance in sync with the crowd's rhythmic movements. Seline lets herself go, feeling the bass throb in her chest, vibrating through every fibre of her being. She dances with abandon, the laughter of people nearby and the symphony of music merging into an intoxicating crescendo that envelopes the room. She takes Charlotte's hands and draws her into the throng.

Michael has been in her life for years, ruining things for her parents, breaking their happiness, ending her father's life. What does she care whether he's her 'real' father or not? It's only useful to her because he's less likely to want her dead if she's his daughter. But that doesn't stop her wanting her revenge on Michael, to make him pay for everything he's done to her family, for everything he's taken away. She wants to take something away from Michael like he's taken some-thing away from her.

They sway amid the sea of people. A sense of euphoria washes over everyone. Seline sees Charlotte join with it. Joy radiates from the dancers, their harmonious movements creating a single, pulsing throng. The weight of the world seems very distant. The heat of bodies pressed close creates a shared warmth that intensifies the experience. With every step, the floor seems to swell, as if the music itself is moving them, a single unified throbbing mass.

Seline returns with more drinks. She spills one in the crowd, but hands the other to a sweaty Charlotte. The room becomes even hotter and the air is thick and clammy.

What does Michael care about? If her mum is right, that he's a psychopath, then maybe he doesn't care about anything. But if he didn't care, why would he put so much effort into destroying her dad? Michael cares about winning, about being number one, about being at the top of the pile. He wants to feel he's in control, and can't bear it when someone does something against his will. The very act of defying him would be a kind of revenge.

The more they dance, the thirstier they get. Seline comes back with even more drink and Charlotte gulps it down. She starts dancing wildly and at one point loses her balance, bumping into a group next to her. It's only really the crush of the dance floor that prevents her from stumbling over and falling to the ground.

Seline has only had one drink for every two she buys for Charlotte, but even she is beginning to feel the effects. The vibrant lights flick on and off erratically, merging into a hazy smudge of colours. The music echoes in a muddy blur. As the crowd undulates in time, it feels like they are dancing on a boat, the floor itself lifting them up and dropping them down, like the breathing of some enormous beast, the ebb and flow, pitching from side to side.

What else does Michael care about? His car? His house? His business? Money and reputation. She could smash his car to pieces, burn his house to the ground. She could turn the gas on in the house he has loaned her and light a match. She could pull the tarpaulin back from one of those diggers and drive it through the estate, smashing down buildings like a child smashing down wooden blocks.

Her thoughts tumble over each other. The dance floor feels distant, as if it's behind a foggy window. Euphoria gives way to confusion. Thoughts turn murky, words become slippery, and she gets the sense of looking at herself from outside, the connection between her body and reality going fuzzy at the edges. Fluid movements begin to stutter, the dance transforming into a more erratic, stumbling sway. She's had more than enough, and Charlotte has had double.

Where is Charlotte? She's no longer here. Seline moves tipsily from the floor, going hand to hand on dancers' shoulders like a passenger steadying herself down the aisle of a turbulent aircraft. It's cooler off the dance floor. She gulps down air and collects her thoughts. She navigates her way to the toilets. As anticipated, she can hear Charlotte throwing up in one of the cubicles.

"Charlotte? It's me, Seline."

Seline goes in through the unlocked door and starts to help Charlotte. The most violent part of the vomiting appears to be over. She wets a clump of toilet paper and begins to clean her up, wiping her face, clearing the hair plastered to her cheek and forehead by sweat or sick or both. The sight of it, combined with everything she's drunk

herself, makes her feel bilious. She hopes she isn't going to
throw up too. Maybe Charlotte actually feels better than her,
now she's been sick.

She gets Charlotte to her feet and walks her unsteadily to
a sink. It's clear Charlotte doesn't feel better than her. She
tries to say something, but it's slurred and incomprehensible.
Washing her face at the sink, Seline can't properly support
the tottering mess that Charlotte has become, and has to sit
her on the floor.

It takes about fifteen minutes, but Seline manages to get
Charlotte out of the toilets and up the stairs, then out of the
club and onto the street. It's freezing and raining hard, but
Seline doesn't worry about that and Charlotte seems oblivious. Supporting her on one side and letting Charlotte rest
her hand against the wall on the other, Seline walks them
slowly down to the end of the road to the disused bus shel-
ter. She sits Charlotte on the bench out of the rain and leans
her head on the glass. Charlotte looks instantly like she is
asleep. A few people are around, but no one takes any notice.
They're all dealing with their own post-club situations,
refugees of the night too absorbed in their own dramas to
pay any attention to hers.

"Wait here." She tells her this in case she can hear, but
really Seline knows Charlotte is going nowhere. She runs
down the road to the taxi rank. The queue isn't too long, the
rain having persuaded most people to walk home fast rather
than stand here and drown. Once in the car, she gives her
destination.

"Oh, can you stop here a moment, please?"

The cab pulls to a halt and Seline jumps out and goes
over to Charlotte. She figures now the driver is mid-fair he'll
have to take them no matter how drunk Charlotte is, or he

won't get paid. Charlotte's a dead weight, but Seline rouses her enough to get her to the back of the cab and flops her in like a sack of potatoes.

"Sorry. I just saw my friend. Thanks."

The driver looks at her through thin eyes in his rear-view mirror, but says nothing and drives on. Fortunately, Charlotte falls asleep and isn't any trouble. She snores faintly as the cab pulls out of the town centre and up the hill.

What else has Michael taken away from her? Family. Everything she thought she knew about her family has been tainted by his manipulation of it, like a kind of anti-Midas, turning everything he touches to shit. And what does Michael care about? His own family. His wife and his daughter Charlotte.

"Are you sure this is right?" The cabbie doesn't understand why they're driving into an unfinished housing development.

"Yes, it's just up here."

He keeps driving and, after a couple of turns, pulls up outside Seline's show home.

Once inside, Seline manages to manoeuvre Charlotte into the dark living room. She turns on a single dim table lamp so she can see what she's doing, and begins to undress Charlotte.

"Let's get you out of these wet things."

Charlotte is sleepy but seems to understand some of what is going on. She lifts her arms and legs heavily as Seline removes her clothes, like a drowsy child who has been carried in from the car by her parents after a night out. She's placid and compliant. Seline notices how young she is, how vulnerable. There are only a couple of years between them, but the events of the last few months have aged Seline immeasurably. In comparison, Charlotte, now naked, seems like a baby.

She slips a nightie over Charlotte's head and then leads her to the bathroom. She opens the medicine cabinet and takes out one of the many unused toothbrushes she still has from Robbie's flat. She peels open the packaging and, recognising that Charlotte is in no fit state to do it herself, begins to clean her teeth.

If Michael turns out to be her real father, he'll gain another child. He'll have won. He'll have finally beaten her dad. Dad. Her dad. She'll never see him again. Michael has taken him away from her. He needs to be made to feel what she's feeling. He needs to lose something in the way she has lost something. How would he feel then?

Michael shouldn't gain a child. Seline is a child who has lost a parent, so maybe it would be natural justice if Michael becomes a parent who *loses* a child.

She leads Charlotte back into the living room and sits her on the side of the sofa, which is already made up as a guest bed. She swings her legs up and onto the sofa as her head falls onto the pillow. She's peaceful now. A faint smile crosses her lips as she sinks back into sleep. She's not aware of what's happening to her at all. Has no idea where she is. Is lost in a dream.

Seline looks down at her. Quiet. Exposed. Defenceless.

She's not a psychopath. She can't hurt someone for no reason, without consequence. Michael *should* lose something. But it's not Charlotte's fault that Michael is her father, just like it wouldn't be Seline's fault if Michael is *her* father. He needs to be made to suffer, but not like this. Not this.

Slowly she tucks the cover around the sleeping Charlotte and turns out the light.

## 50

---

She can't remember the last time it wasn't raining. Her life moves to the soundtrack of its nagging, the raindrops tapping on the windows like the drumming of restless fingers. The day is dull, and feeble sunlight barely forces its way through the curtains, casting patchy smudges of shadow across the floor as she navigates her way around the house, undertaking a series of seemingly mundane tasks. There's a quiet restlessness in the air, a tension she tries to put out of her mind.

She starts in the bedroom. She puffs up the duvet and strokes the cotton cover, her palms smoothing out miniscule wrinkles. She arranges the throw pillows with meticulous care. She gazes at the framed photographs on the wall – lush green fields, ice-smooth lakes and sun-dappled meadows, each an idyllic moment frozen in time. Shop-bought, not hers. Then to the bathroom, where she organises the towels, folding them over the rail in perfect symmetry. She runs the tap and wipes around the sink, then dries it with some toilet tissue and flushes it away. She gazes at herself in the mirror before moving on, like a ghost flitting briefly through the room.

With each task she undertakes, there's a palpable sense of avoidance. The whole ritual is a studied exercise in prevarication.

Then down the stairs and on to the living room, straightening cushions that are already perfectly aligned, pausing to reflect on the volumes of unread books on the bookshelves. The TV remote catches her eye, and she spends a while scrolling through channels, not really taking anything in. The minutes slip away as she loses herself in the mundane world of morning shows and advertisements, before she switches the screen off again. She strokes the sofa where she has perched momentarily, smoothing away any trace of her presence. With every room she passes through, she eradicates any sense of her temporary occupation, any indication that she has ever been here at all.

She moves past her suitcases in the hallway, still packed and ready for her departure. She sighs as she enters the final room of the house, the kitchen. Nothing is out of place, except the book she has been reading for the last couple of days: *Evolving Shadows: Exploring the Genetics of Psychopathy.* If Michael is a psychopath, as seems increasingly likely the more she learns, and if Michael is her biological father, then what does that mean for her? Are the traces of him inside her, tainting her, like a genetic ticking time bomb? Bits of him snaking through her, corrupting her fibres and tissues and organs, zigzagging through her brain like malignant lightning?

She puts the book in her bag. She checks the potted plant by the window, adjusting a drooping leaf. She scans the room one more time. Everything is exactly as she found it the day she moved in.

Just one thing remains: the envelope on the kitchen table. It arrived in the morning post and she left it here, unopened. She pulls out a chair and sits down. The envelope rests there, seemingly innocuous. Her pulse quickens with a mixture of anticipation and fear. She picks it up, then hesitates, her fingers tracing the edges, the paper cool against her touch. She looks at the printed logo above her name and address: *MyDNAPath.*

She takes a deep breath and slides her finger under the flap. The seal gives way, and the envelope opens. She slips her hand inside and slides out the contents, a folded sheet of A4 paper and a second sealed envelope. She unfolds the paper and reads.

**DNA Paternity Testing: Understanding Your Results**
*Congratulations on completing your DNA paternity test. We understand the significance of this journey and are here to provide you with a clear understanding of your results.*

**The Power of DNA Testing**
*DNA testing stands as the pinnacle of modern technology in determining parentage with unparalleled accuracy. In a DNA paternity test, the outcome is presented as the 'probability of parentage.' This probability is measured at 0% when there is no biological connection between the alleged parent and the child. Conversely, if a biological relationship exists, the probability of parentage typically soars to 99.99%.*

Seline knows all this. She read all of the information enclosed in several tests, over and over, before going ahead with her plan. And yet she reads it again now, knowing that the other sealed envelope on the table will reveal the actual result. She isn't ready to look at it yet.

### Your Journey Continues
*Your test results are presented in the enclosed tamper-proof sealed envelope.*
*As you digest this information, remember that these results hold immense significance. Whether your path leads to confirmation or revelation, DNA testing serves as a guiding light, unravelling the mysteries that weave through our shared genetic tapestry.*

That's it. Everything tidied away, every other task completed, nothing left now but to look at the results. She closes her eyes briefly, letting the weight of the moment settle within her.

She picks up the envelope and looks at the seal on the reverse.

Not now. Not here.

Not quite yet.

# 51

---

The room is buzzing with anticipation. People stand talking in small groups, dressed in their finery. One woman wears a red velvet coat trimmed in white fur and heavy mayoral chains over an extravagantly ruched shirt collar. There's a general level of animated chatter, punctuated by the occasional laugh. Sombrely dressed young men and women glide through the room between the groups, carrying silver trays of bubbling drinks and morsels of food: truffled mushroom tartlets, prosciutto-wrapped asparagus, mini crab cakes, grilled shrimp with mango salsa.

Seline observes from the edge of the room. It's all very civilised. She's aware the occasion is primarily social, though she does spot the odd person turn away from the throng now and then to gaze for a while at the paintings which adorn the walls of the magnificent gallery space. The shadowy rooms peopled with passive, blank-faced girls, inert, enduring, acquiescent. *Her* paintings. Her exhibition, to mark the official opening of The Lockwood Arts Centre.

Seline feels a touch at her elbow and turns to see the

centre administrator, who smiles at her and nods towards a microphone stand on a small raised wooden platform, indicating that it's her turn to make one of the many speeches that evening. Seline walks to the microphone and takes out her notes, waits for the crowd to hush. Someone somewhere taps the side of a champagne flute with a knife and slowly the room falls silent. People turn towards her expectantly.

"Ladies and gentlemen, esteemed Lady Mayoress, distinguished guests, dear friends, and cherished family, thank you from the depths of my heart for gracing us with your presence tonight. Your attendance here brings life and meaning to this exhibition, and I am truly honoured to have you all gathered to share in this very special moment. Special for me personally, of course, but also for the town of Statheley Bridge on the opening of this magnificent arts centre."

She takes a moment to pause and look up from her notes, looks around the room at the many faces, several she knows but most of them unfamiliar to her. She notices someone has thoughtfully placed a full glass of champagne on a table next to the microphone stand. She lifts it and takes a sip.

"Nervous. Dry throat."

A warm and supportive laugh ripples round the room, encouraging her to continue.

"It's wonderful to see so many friendly faces here, and also so many new people I hope to have the opportunity of meeting this evening. But I'd also like to take a moment to acknowledge some important people who aren't able to be in the room with us tonight, without whom this evening, this exhibition, and even this building itself wouldn't have been possible. First on that list, of course, is Michael Lockwood, after whom this arts centre has so very rightly been named."

A round of applause fills the room. She doesn't need to say much about Michael. The village has been awash with rumours and theories for the last nine months. His car found unlocked and abandoned on a remote country lane out of town, still in working order, still with half a tank of petrol, miles from anywhere. Why would someone stop here, and get out? Why would they walk here, and where would they be walking to? Were they meeting someone, and why?

THE CAR ROUNDS the corner and turns off the road, tarmac giving way to gravel and the seasick undulations of a track designed more for lorries and diggers than a limousine. Michael doesn't seem fazed, navigating this way in the dark, as he splashes the car through crunching potholes, pitching it left and right like a cork on a sea, coming to a halt by a high fence and a gate made of thick, corrugated metal streaked with rust. He keeps the engine running. A Portakabin sits to the right of the fence, its windows black and featureless, and Michael has angled the car so he can flash his headlights at it.

Seline watches from the passenger seat, anticipating that the lodge will light up and a security guard will be obliged to switch off his television or put down his hot cup of tea, emerge from the warmth of the cabin into the cold and rain, pulling the hood of his thick Day-Glo yellow jacket up as he does so, and scamper out to greet the big boss.

But no light goes on.

"I gave the guys the night off. I just wanted to check."

So they're all alone out here, in the middle of nowhere. Seline's pulse quickens a little.

"Hang on." Michael gets out of the car, walks briskly to the gate, stands in the beam of the car's lights and fiddles at the lock with some keys. He leaves his driver-side door open as he does so, presumably with the idea that he can get back in fractionally quicker, prevent himself from getting more wet than necessary. Seline watches the rain coming into the car at an angle, spattering the steering wheel with flecks of water. She turns and looks at his coat on the back seat of the car. He should have put it on. He's misjudged quite how heavily it's raining.

Michael swings open the gates and hurries back to the car, pulls the door closed with a heavy thud and wipes some of the rain from his face with his hand. Beads of moisture cling to the coarse fibres of his suit like drops of dew on a spider's web.

"We've picked a nice night for it."

He swings the car round and through the gates, then further along the rough track, up to the crest of the hill. She can see immediately that a lot of work has happened since they were last here. The footprint of the arts centre seems even bigger than before, the groundwork spreading out across the field like crooked fingers lined with heavy machinery, diggers for excavating the foundations and trucks for clearing away the soil. Thin strands of steel burst out of the ground like sick weeds.

The car comes to a stop in an open area that gives a clear view across the entire site and then down the valley to the lights of Statheley Bridge below. Michael turns off the engine. He reaches to the roof and flicks a switch for the interior light. The two of them sit there in the anaemic gloom.

Michael breaks the silence. "I hope you don't mind us meeting here."

"Not at all," she says, as calmly as she can manage. But Seline *is* nervous, being here. If the results show she's not his daughter, it would be the perfect place for him to finish her off.

"Like I said," she continues, "I have the test results. I wanted us to open them together. Here's as good a place as any."

Seline keeps her gaze fixed ahead. She tries to make it look like she's admiring the view rather than avoiding eye contact. Outside the car, the world seems normal and at peace, like nothing is going on. She tries to take reassurance from the solidity of the rain-soaked horizon where the darkness of the field meets the lights of the town.

"This feels like a perfect place to find out."

He looks at the site ahead. "It will soon be finished." She isn't clear if he means the building or the business between them. She's aware of the suggestion of menace that still hangs in the air.

"Let's get out." She can feel her nerves, the quiver in her voice, the goose-flesh on her arms. She doesn't want him to see her hands trembling and thinks if they're outside, in the cold, there will be a legitimate reason to shiver and he won't be able to tell how scared she is.

Michael gets out of the car and opens the back door, takes out his coat. He pops the boot and then comes round to her door and opens it. He's holding a large black golf umbrella. Seline gets out, folding her own coat around her as she does so, digging into her pockets and pulling on her warm gloves. They step away from the car and walk towards the site of the building works. It's raining more heavily now, and the patter of droplets drum on the fabric of the umbrella. To stay dry, they have to keep very close together as they walk. At one point Seline slips on a clod of earth and stumbles, instinctively grabbing Michael's arm to stop herself from falling.

They reach the edge of the building works proper. It's a sprawling, deserted space, but up close it's easier to make out the channels of trenches that form what will be the foundations of the arts centre, their grid etched into the ground like a shadowy negative of what the structure will soon become. The dim glow of security lights illuminates the area, casting malformed shadows over the construction machinery and towers of building materials. She can feel the ground under her feet, loose and muddy. She looks down into the darkness of the waterlogged trench before them, like a moat separating them from the town.

Drawing a deep breath, she reaches into her pocket and pulls out the envelope, hands it to him. She knows the only reason she's still alive is because there's a possibility she is his daughter. He looks briefly at the *MyDNAPath* logo, but he already knows what she's asking him to look at. She takes the handle of the umbrella and holds it over them both while he notes the untouched tamper-proof seal on the envelope, then rips it open and takes out the test results. She can see his eyes scanning the page, and his mouth moves slightly as he reads to himself. A thin wisp of condensation escapes from his lips and disappears into the cold night air.

"99.99% probability of paternity...?" He looks up at her from the paper in his hand, passes it to her to read.

She looks at their names at the top of the form, the

columns of figures echoing each other, and the summary at the bottom. It's irrefutable proof.

"You're my father."

Michael looks back at the view. He's entirely still for a moment – and then lets out a sigh. It's an extraordinary sound. Not a normal sigh. He sounds like the air is being pulled from somewhere deep within him. Finally he finishes and is silent. He swallows, gathering himself.

"All these years... All these years..." He's speaking to himself, to no one.

The gravity of the information sinks in.

Seline turns to him. "Whatever else has happened, or hasn't happened, this is where we are now. It makes sense somehow, why I felt so connected to you when we met, why you did too. Something linked us together all the time... and it's this. It isn't chance, you inviting me here, you offering me the exhibition of my paintings. You're *in* my paintings. You've *always* been part of them. You've always been part of *me*."

He sighs again. "These years I've been focused on Colin. Trying to win. And all the time he's been bringing up *my* daughter. I *have* won. I'd *always* won."

He laughs to himself.

"You know, I never really liked art. This place, this building – it was just about money. Government grants, lottery funds. An easy way to land some local council contracts. But there's a reason it's happened. For the first time I feel like I'm building something real, more real than money. For my daughter."

He looks at her and smiles. It's not his usual smile, a mask of control, hiding everything. He's smiling artlessly. He's happy.

"It's a relief, you know? To stop. To know it's over. So much wasted time."

She can hear it in his voice, the relief, like he's let something go, like he's let the grudge go, like he's somehow at peace. She feels a surge of empathy for him. In that moment, as he exhaled that sigh, Seline felt the extraordinary power of release.

"Beautiful, isn't it?" He steps forward a little, out from under the umbrella, to better see the view – the building site and the valley and the town. The rain falls on him, but he doesn't seem to notice it, or doesn't care. Seline steps back and lets the umbrella fall to one side, lets the rain fall on her hair as well. She looks at Michael, silhouetted against the lights of the town. He's right. She feels it too. The romance of the light and the shadows. The sense of something in the emptiness. The drama of it all. It's all she's ever painted, really. It's bewitching.

The rain continues to fall. Michael takes it all in.

"I always think it's magical up here. The security lights and the lights on the fences. The streetlights and the houses. The night. Who needs the stars?"

At peace, he turns to share the moment with her.

She's no longer holding the umbrella. She has something else in her hand, cold and hard and heavy – a discarded length of scaffolding pole. It makes contact with his head with a sickening crack. She doesn't even see his face as he falls backwards. His face is just a shadow, silhouetted against the town as he falls backwards like a dead weight and disappears into the foundation trench with a splash, like a large rock tossed in a pond.

Then nothing.

She stands utterly still. She doesn't move for at least a minute.

She listens for a noise, anything, a grunt or a moan.

But there's no sound other than the faint spattering of raindrops on the muddy ground.

"Michael is a big part of this arts centre, which has been a passion project for him for a long time. I feel incredibly lucky to have received the encouragement I did from him, and of course, the amazing opportunity to put on this opening exhibition. I genuinely feel that his influence permeates the very essence of my work. This exhibition literally would not exist without him. I know that you, like me, wish him well wherever he is and we hope he comes back to us very soon. In a very real sense I feel he's with us now and none of us would be standing here without him."

She looks down at the floor.

She waits a full five minutes, listening for any sound at all, before taking out her phone, switching on the torch and moving carefully to the edge of the foundation to look into the trench below. She can vaguely see the shape of what she assumes is Michael's body, almost fully submerged in the water. She remembers everything Robbie said about pouring foundations, the time they'll start in the morning, before it's properly light in winter, before anyone can see anything in the gloomy shadows of a dark muddy trench. She recalls the shortcuts they're likely to take on one of Michael's projects, desperate to avoid late completion penalties, ignoring the rain, compensating for the waterlogged groundworks with cement dust and a less watery mix of concrete. She's banking on the likelihood that in this massive rabbit warren of foundations, no one will look into this particular trench before the concrete gets poured.

She is careful to look for security cameras as she drives the car out of the building site. They are pointing outwards at the gate and on the perimeter fence but not, as far as she can see, inwards on the site itself, so all that will be on film is his car arriving and then leaving, and Michael opening the gate. She won't be seen at all. In any case, she is pretty sure that if he had his own plan to kill her that evening, he'd have disabled the cameras when he gave the security guards the night off, keeping anything he did well away from the gaze of prying eyes.

She drives the limo to a remote stretch of road Robbie took her along once, miles from any houses and with very little traffic, parks the car, leaves the keys still in the ignition and then makes the long walk back into town. She's kept her gloves on throughout – though in all honesty she's been in his car so many times before that there wouldn't be anything suspicious in her fingerprints and DNA being found.

She waits to hear news that Michael's body has been discovered, but after a day she knows he's encased in concrete and won't be seen again. She gets a call from the police one day, and is certain they know she's killed Michael – but the call is to tell her that her drugs test from all those weeks ago has come back negative. For weeks after that she's expecting to be caught, and any knock at the door or ring of the phone fills her with panic. But the bad knock and the bad call never come. In the weeks and months that follow, she occasionally drives past the building site and sees the structure sprouting out of the ground, layer upon layer of cement bolstering the heavy sarcophagus that houses his corpse. He's buried. He's gone. He isn't coming back.

"I CAN'T EVER COME into this space without feeling his support." She looks up from the floor. She takes another sip of her champagne and catches her mother's eye in the audience. Seline puts her notes to one side.

"There's just one more thing I'd like to add. Someone else important who isn't here this evening, who I'd like to say a few words about, who didn't always understand my art and what I was doing pursuing a precarious career as an artist, but who offered all of his support when it really mattered, the best way he knew how. My father."

Her father. Not Michael. Colin – her *real* father.

Of course, it was certainly possible Michael was her father, the two of them sitting in her kitchen, rubbing those swabs inside their cheeks, sealing them up, sending them off. For days Seline was haunted by the sickening thought that the monster Michael might be a part of her. Then, when the results came back, she could hardly bear to think of what they might say; toying with the envelope, putting it off... then getting up the courage to rip it open – and reading, with relief, that there is a 0.00% chance that she and Michael are related.

The euphoria of it! Definitely not Michael. No part of her at all. Nothing but a shadow in the background of her life.

Then exhilaration giving way to fear, the certain knowledge that once Michael finds out she's not his daughter he'll have no use for her, she'll be a threat and a danger to him, and he'll want her dead and gone. The terrible danger she is in.

The thought of it running through her mind on her night out with Charlotte. Taking Charlotte out, getting her drunk, helping her out of her clothes, washing her face, and cleaning her teeth. And once Charlotte has drifted into unconsciousness, taking Charlotte's toothbrush, rubbing the cotton-wool swabs on it, sealing them in the tube, writing the names on the paperwork, Michael's name and her own name – Seline, not Charlotte – sending off the test and knowing, days later, that when *these* test results arrive in their sealed envelope they will 'prove' to Michael that he is Seline's father, and keep her safe.

And she *was* safe. She knew it, seeing Michael open the envelope, the unguarded look on his face, the tone of his voice, hearing how happy he was.

Happy.

His happiness, after all he'd done. His unbearable, unacceptable happiness, surprising her more than she'd anticipated, shocking every fibre of her being, filling her with so much rage that, before she knew it, she lunged at him, hitting him hard, smashing him out of her life, down into that dark hole, pushing him back into the shadows, never to return.

# EPILOGUE

"Well done, darling. I'm so proud of you. Your dad would be too." Her mother hugs her, hard, and for a long time.

"Thanks, Mum."

"Your speech was amazing. The paintings are too. You know I love them."

"Aw, thanks."

"It's a real achievement, luv. Especially after the year you've had."

The monumental weight of the thought hangs heavy in the air. Her mum doesn't know the half of it.

"Yeah." Seline considers. "I guess it feels like it kind of draws something to a close."

"So..." Seline knows her mum has been building up to asking the question. "What are you going to do next?"

Seline looks round the room. All these people, chatting, moving around, looking so effortless. That's what people look like from the outside, isn't it? Joined-up. Effortless. Like they know what they're doing. No one knows what's really going on, what a terrible chaotic muddle they might be inside.

"I think I'm going to stay here for a bit. Keep painting. Keep teaching. Just see what happens next, I guess."

Her mum smiles a sad, thin smile. Seline knows it must be bittersweet, having kids grow up okay, having to hide just how desperately you love them, learning to let them go. Probably to change the subject back to safer ground, her mum goes back to looking at the exhibition.

"Well, they really are lovely paintings. I particularly like this one. Have I seen it before?"

Her mother points towards the entrance of the gallery, on the rear of a free-standing wall. It's the last painting you'd see in the exhibition before leaving.

"No. It's called *Evolving Shadows*. It's new."

It's a large canvas, larger than the others. The image is of a room, like the other works – but in this one the room is empty and without any shadows at all. The window high on the wall has a thin lace curtain that seems to stir softly in a breeze. The window itself is crisp and white and frames a dazzling cloudless blue sky. The door to the room is thrown open wide and sunlight blazes into the space. There is no figure of a girl. It's as if she has just risen and stepped out for a while.

She's gone.

# THANK YOU FOR READING

Did you enjoy reading *The Girl in the Painting*? Please consider leaving a review on Amazon. Your review will help other readers to discover the novel.

# ABOUT THE AUTHOR

Caleb Crowe is a British writer of psychological thrillers, and is fascinated by stories where extraordinary things happen to ordinary people, and the mundane is transformed into the menacing.

He's afraid of the sea, fearful in the countryside, panicky in large open spaces and terrified of small, confined spaces. He finds eerily quiet villages and bustling impersonal cities equally unsettling. There's nowhere, and no one, that doesn't possess some kind of dark, brooding anxiety just waiting to have the lid prised open and turned into a twisty, suspenseful, nerve-shredding story.

He lives in Manchester with his partner, two children and two cats, who probably have their own mysterious agendas. Whether he's navigating the urban jungle or wrestling with the daily challenges of family life, Caleb draws inspiration from the unpredictability of everyday existence.

Find Caleb on his website: www.calebcrowe.com

# ALSO BY CALEB CROWE